Risky Undertaking

Books by Mark de Castrique

The Buryin' Barry Mysteries
Dangerous Undertaking
Grave Undertaking
Foolish Undertaking
Final Undertaking
Fatal Undertaking
Risky Undertaking

The Sam Blackman Series
Blackman's Coffin
The Fitzgerald Ruse
The Sandburg Connection
A Murder in Passing

Other Novels
The 13th Target
Double Cross of Time

Young Adult Novels
A Conspiracy of Genes
Death on a Southern Breeze

Risky Undertaking

A Buryin' Barry Mystery

Mark de Castrique

Poisoned Pen Press

Poisoned Pen Press
6962 E. First Ave., Ste. 103
Scottsdale, AZ 85251
www.poisonedpenpress.com
info@poisonedpenpress.com

Printed in the United States of America

For Linda

Chapter One

"Read them and weep, gentlemen. Read them and weep." Archie Donovan Jr. flipped over his cards and spread them with all the puffed pride of a peacock fanning his tail feathers.

Mayor Sammy Whitlock threw in his hand. "You drew that inside straight, didn't you?"

"I'll never tell." Archie raked the pile of quarters, dimes, and nickels across the surface of the round oak table and dumped them into the purple cloth Crown Royal bag he used to transport his poker stake. "Let me just say you can't be afraid of risk if you want reward."

"My deal." Luther Cransford motioned for the five of us to pass him our cards.

I glanced at my watch. Nearly eleven. "I'm afraid I have to bail out."

"Funeral tomorrow?" Pete Peterson, the town's barber, looked confused as if somehow a citizen of Gainesboro had died and the news had escaped him. P's Barbershop was the nexus of Main Street communication for the local men, just like the back booths of the Cardinal Café was gossip central among the women. Like his father before him, PJ, as everyone called him, was a central character in the day-to-day drama of small-town life. If you wanted to know who was on the outs with whom, you only needed to get a haircut.

"No," I said. "I'm on duty tomorrow. We've got the fall craft show out at the fairgrounds. Tommy Lee wants a couple of deputies on hand in case traffic backs up."

Mayor Whitlock nodded with the exaggerated enthusiasm of a bobble-head doll. "And guess who's giving the opening speech?"

"I have no idea," Mack Collins said. "Any speech you give would automatically be the closing speech."

Collins owned a construction company and was one of the wealthier residents of Gainesboro. He was also a North Carolina state senator and one of the mayor's major campaign donors, and so the thin-skinned His Honor had to laugh along with the rest of us.

I stood from the table. "Thanks for the invitation. I enjoyed losing my money to Archie. But then I've been doing that for years."

The group laughed louder. Archie had taken over his father's insurance and investment business and knew no shame when it came to pushing his policies and annuities. He and I had a history going back to grade school; Archie had been the wise-ass in junior high who called me Buryin' Barry, a nickname that stuck to this son of a funeral director like white cat fur on a black sweater.

Archie and I were the youngest of the mayor's Friday night poker gathering. The other men averaged a good twenty years older, each at least somewhere in his fifties or sixties. Archie must have inherited his father's seat at the table. I was there for the first and probably only time, a last-minute substitute when Taylor Hobbs, the president of my archery club, had to travel to Charlotte when his daughter delivered his new grandson prematurely.

"Tell Susan thanks for letting you out on a Friday night," Archie said.

"Don't tell us the romance of newlyweds has worn off already?" Mayor Whitlock winked at his cohorts.

I didn't tell them my wife of six months had been the one who encouraged me to join them. As a surgeon, Susan was on call this weekend in the ER and she thought a night with the boys would do me good. "Susan and I have an open and honest understanding. She tells me what to do and I do it."

Luther Cransford laughed the loudest. "Sounds like our Eurleen, right, Sammy?" He slapped Whitlock on the back. "She's the one in the family who should have gone into politics." He elbowed Senator Collins. "She'd be governor by now, right, Mack?"

"No two ways about it," Collins said. "I wouldn't want to run against her."

Luther was Whitlock's brother-in-law and everyone in town agreed the mayor's sister Eurleen got the brains in the family.

Mayor Whitlock forced a smile. "That's why I always listen to her advice." He returned the good ole boy backslap. "And you, Luther, are proof she doesn't listen to my advice."

For Mayor Whitlock, the retort was uncharacteristically glib. Luther looked dumbfounded as it took a second for the insult to sink in.

"Just kidding, Luther." The mayor stood. The game was over. "Thanks, boys. It was a fun evening." He turned to me. "Barry, you think Susan would let you stay out a few minutes longer? I've got a little town business to discuss."

"Sure." I smiled, trying to disguise the dread of being trapped alone with someone who loves nothing better than the sound of his own voice.

"Excellent." Mayor Whitlock glanced over his shoulder at the men climbing the stairs. "Let me say good night to the others and I'll be right back. Make yourself at home."

I looked around the room, at a loss for what I should do to make myself at home. The poker club met in what the mayor called his "man cave." Actually, it was his basement, and the unpartitioned room sported every decor cliché imaginable.

In addition to the poker table, the mayor had a wide-screen TV mounted on the wall in front of an oversized leather sofa and two matching recliners, a well-stocked wet bar, a refrigerator, a pool table, four deer heads that he probably bought at a yard sale, and a NordicTrack treadmill that the mayor only set foot on when taking a shortcut from the refrigerator to the sofa. The treadmill also gave him an excuse to wear his favorite wardrobe item, a Clemson University warm-up suit that must have been altered to fit his rotund body. Its bright orange color turned His Honor into a pumpkin of planetary proportions.

I sat down at the poker table, choosing a seat that would keep me closer to the stairs than the mayor.

Within a few minutes, I heard multiple footsteps descending. I turned around and was surprised to see Sammy Whitlock followed by Archie and Luther. One of them might have forgotten something, but not both of them. I realized I'd been ambushed.

The mayor waddled up to me and placed his pudgy hands on my shoulders. Pinned in my chair by a giant pumpkin.

"Barry, this community just doesn't appreciate all you do for it. Archie, Luther, and I were talking about that earlier, right, boys?"

Luther nodded.

Archie took the seat next to me. "That's right, Barry. You guard us while we're alive and you bury us when we're dead."

I must confess I suddenly looked forward to providing Archie with the second service.

"And Archie's insurance policies make sure I get paid," I said, trying in vain not to be the center of their attention.

All three laughed too loudly.

"Why, we were even talking about having Gainesboro declare a Barry Clayton Day," Whitlock effused, and gave my shoulders an extra squeeze before turning me loose.

I wondered how much this Barry Clayton Day was going to cost me—not to have it.

"We all do our part," I said.

Mayor Whitlock's head bobbled. "That we do. It's about taking a village."

He mangled the quote, but perhaps it more accurately reflected his take-what-I-can-get philosophy.

"And you've been a big help to the three of us," Archie said. "Right, Luther?"

"Right," Luther grunted. Luther stood six foot five, and even sitting down was as tall as the mayor.

"How?" I asked.

"Why, Heaven's Gate Gardens," Whitlock exclaimed. "You always recommend it to plotless families. And we appreciate it."

I felt my stomach tighten. Heaven's Gate Gardens was a cemetery atop Bell Ridge on the outskirts of town owned by the three men. We'd already run into a conflict a few years earlier when Archie pressed me to recommend the cemetery before adequate landscaping had been completed.

"You've done a nice job with it," I said. "Fletcher and I are pleased to offer it as one of the options for the families we serve." I brought in the name of my partner, Fletcher Shaw, to underscore I wasn't making any under-the-table deals for pushing their plots.

"Yes," the mayor agreed. "And we especially appreciate that you've never asked for any referral fees."

The mayor's selective memory seemed to have forgotten they had been the ones to make that unsolicited offer, an offer I'd vehemently declined.

"That's why we wanted you to be the first to know."

"Know what?" I asked.

Whitlock nodded to Archie. "You tell him. He's your best friend."

Archie clutched my forearm like I was his only friend. "Great news, Barry. We've bought more of the ridge and we're expanding Heaven's Gate Gardens. Heaven's Gate Gardens South. It's doubling the size. If the whole town died tomorrow, we could bury everyone."

"That's comforting," I said. "I guess Asheville could supply the gravediggers."

"Great idea, Barry," Whitlock said. "I'll draft a memo for the town clerk's emergency action file." The man was serious. "And we'd be honored if you'd attend the ribbon-cutting. We're building an entrance to the new section. It overlooks I-26."

"Ah, life passing by at sixty-five miles per hour," I said.

"Exactly," Whitlock agreed. "Mention that phrase when you're consoling families."

I stood. "Well, I'll certainly be there if my schedule permits."

Mayor Whitlock clapped his hands. "We thought you'd say that. So, I took the liberty of talking to Tommy Lee about your schedule. He said he'd be happy to free you up Monday afternoon."

I made a mental note to pay Sheriff Tommy Lee Wadkins back for his kindness. Sugar in his gas tank seemed appropriate.

"Fine. Although we might have a funeral."

The mayor beamed. "We've been over that with Fletcher. He said even if someone died tomorrow the earliest burial day would probably be Tuesday. But if they want to be buried Monday afternoon, hell, we'll give 'em a great deal. Fifty percent off for a plot in the new section." The idea made him giddy. "A real funeral would be a nice backdrop for the ribbon-cutting."

The idea—and their audacity—took my breath away. In fact, the man cave seemed to close in on me. I was anxious to leave. "OK. When on Monday?"

"Two o'clock," Whitlock said. "We want the *Gainesboro Vista* to have time to get an article and photographs in before deadline."

I could see their ideal caption: "Funeral Director and Deputy Sheriff Barry Clayton Endorse Cemetery Expansion."

"Wear your uniform," Archie said.

"No. I'll be off duty. The mayor saw to that."

Archie laughed. "I mean your other one. Your black suit. You're the only guy I know with two jobs and two uniforms. An undertaker and a deputy. What'll you be next, Barry? A bus driver?"

"Someone must have incriminating photographs if they got you up here." Melissa Bigham shook her head with exaggerated disappointment.

I'd just gotten out of my jeep when the feisty reporter hustled over, her Nikon bouncing on the strap around her neck.

"And I see you're covering another Pulitzer Prize contender. Your editor must be holding the front page."

"Jonah Tugman should be holding his nose, wasting resources on a cemetery opening."

"Wouldn't have anything to do with the Heaven's Gate Gardens ad that runs on the obituary page, would it?"

Melissa laughed. "Of course not. Jonah's journalistic standards are the best money can buy."

We started walking down the newly graveled road. Melissa stood about a half foot shorter, maybe five two, and her brown hair was cut in a simple, no-nonsense style that said "shower and towel dry." She wore tan slacks and a light-green windbreaker. Melissa was always neat, but never overdressed. She looked like a young elementary schoolteacher, which disguised the brain of a barracuda searching for prey. We'd broken several national stories together, and her greatest asset was that people underestimated her until they felt her teeth in their flesh. I knew she'd turned down numerous big-city job offers, and although journalism was her passion, it was trumped by her love of the western North Carolina mountains.

About twenty yards down the slope, a group of men milled around a stone wall. Archie, Mayor Whitlock, and Luther stood with their backs to us, engaged in conversation with two men wearing bib overalls, in stark contrast to the dark suits of the cemetery owners.

"At least it's a pretty day," Melissa said. "I could be in my cubicle writing obituaries."

The September sunshine had warmed the afternoon air to the high fifties. A light but steady breeze blew across the ridge, or maybe it was the wind from the eighteen-wheelers rolling along I-26 on the valley floor.

"Life passing by," I muttered.

"What?"

"Nothing." I looked ahead. "Are those the Tucker brothers?"

"Yeah. Barney. I forget the other one's name."

"Me too. Barney does all the talking anyway."

The Tucker brothers owned a backhoe and worked as gravediggers and performed odd jobs around the county. They'd had the misfortune of uncovering an unexpected skeleton when we were moving a grave several years ago, a skeleton that turned out to be an old boyfriend of my wife.

"Evidently they're still building the entry sign," Melissa said. "They aren't ready for the ribbon-cutting."

"Are they postponing?"

"Hell, no, Barry. It's just you and me. And the Tuckers. I can guarantee you Whitlock won't want them in the shot."

As we drew closer, I heard Barney say, "But the cement will need to set up before we put any weight on the post." He pronounced the word, "SEE mint."

"That's right," the nameless Tucker brother chimed in.

"Well, we can't have a picture of Heaven's Gate Gardens South without a god damned gate." The mayor jumped up and down with each word.

It was then that I understood the origin of the phrase, "hoppin' mad."

"What if we hold the gate up while you take your picture?" Barney asked. "People will just think we're some of the dignitaries."

Sputtering noises came from the mayor like he was being waterboarded.

The sound of our footsteps on the gravel filled the space between his gasps.

Archie turned around. "Hi, Barry. We've got ourselves a situation."

Everyone faced me. I looked beyond them to a white wrought-iron gate on the road behind them. Two cherubs were fixed to the bars. White gateposts lay flat on the grass on either side. To my left I saw the rock wall with a bronze plaque embedded in the stonework. HEAVEN'S GATE GARDENS SOUTH were the words in relief.

"Everything's ready but the posts?" I asked.

"Yes," Barney said. "It rained Friday so we had to stop work on the wall. We come here early this morning and finished it less than thirty minutes ago. The gateposts got to have a solid anchor."

I nodded like I planted posts every day. "I understand. How long would it take you to dig holes that you had no intention of filling with concrete but would temporarily keep the posts erect?"

Barney scratched his grizzled chin. "I see. Just something snug for the picture, and then we could widen the holes for the permanent placement."

"Right."

"I reckon about fifteen minutes a hole."

I turned to Melissa. "You OK with that?"

"For a story of this magnitude? Sure."

I alone appreciated her sarcasm.

"That's great," Mayor Whitlock said. "You got a good head on your shoulders, Barry." He clapped his hands. "Well, let's get to it, boys."

For the next five minutes we watched the Tucker brothers trade off as they buried the manual posthole digger deeper into the ground with each thrust. It ranked up there with watching PJ give haircuts.

Then a muffled clank rose from the hole as the blades bit into something harder than earth. Barney lifted up the dirt and when he dumped it to the side, we saw shards of pottery mixed with the soil.

"What's that?" Archie asked.

I saw Melissa's eyebrows arch as she studied the pieces.

Barney lifted the digger higher. "Probably some ol' jug." He brought the tool down like he was smashing through granite.

Another crunch. He extracted the digger and opened its jaws. More shards of pottery.

And I saw something else. Pieces of bones. What looked like human bones.

Barney stared at me, his grizzled face pale as chalk. "Oh, man. Not again."

Melissa's camera whirred like a machine gun.

Chapter Two

Melissa Bigham's photograph made the front page of the *Gainesboro Vista* the next day, but neither the mayor nor a severed ribbon were in the shot. Above the close-up of pottery shards and bone fragments read the headline, "New Cemetery on Cherokee Burial Ground?" At press time, no one knew the answer to that question.

To the horror of Archie, Luther, and His Honor, I'd cleared everyone away from the posthole, first concerned we had unearthed a crime scene. Melissa said the pottery showed Cherokee markings, and Mayor Whitlock jumped in, claiming the bones were only from an old Indian.

Melissa smiled as she scribbled because she knew what was coming next.

I agreed with the mayor and so did the government of North Carolina. I told everyone all construction and development would stop immediately. State law required notification of archaeologists and tribal representatives to insure any remains were dealt with respectfully and thoroughly. I had no idea how long the process would take, but I was obliged to enforce the legal statutes. My quotes, along with the mayor's, appeared accurately in Melissa's front page article, an article Sheriff Tommy Lee Wadkins reviewed again as we sat in his office the following morning. I watched his face closely. His good right eye scanned quickly down the page. A black patch covered the left, intersected by a curving scar that ran underneath it and across his cheek to his chin. Tommy Lee's heroism in Vietnam had come at a cost, but a cost I knew he would pay again for the safety of his men.

He tossed the paper aside. "Statute Seventy, Article Three."

"What?"

"It's what you should have said if you really wanted to look smart. The law contains the specific procedures for when human bones are accidentally discovered."

"Should I have done something differently?" The sheriff's approval was important to me.

Tommy Lee laughed. "No. When you called it in, I set everything in motion."

"Why didn't you bring me in?"

"Because you had the afternoon off. Thanks to me."

"And the mayor. Why'd you let him talk you into changing my schedule?"

Tommy Lee stood and refilled his cup from the Mr. Coffee in the corner of his office. "And if you hadn't been up there?" He let the question hang.

"How'd you know there'd be trouble?"

"Come on, Barry. Archie and the mayor in a scheme together? I didn't know what would happen, but I sure as hell figured some fallout would wind up in this office."

I couldn't argue. "Where do things stand now?"

Tommy Lee sat on the corner of his desk and looked down at me. "The bureaucratic machinery has started. I notified Mack Collins. He's on the state senate's committee for Indian affairs." He paused and took a sip of coffee. "And that's a good thing because there's nothing I can do to circumvent the process and I can tell the mayor to whine to Mack."

"Are we out of it?"

Tommy Lee shook his head. "No. After Reece took statements at the scene, I sent Wakefield up for overnight security. We're responsible for making sure the scene is protected."

Reece Hutchins was one of Tommy Lee's more experienced deputies. He took his work seriously, second only to how seriously he took himself. He resented my part-time role with the department and my close relationship with Tommy Lee. Before my father's Alzheimer's forced my return to Gainesboro to run our family's funeral home, I'd served three years with the Charlotte Police Department and loved to hang out with the detectives. Tommy Lee considered me his best investigator, a position Reece coveted but for which he had no aptitude.

Tommy Lee set his cup on the desk beside him and crossed his arms over his chest. "Even though you speculated the bones were Cherokee, and the mayor, God bless his greedy little heart, unwittingly gave his endorsement of respecting Native American remains, we still have yet to rule out foul play. I'm meeting the ME from Buncombe County at nine."

Laurel County, the sheriff's jurisdiction, was too small for anything but a coroner. I looked at my watch. Eight fifteen. "I'll be surprised if they're not relics."

"Me too. But he has to sign off. Then an archaeologist comes from the state and if he or she says they're Cherokee, the executive director of the North Carolina Commission on Indian Affairs is notified."

"What kind of say do the cemetery owners have?"

"They can either agree to protect them, or request they be removed."

An image of Archie Donovan replacing the bronze Heaven's Gate Gardens plaque with one reading Happy Hunting Grounds flashed through my mind. "They'll do whatever they think will make the most money. Is their request for removal of the remains only that, a request, or is it an unchallengeable demand?"

"That's the potential problem. Usually if it's a development project, the owners and state archaeologist confer as to whether there are prudent steps the owner can take to preserve the burials."

"What's more prudent than leaving a burial in a cemetery?"

The somber expression on Tommy Lee's face transformed to a wide grin. "Which is why our illustrious mayor and his partners should be as cooperative as they can be. The ME rules out homicide, the remains do just that—remain, and the cemetery designates the spot as an existing grave."

"How do the Cherokee fit in?"

"If the archaeologist confirms the remains are Cherokee, then the Commission of Indian Affairs notifies tribal leaders and the Commission and tribe work together to insure the remains are treated respectfully."

All the steps sounded logical and orderly. And if something was logical and orderly, I was confident Archie and the mayor would screw it up.

Tommy Lee asked me to join him for his meeting with the medical examiner. We found Deputy Wakefield with his patrol car parked across the new entrance to Heaven's Gate Gardens South. He wasn't alone. Three other vehicles were lined up single file, as if waiting for the deputy to pull aside so they could enter.

"Oh, boy," Tommy Lee muttered. "Curly, Moe, and Larry are already here."

The sight of Archie's BMW told me Tommy Lee wasn't comparing the ME to the Three Stooges. Archie, Mayor Sammy Whitlock, and Luther Cransford had all driven up to protect their investment. They clustered around Wakefield and turned to face us as Tommy Lee pulled onto the shoulder of the gravel road, clearly giving room for our unwanted friends to exit.

The cemetery investors came hustling to meet us, Luther in the lead followed by Archie and then the huffing-and-puffing mayor.

"How much longer is this nonsense going to go on, Tommy Lee?" Luther stepped close to the sheriff, an effort to use his height as a physical intimidation.

Instead of backing up, Tommy Lee leaned in and rose on his toes, putting his face inches away from the bigger man. "If you mean by nonsense that you're trying to tell my department or the state of North Carolina how to do our jobs, then this nonsense could go on quite a while, and this so-called gate to heaven could be closed till Gabriel blows his trumpet, for all I care."

Luther couldn't take staring into Tommy Lee's scarred face and eye patch. He blinked and retreated. "We're just frustrated.

I mean we got the Tucker brothers to deal with." He glanced at the backhoe still parked on the cleared slope. "And we got interest in the plots already. Nobody knows when they're going to die." He turned to me. "How long can we keep somebody in your refrigerator?"

The image of bodies stacked with "sell-by" dates left me speechless. I was saved from concocting a suitable response by the crunch of gravel as a black Land Rover pulled behind Tommy Lee's patrol car. Close on its bumper came the Buncombe County mobile crime lab.

Tommy Lee shouted instructions to the arriving team. "Hold up. We'll clear these cars so you can get closer." He turned to the hapless trio. "OK. Either move your vehicles to the shoulder below the crime lab or park over the hill at the original cemetery."

"We can stay?" Archie asked.

"Yes. As long as you stand where I tell you and don't interfere." The three men scurried to their cars.

Deputy Wakefield laughed. He was a long, lean man in his forties, quiet and competent, but not particularly ambitious. "They were up here at the crack of dawn. I think if I hadn't been on site, they would have pulled some stunt. God only knows what."

"Probably planning to substitute chicken bones and the remnants of a picnic basket," Tommy Lee said. "Or something equally hare brained."

"What's this about chicken bones?"

We turned to face a small man wearing jeans and a blue flannel shirt. A neatly trimmed gray goatee framed a welcoming smile.

"If you expect me to know the difference between chicken and turkey bones, then I brought the wrong equipment." He lifted a black bag in his left hand and extended his right to Tommy Lee.

"Good morning, Howard." The sheriff grasped the offered hand in a firm grip. "Nice of you to make the trek to our humble county. These are two of my best deputies, Barry Clayton and Steve Wakefield." Tommy Lee gestured to the diminutive man. "This is Howard Tuppler. He's forgotten more about autopsies than the big-city boys will ever know."

"Simply a product of growing old," Tuppler said. "Well, what have you got for me today that your coroner couldn't handle?"

"More a case of history than mystery," Tommy Lee said. "We're pretty sure it's an Indian burial."

"Then I'll keep the lab men back till I've made a preliminary exam." He held up a hand to two techs standing by the mobile crime lab, signaling them to wait. "OK. Lead on, Kemosabe."

Tommy Lee gave instructions to Wakefield to stay with Archie, Luther, and the mayor at the newly constructed gate. That would put them close enough to observe without being in the way.

I followed Tommy Lee and Tuppler to the spot where the post-hole digger unearthed the bones.

Tuppler didn't bother to bend down for a closer look. "Cherokee. No doubt about it."

"How can you be sure?" I asked.

"The pottery. The blackened coloration is indicative of the way the Cherokee fired their clay." He surveyed the round curve of the cleared ridge. "Beautiful spot." He rolled on latex gloves and knelt beside the relics. "Yes, a beautiful spot. I wager our friend here isn't the only resident."

"There's more of 'em?" Mayor Whitlock wailed the question from behind Wakefield's outstretched arm. Luther and Archie peered over the deputy's shoulder.

"That's my guess," the ME said. "The state archaeologist will give a more accurate assessment, but if I were you, I'd plan on selling these plots as pre-owned."

"What's the next step?" Tommy Lee asked.

"The archaeologist should be here within a few days. Maybe even sooner. Once he makes the official determination of their origin, then the state, the tribal representatives, and the property owners will have a powwow."

The sound of a damaged muffler roared up the hillside. Tuppler got to his feet as we watched a battered pickup brake to a sudden halt behind Wakefield's patrol car.

The driver's door flew open and a man jumped out. He wore faded jeans, a yellow tee shirt with the words Preserve the Qualla Boundary printed in red on the front, and a checked blue bandanna tied across his forehead. Black stubble of a buzz cut sprouted above it. He jogged toward us.

A man and a woman emerged from the passenger door. Both wore jeans, with the second man in an untucked green flannel shirt and the woman in a loose-fitting, rust tunic. Her hair hung in two long braids. His was covered by a John Deere cap. They approached slowly, eyeing their companion more than watching us.

Wakefield raised his hand. "Hold up."

"What's going on?" the driver demanded.

"A lawful investigation."

The man grunted. "We'll see. Who's in charge?"

"I am." Tommy Lee walked toward the gate. "Sheriff Tommy Lee Wadkins."

Archie, Luther, and the mayor stepped aside.

"And you are?" Tommy Lee asked.

"Jimmy Panther."

His two companions stopped behind him, one at each shoulder.

"You're from the tribal council?"

Jimmy Panther crossed his arms and stared at Tommy Lee. "We represent preservation, not termination."

"I'll take that as a no."

"Take it how ever you want." Panther looked beyond the sheriff to Tuppler. "Who's he?"

"The medical examiner. He's determined we're dealing with Cherokee remains. We're notifying the state archaeologist."

Panther dropped his hands to his side and started forward.

Tommy Lee blocked his path. "Sorry. We're protecting the site."

"I'm Cherokee."

"But not an authorized tribal representative."

Jimmy Panther took a deep breath. He scanned the hillside. "This is sacred ground. Remember that."

He pivoted and jogged back to his pickup, leaving his passengers to chase after him.

The truck backfired once and rattled down the mountain.

Mayor Whitlock edged closer to the sheriff. "What do you think, Tommy Lee? Is that Indian going to make trouble?"

"Hard to say. There are people who make trouble, and there are people who are trouble."

"He sure got here fast," Luther said. "Must have driven from the reservation as soon as he saw the morning paper."

Archie Donovan looked at me with wide eyes. "He said this was sacred ground, Barry. I hope we haven't let loose some curse."

Luther kicked the ground in frustration. "God damn it, Archie. You spread that foolishness around town and we'll be lucky if we sell someone a plot to bury their dog. Indian curse, my ass. I've got too much money tied up in your expansion scheme to let a pile of old bones get in the way."

That afternoon our funeral home got the call. Luther Cransford's wife had dropped dead.

Chapter Three

"And he found her facedown in a bowl of Cool Whip." Archie Donovan described the bizarre scene as if he'd been an eyewitness, and then he glanced around Mom's kitchen like she might have an identical deathtrap on the counter.

"You sure it wasn't whipped cream?" my uncle Wayne asked. "Eurleen looks like she chowed down the real stuff."

"Wayne, don't talk nonsense," Mom said. "She was probably icing a sponge cake."

"Maybe. One she was going to eat single-handedly. Connie, last night it took four of us to get her onto the embalming table."

"I won't hear it. The poor woman's dead." Mom rose from her chair. "Archie, would you like more coffee?"

"No, thanks, Mrs. Clayton. I'm jittery enough. Who knows where the curse will strike next."

The four of us, Mom, Uncle Wayne, Archie, and I were in the kitchen of the funeral home the day after Luther Cransford walked into his house and found his wife dead at their kitchen table. At eight o'clock in the morning, Archie had stopped by unannounced, anxious for any assurance that he wasn't facing imminent doom.

"Eurleen had nothing to do with those remains," I said. "If there's a curse, why her?"

Archie made his case to my uncle. "Don't you see, Wayne? Who's the one person the curse could kill and hurt both Luther and the mayor?"

"The woman who was Luther's wife and the mayor's sister," Wayne said, actually giving Archie's theory serious consideration.

"Come on. That's ridiculous." I pointed at my uncle. "You just said Eurleen was overweight. She was in her sixties with heart and blood pressure issues. Susan said she was the poster child for a coronary."

My uncle cocked his head and eyed me with undisguised skepticism. "But at the same time this Cherokee proclaims a curse?"

"He didn't proclaim a curse. He urged us to respect the dead. You of all people should appreciate that."

Uncle Wayne straightened in his chair. He was tall and lanky, a distinct contrast to his sister, my mother, who struggled to keep weight off her short frame. The one trait they did share was their curly, cotton-white hair.

My uncle ran his gnarled fingers through his thick locks. "My point exactly. Digging up those remains might bring a curse from the dead, not the living. Imagine a bunch of Indians planting a post through your father's grave."

"Wayne! That's enough." My mother turned from the counter, her eyes welling with tears. "Jack would never kill anybody."

My uncle took a deep breath. He knew he'd crossed a line. Although my father had died from complications of Alzheimer's more than a year ago, his loss was still raw.

"I'm sorry," Uncle Wayne said. "Of course he wouldn't." He stared at Archie. "But I'd look twice before crossing the street, if I were you."

The blood drained from Archie's face. He'd come for reassurance and received my uncle's death sentence. Well, if Archie was foolish enough to believe that, I wasn't going to waste my breath trying to change his mind.

"Think what you like, Archie," I said. "But don't go spreading such talk between now and Saturday's funeral. You'll only upset Luther and his family." Then I hit him below the belt. "And you may encourage whatever spirit's behind this to strike again."

The next few days passed without incident. The investigation of the Cherokee burial ground in the new section of the cemetery followed the prescribed protocol, and the state archaeologist and tribal representatives worked on site under the watchful eye of a deputy.

Eurleen's death kept Luther and the mayor occupied with funeral arrangements. Archie took my words to heart. He was neither seen nor heard.

By seven on Friday, the night of the official visitation, the line of visitors stretched out our front door and back to the parking lot. I knew what had been scheduled for two hours would stretch to three. Fortunately, the evening sky was clear and the temperature hovered in the mid-sixties.

My partner, Fletcher Shaw, stayed close to the family's receiving line, gently nudging people along who tended to talk beyond the appropriate expression of sympathy. Uncle Wayne stood near the casket, prepared to assist anyone who might be overcome with emotion and need an escort to a nearby chair. During his long life, Uncle Wayne had seen women and men collapse at the sight of the deceased, and although my uncle couldn't move as fast as he once did, he adamantly refused to give up his post.

Our part-time assistant, Freddy Mott, worked the parking lot. He wore a yellow and orange vest and tried to manage the traffic flow as parking spots emptied and filled. I hired Steve Wakefield as an off-duty deputy to insure vehicles didn't clog Main Street. He also worked the crosswalk for the safety of pedestrians who found side-street parking.

My wife Susan wasn't on hospital call for the weekend and she helped Mom in the kitchen by providing lemonade and snacks for the family.

I was the floater, the troubleshooter who moved along the human stream from parking lot to viewing room, looking to head off any glitch.

I eased my way through the throng to the thermostat in the front parlor. The body heat generated by the multitude must have raised the temperature at least ten degrees. I lowered the setting to sixty-five, knowing the air conditioning unit was already over-taxed and would probably freeze up before the night was over.

"Barry." The whispered shout cut through the rumble of unintelligible conversation.

Susan stood in the doorway of the hall to the kitchen. I could tell from her expression something was wrong. She motioned me to join her.

"What is it?"

"Archie." She rolled her eyes in exasperation. "He's on the back porch demanding to see you."

Susan was the calmest person I knew. As a skilled surgeon, she routinely faced tense, pressure-filled situations with unflappable poise. No one lasts long running an operating room otherwise. But Archie stretched her patience beyond her self-control.

"Well, why didn't he come around front?"

"How the hell should I know? He's your friend." She bit her lower lip, as if to seal her mouth shut.

"OK, OK."

Susan took a deep breath. "I'm sorry. It's just that he's upset your mother. He won't come in, but claims it's a matter of life and death."

"With Archie it always is." I nodded toward the parlor. "Would you keep an eye on things while I sort this out?"

"Yes. And whatever it is, keep your cool."

"Thanks for the advice. Try it some time."

She smiled. "Smartass."

I found Archie pacing a tight circle on the back porch. His head jerked around as I opened the kitchen door.

"Come in, Archie."

"No. Fetch Luther and the mayor. There are too many people inside."

I stepped out onto the gray floorboards. The old wood creaked beneath my weight. The porch served primarily as a shelter for Mom's work sink where she could wash vegetables and her garden utensils. Overhead, several moths fluttered around the yellow light bulb—a bulb advertised not to draw bugs.

"I can't just yank them out of the receiving line."

"Even to save their lives? I mean, you don't even have a metal detector at the door."

"It's a damned visitation, not a presidential address."

Archie thrust his hand inside his sport coat and pulled out a white envelope. "Yeah. And what would the Secret Service do with this?" He shoved it toward my face.

On the front, ARCHIE DONOVAN JR. and his address had been scrawled in block letters by a blunt pencil.

"Go ahead. Open it."

The back flap had been torn loose. I extracted a single sheet of double-folded white typing paper. A bent, brown feather glided to the floor.

I picked it up. The vanes were still smooth but the shaft had been snapped midway down its length. Unbroken, the feather would have been five or six inches. I unfolded the paper. Five words, one per line, appeared to have been written by the same hand that addressed the envelope. STAY AWAY FROM BELL RIDGE.

"See." The fear in Archie's voice turned him into a boy soprano. "A broken eagle feather. You know what that means."

"No, I don't. And this is from a turkey." As an archer I had fletched my own arrows and knew something about feathers.

"Well, it's clearly a threat," Archie insisted. "I've sent Gloria and the girls to stay with Gloria's mother in Weaverville."

I looked at the feather and the note a second time. "I think you're overreacting. If the mayor got one, you know he'd immediately come running to Tommy Lee."

Archie seemed to consider this. "Maybe he did, but with all the sympathy cards coming in, he hasn't seen it yet. I found it in my mailbox when I got home from work."

"There's no return address."

"That's right. Someone doesn't want to be known."

I refolded the note around the broken feather and stuffed both back in the envelope. "If it makes you feel better, I'll hold onto this."

"Are you going to warn Luther and the mayor?"

I shook my head. "They have enough to worry about. It's probably a prank played on you by someone here in town. That's why there's no return address. And everybody knows about the bones."

Archie relaxed. "OK, Barry. If you say so."

"I say so. Now come in and have some of my mom's lemonade." I lifted the envelope in front of his eyes. "And not another word about this."

"Will you be driving us?" Luther asked me the question as he watched the pallbearers load the casket of his wife in the hearse.

"Yes. We should go ahead and get in the car."

"All of us?"

"Just you and your son and daughter."

I'd gone over everything with Luther earlier before the funeral service, but it was not uncommon for the family of the deceased to be living moment to moment, events unfolding within a blur of disjointed activities.

"OK," Luther mumbled. Then he looked at me, eyes moist but sharply focused. "Thanks for all you're doing, Barry. I don't know how I'd have gotten through these past few days without you."

"You're doing as well as can be expected, sir." I turned to the family limousine directly behind the hearse. "Allow me to get the door."

Luther took the arm of his daughter, Sandra, and escorted her to the car. His son, Darren, followed. Both children were grown. Sandra was the older, probably in her early forties and working in Atlanta. Darren was still in his thirties and had a job in DC.

I nodded to Fletcher. He was driving a second limo with the mayor and his family. We could have squeezed them into one, but that would have been the operative word—squeezed. And emotions run high during times of grief. Family rifts can be exacerbated into ugly scenes. I didn't think such a history existed between Luther and the mayor, but why take a chance?

Attendees got to their vehicles quickly. Uncle Wayne started the hearse. I signaled to Tommy Lee that we were ready. Instead of a deputy, the sheriff was driving the lead patrol car for the procession. Deputy Reece Hutchins would trail, but then he and the sheriff would leapfrog through intersections until we were outside the town limits.

The journey from the First Presbyterian Church of Gainesboro to the cemetery on Bell Ridge was about five miles. Our community was one where oncoming traffic still pulled to the side of the road out of respect. We would keep our speed below thirty-five miles per hour to give time for those maneuvers.

We traveled in silence down Main Street until we reached the outskirts of town.

"It was a lovely service," Luther said.

I glanced in the rearview mirror. Luther was speaking to his daughter seated beside him.

He put his arm around her. "Your mother would have been very pleased."

"So many people came," Sandra said. "Almost the whole town."

"She had lots of friends," Luther said, his voice choking.

"Then why would somebody send that note to stay away from the cemetery?" Sandra asked.

"What?" The question popped out of my mouth before I could stop it. A tingle ran down the back of my neck.

"I was going to mention it later," Luther said. "This morning, we found a plain envelope mixed in with the sympathy cards. There was a broken feather and an order to stay away from Bell Ridge. Must have come yesterday."

"Was it signed?"

"No. But it had to be that Indian. Can you believe it? My wife's not even in the ground and he's making threats. I was going to tell you later. Right now I don't need the aggravation."

"Dad, we don't know who did it," Darren said. "It's not worth getting upset."

"Did one go to the mayor?" I asked.

"Not that I know," Luther said.

I wondered if that letter had been intercepted by someone in the mayor's household who would have known the mayor would overreact. I decided not to mention that Archie had received the same message.

"Did you save it?"

"Yes," Luther said. "It's at the house."

"I'll talk to Tommy Lee. We should look at it."

"OK. Thanks, Barry."

We began the climb up Bell Ridge. As we neared the top, the brake lights on the hearse flared. I made a quick stop and skidded a few yards on the gravel.

"Can't you get us any closer?" Luther asked.

We were a good fifty yards down the hill from the original Heaven's Gate Gardens. I craned my neck to look beyond the hearse and saw that Tommy Lee's patrol car had also stopped. He was getting out.

"Maybe something fell across the road," I said. "Tommy Lee's checking. I'll see if he needs help. Stay here."

I got out. Uncle Wayne was opening his door. I heard drums. And then I saw the picket line.

Six marchers walked counterclockwise in an elliptical pattern over the width of the road. Their steps crunched the stones in time to the beat of two small drums played by two men standing at either side of the formation.

Jimmy Panther held the largest sign, "Respect Our Dead As Well." Other signs read, "Dignity in Death" and "Cherokee Rites Are Rights."

I recognized the man and woman who had been with Panther earlier in the week. The others, a mixture of men and women, appeared to range in age from late twenties to mid-thirties.

They walked solemnly without speaking. No chanting. No native garb. No ceremonial paint. The men wore dark suits and the women, dark slacks and white blouses. They could have been attending a funeral themselves. I realized they were making a point of being respectful, drawing a comparison between Eurleen's interment and the burials that may have occurred here centuries before.

"Are those the Indians?" Uncle Wayne caught my arm to steady himself on the slope.

"Yes. The tallest is Jimmy Panther. The Cherokee who scared Archie."

"Well, we've got a burial to tend to. Eurleen can't stay in the hearse all day."

I wanted to say Eurleen could stay in the hearse for eternity, but instead I said, "You're right. Stand guard. I'll help Tommy Lee."

I quickly walked away before my uncle could object.

"I'm asking you to stand aside." Tommy Lee spoke in a calm voice, loud enough to be heard above the drums without becoming a shout.

I stopped a yard behind him. The protesters kept marching. Panther let his gaze linger on me long enough to show he recognized me out of my deputy's uniform.

"You are on private property," Tommy Lee said. "If you don't stand aside, I'll arrest you for trespassing."

Panther shifted his gaze behind me. His thin lips hinted at a smile. I heard the sound of feet running up the gravel road. Then a familiar whir. Melissa Bigham was beside me, her breath coming in gasps almost as rapid as her camera shutter.

Panther raised his sign high over his head. Drums and marchers halted.

"Who is trespassing?" he shouted. "Those who disturb the dead."

"We're headed to the original cemetery," Tommy Lee said. "Not the site of the remains. Remains that the tribal representatives have successfully and respectfully reinterred on the reservation. Nothing and no one will be disturbed."

"We are disturbed. What guarantees are there that sacred ground stops where you say it does?"

I thought of ME Howard Tuppler's comment that the beautiful ridge was probably the site of multiple Cherokee burials.

Tommy Lee gestured back to the hearse. "This woman's grave has been carefully dug. There was no evidence of any Cherokee remains. I made sure."

"And if there had been, you would have boxed them up and shipped them off to the reservation. No preservation, just the termination of an inconvenient problem."

I heard car doors slamming behind me. People were getting out to see what was happening.

Tommy Lee took a step closer to the protesters. "You've made your point." He nodded to Melissa. "And it will be duly reported. But you'll lose any sympathy for your cause if you keep a grieving family from burying their loved one."

Panther stared at the sheriff, stretching out the tension of the moment. His followers looked at their leader for a signal of what to do next.

"What the hell!" Luther Cransford rushed by me like a line-backer pursuing a quarterback. He lunged at Panther before either the sheriff or I could stop him.

The Cherokee brought his sign down as a shield. Luther punched through it with a roundhouse swing aimed at Panther's face. The blow missed, but the sheer force of Luther's assault knocked Panther to the ground. Luther drew back his right leg, preparing to kick the man.

Tommy Lee hurled himself through the air and drove his shoulder into Luther's side. Both men tumbled in a melee of flailing arms and legs. I rushed to assist.

"Sit on him," Tommy Lee ordered as he rolled off Luther.

I straddled the big man. He was sobbing and made no effort to get up.

Jimmy Panther rose and brushed off his suit. Then the Cherokees split into two groups lining the edge of the road. They bowed their heads. The drums started a slow rhythm. Two beats and a pause. Thump thump. Thump thump. I recognized the sound of a human heartbeat.

Tommy Lee brought Luther's son and daughter over. We helped their father to his feet and I guided him to the family car.

The funeral procession resumed up the ridge, each vehicle passing between the silent protesters, each mourner hearing the ancient sound that had once echoed through these hills while their own European ancestors lived and died an ocean away.

Chapter Four

"He's back." Fear vibrated in Archie's voice.

I'd answered the call without looking at my cell phone because I assumed it was Susan. She'd left fifteen minutes earlier to perform a Monday morning surgery and she often phoned en route to the hospital with some "Honey, please do this" item she'd forgotten to mention.

So, ignorance was bliss as I enjoyed a second cup of coffee on my deck. The mist was lifting from the valley below, cardinals hovered around the sunflower feeder, the debacle at the cemetery lay two days in the past, and all was right with the world. My yellow lab, Democrat, and I were lords of the manor, five acres of hardwoods surrounding a home reconstructed with the logs of four Blue Ridge cabins that once housed mountaineers in the eighteen hundreds.

Now, I had inadvertently let Archie invade my sanctuary.

"Who's back?"

"The Panther." Archie spoke the Cherokee's surname as he might have that of the assassin Carlos the Jackal.

I checked my watch. Seven thirty. "Are you at the cemetery?"

"Yes." His voice dropped to a whisper. "I promised Luther I'd come up and make sure the grave had been covered and seeded properly."

"And Panther's there already?"

No answer.

"Archie?"

"Sorry, I was nodding my head."

"Well, the connection's not strong enough for me to hear the rattle. What are they doing?"

"I don't see anyone. His truck's parked on the road. You know, where they had the protest."

I stood and walked into the cabin. "Don't look for them. They're probably down at the site where we found the remains."

"Do you want me to block their escape?"

I moved quickly to the bedroom and pulled a clean uniform from my closet. "No. Just leave. I'll be there as soon as I can."

"OK. But hurry. I hate to think they're desecrating Eurleen's grave."

"Archie, whatever you do, don't tell Luther. That's an order."

I called into the dispatcher to tell her I was checking out a report of trespassing on Bell Ridge. I didn't mention the cemetery or Panther's truck. Within twenty minutes, I pulled my jeep behind the rusted vehicle. As I stepped onto the gravel and adjusted my duty belt, Archie rose from behind a stand of rhododendron.

"What the hell are you doing here?" I asked.

"I parked off the state road and walked up. How else was I supposed to know when it was safe to return?"

"You could have called me on your cell phone."

"Oh."

I sighed. "Come on. We'll see where they are and then you can check on Eurleen's grave."

Archie followed me down the southern slope to the new section. The ground was bare where the archaeologists had conducted their exhumation after Mayor Whitlock enlisted the aid of his poker buddy, State Senator Mack Collins, to broker a deal to return the bones to the reservation.

The site was empty.

I cupped my hands around my mouth and shouted into the air. "Jimmy! It's Deputy Clayton. You need to leave right now."

Silence.

"Maybe they camped out," Archie said. "And they're still sleeping."

"Why do you think that?"

"Because the truck was covered with dew."

I hadn't noticed. "Good observation."

"I'm scared, Barry. Not blind."

For once, Archie had a point. "Then let's check on Eurleen," I said.

We walked up the ridge and through the gates of the original cemetery. The grassy slope opened on the eastern exposure and the morning sunlight brought the colors vibrantly to life. None more brilliantly than the red of the shirt of a man stretched out on the fresh earth of Eurleen Cransford's plot.

"He's sleeping on Eurleen's grave," Archie whispered.

I said nothing. My eyes were sharper. Sharp enough to see the flies buzzing around the man's head.

"Oh, my God." Archie jumped back like he'd stepped on a rattlesnake.

Jimmy Panther lay with one side of his face flat against the dirt. Behind the upturned ear, a circular hole of dried blood marked the entrance of the bullet that had taken his life. A white piece of paper lay under a stone beside his outstretched hand.

I pulled a clean handkerchief from my hip pocket, set the stone aside and lifted the folded paper. Inside were four pencil-scrawled words: "The only good Indian."

"Is a dead Indian." Tommy Lee completed the old racist phrase and then dropped the paper in an evidence sleeve. He looked down at Jimmy Panther's body. "What do you think he was doing at Eurleen's grave?"

The sheriff and I stood inside a perimeter of yellow crime tape and waited on the arrival of ME Howard Tuppler and the mobile crime lab. My fellow deputies had set up a roadblock at the base of the cemetery road and secured the immediate area around the pickup.

"I don't know," I said. "There's no sign of vandalism. Maybe someone saw him here and thought the worst."

Tommy Lee knelt down by Panther's head. "This was an execution. You can see the muzzle was placed against the scalp. All six tells of a contact shot." Tommy Lee circled his finger around the wound. "We've got skin abrasion, unburned gunpowder, soot, seared skin from the heat, triangular skin tears from gas going into him, and I can see the muzzle contusion from the expanding gas pushing the scalp back against the barrel. From the shape, I'd say a semiautomatic twenty-two."

"Small caliber for a pistol."

"Not for a close range execution." Tommy Lee rose. "Surprised it was just a single tap. Either the killer was confident or he fired a single shot in anger and fled."

"Someone angry like Luther?"

Tommy Lee nodded. "But how did he get so close? And how did he know Panther was up here?"

"What do you want me to do?"

He fixed his one eye on me. "What do you think? Lead the investigation, of course. Reece can secure the scene here. I'll work with Tuppler and the lab boys. You get your butt to Luther's house and find out where he was last night."

I looked down at the body. "And notification?"

"I'll take care of contacting tribal police. We could be facing a jurisdictional mess and a political nightmare." He held up the sleeve with the note. "No word about this. Not only is it inflammatory, but I want it withheld so we've got a piece of evidence to corroborate any confession. We'll analyze it for comparison to the messages Archie and Luther received."

"OK. So, I'm off. Alone."

Tommy Lee grimaced. "Ah, hell, what was I thinking? If Luther shot Panther, he might do anything. Take Wakefield as backup." He flashed a crooked smile. "But be careful. I'd hate to lose Wakefield."

Luther Cransford lived in a gated community called Glendale Forest that was two miles on the other side of town. I took a patrol car from the murder scene and the guard at the gatehouse waved us through without asking for our destination. I wouldn't have given it to him if he had.

Wakefield and I parked a half a block away so that Luther wouldn't see our vehicle. The white, two-story house bore a striking resemblance to our funeral home, except instead of being antebellum to the Civil War it was one of those faux plantation houses antebellum to the Iraq War and more suited to a studio backlot.

A wide, cement driveway curved in front with a split on the right that ended in a two-car garage. Luther's Cadillac was parked in front of a closed garage door.

"He's home," Wakefield said.

"Maybe. Or maybe he's with one of his children if they drove from Atlanta or DC."

"Only one way to find out." Wakefield stepped up on the veranda and headed for the front door.

"Wait a minute," I said. "Let me be the first person he sees. I've spent more time with him over the past few days."

"Right." Wakefield retreated a few yards to the left. "And this way he can't get both of us with one shot." He winked at me. "Don't worry, Barry. If he shoots you, I'll shoot him."

I wiped my perspiring hands on my pants and rang the bell. "Thanks."

Somewhere inside a heavy chime sounded. Behind me I heard Wakefield unsnap the holster strap securing his pistol. He wanted no impediment should he need to draw it.

A few minutes passed. I rang the bell again.

"Coming." A tired, gravelly voice trailed the echo of the chime.

The bolt clicked, the door swung inward, and Luther Cransford squinted as the morning sun struck him full in the face. Dark bags puffed beneath his eyes. Gray stubble covered his jaw. He seemed to have aged ten years and shrunk ten inches.

"Barry?" His confusion grew when he saw Wakefield.

"Hello, Luther. Is it OK if we come in for a few minutes?"

He pondered the question like I'd asked him to name the capital of Lithuania.

I pressed with an explanation that sounded innocent. "We want to talk to you about the feather you received. The one Sandra mentioned Saturday."

The vacuous look in his eyes hardened into a flinty glare. He stepped back. "Yes. Come in. Maybe you can find a fingerprint or something to nail the bastard."

We followed him through the foyer and into a living room decorated by someone who never met a knickknack she didn't like. I took a floral-upholstered armchair, Wakefield sat on a beige chintz sofa, and Luther hovered by a hardwood rocker, uncertain whether to sit or stand.

"I would offer you some coffee, but I haven't brewed any this morning." He looked away. "I don't like going in the kitchen."

"We're fine," I said. "Have you been able to get any sleep?"

He shook his head. "I'm exhausted, but when I lie down, my mind just races."

I started fishing. "Have you been able to leave the house?"

"Yeah. Darren, Sandra, and I went to the club for lunch yesterday. But we could hardly eat for people coming up to pay their condolences. And they all brought up the fight with the Indians and how they didn't blame me for losing control."

"Are your children still here?"

"No. They left yesterday afternoon."

"Did they fly out of Asheville?"

"They drove. Sandra's trip wasn't so bad to Atlanta, but Darren had a good eight hours to DC. I tried to get him to stay over, but he said he had to be at work this morning. He's a junior account exec in a PR firm and it's all about billable hours."

"So, you were here by yourself last night?"

"Yeah." His eyes filled and again he looked away. "Last night. I guess every night from now on."

I backed off the questions. Luther didn't seem suspicious that we were there for more than I'd claimed. "I'd like to see that letter you got."

Luther jerked his head around. "Right. Sorry. I'll be right back." He went to the foyer and ascended the stairs.

Wakefield leaned forward. "Man, if he killed that Indian, he's giving a hell of a performance."

I touched my forefinger to my lips. Air vents and corridors could carry sound in unexpected patterns. But Wakefield was right. Luther appeared to be a grieving husband and nothing more. He was soon back.

"Darren suggested I put it in this." Luther handed me a nine-by-twelve manila envelope. "He thought maybe you could find some fingerprints."

The end flap was sealed with a metal clasp. I set the envelope on the floor beside my chair.

"Aren't you going to open it?" Luther asked.

"No. It will go straight to the lab. Your son was smart to take the precaution."

For the first time since Wakefield and I entered the house, Luther smiled. "Darren's always thinking."

"What's the company he works for in DC?"

"Wilder and Hamilton. It's one of the larger PR firms."

I pointed to the rocking chair. "Why don't you sit down. We've got a few more questions."

Luther glanced at Wakefield and then back to me. "About what?"

I waited until he settled in the chair. "Did you know Archie Donovan also got a note and a broken feather?"

Luther's eyes widened. "No. When?"

"Friday."

Scarlet exploded on his unshaven cheeks. "God damn it. I'd like to get my hands on that son of a bitch."

In my peripheral vision, I saw Wakefield cut his eyes to me. Faking blood flow to the face would be an incredible acting achievement and we both knew it.

"Was Jimmy Panther one of the reasons you couldn't sleep?" I asked.

"Yeah. He ruined Eurleen's funeral. There was no call for that. We did everything the law required us to do." Luther paused. "Did my brother-in-law get a feather note?"

"Not that we know. Have you seen the mayor since the service?"

"No. He offered to come by yesterday, but I just wanted to be alone with the kids."

"And last night, after Darren and Sandra left and you couldn't sleep, did you go out?"

Luther tensed, wary of a question that clearly had a tone of interrogation. "Why do you want to know?"

I shrugged. "Like you said. Your mind was racing. I find it hard to stay put when that happens to me."

He leaned forward in the rocker. "Don't bullshit me, Barry. I've seen you play poker and you don't have the face for it. Now what's this about?"

"Someone crossed paths with Panther last night."

"Crossed paths?"

"Yes. Except Panther's path didn't go any farther than Eurleen's grave."

Luther's jaw dropped. "He went to my wife's grave?"

"Went or was forced. Someone shot him in the head. We found him this morning."

Luther bolted from the chair. "I've got to get up there."

"No. Nothing about the grave was damaged. But it's a crime scene. I'll let you know when we've finished."

I stood and Wakefield eased around us to stand between Luther and the front door.

I stepped closer to Luther. "I'm sorry, but I have to ask. Where were you last night?"

He licked his lips. "I was here, Barry. All night."

I might not be the best poker player in the game, but at that moment, I could read Luther's face like an open book.

He was lying.

Chapter Five

Wakefield buckled his seatbelt. "What do you think?"

I waited until we pulled away from the curb before answering. "I think we have some leads to follow."

"Yeah, but what about Luther? Seems obvious he's in the clear."

"I'll grant he looked surprised at the news. But if he's guilty he had to know he tops our suspect list. And rekindling his anger could have created that believable outburst."

Wakefield whistled through his teeth. "I don't know. If so, the guy deserves an Oscar."

We neared the gatehouse. The bar on the exit lane was up, but I stopped the patrol car on the grassy shoulder. "Wait here," I told Wakefield.

The guard stepped out when he saw me approach. "Good morning, officer. How can I help you?"

"When did you come on duty?"

"Seven." He frowned. "Has there been a break-in?"

"No. Nothing like that." I looked for a nameplate but the patch on his generic uniform only read Hendrick Security. "Was there someone on duty overnight?"

He nodded. "The eleven-to-seven shift. Joey Abbott pulled last night's."

"Would you happen to have his number?"

"Sure. We keep a phone list in case a guard gets sick or has an emergency." He glanced at the patrol car. Two deputies signaled we were doing more than a routine court summons. "Is it an emergency?"

"No. Simply checking out reports of someone driving erratically last night. Thought you guys might have seen something."

He grinned. "Somebody celebrating the weekend all the way to Monday morning, huh? More than once a resident's come home liquored up and crashed right through that lane bar." He pointed to the entrance's crossarm.

I gave him my sternest deputy look. "If they're headed out of here that way, you call us."

"Yes, sir." He stiffened as if awaiting further orders.

"Joey Abbott's number," I prompted.

"Yes, sir. Right away."

When I returned to the car, I asked Wakefield to drive.

"Where are we headed?"

"Back to the cemetery, but I want to talk to the guard who was on duty last night." I pulled my cell phone from my pocket.

Wakefield turned onto the main highway. "What's his name? Maybe I know him."

"Joey Abbott."

"Nah, doesn't ring a bell. Maybe he moved here. But Abbott doesn't sound like a Yankee name."

"What's a Yankee name?"

"You know. Six times more consonants than vowels. Like Coach K from Duke. Hell, I can't even pronounce his name let alone spell it."

"Not like Roy Williams of Carolina."

Wakefield slapped the steering wheel. "Exactly. And Roy's from Asheville. He's one of us."

I punched in the number. "Well, whether Joey's a Yankee or not, I'm probably waking him up."

The line rang nearly ten times before a sleepy voice muttered, "Hello."

"Joey Abbott?"

"Yeah." He coughed and I heard smoker's phlegm rattle in his throat.

"This is Deputy Barry Clayton of the Laurel County Sheriff's Department."

"What's wrong?" A note of panic rose in his voice. A call from a deputy usually wasn't good news, especially for parents whose kids were driving or away at school.

"Nothing. Sorry to bother you, but I understand you were on duty at Glendale Forest last night."

"That's right."

"Did you notice anyone going out or coming in late?"

The line was silent a moment and then Abbott asked, "You mean a visitor?"

"Not necessarily. Could have been a resident."

"Sunday night's pretty quiet, especially after the Baptists finish services. I don't remember anything unusual."

"You sure? We had a complaint about a car knocking over some mailboxes on the county road near your entrance."

"No. The only late night driver was Mr. Cransford."

"Luther Cransford?"

"Yes. The man whose wife died. I was working dayside last Monday when the EMTs rushed through."

"When did you see him last night?"

"About three thirty."

"You sure?"

"Oh, yeah." Abbott laughed. "Between you and me and a fencepost, it's the time of the graveyard shift I have the most trouble staying awake. I was close to nodding off when that big Caddy of his came in with the high beams on. Liked to blind me."

"Had you seen him leave?"

"No."

"I'm not trying to get you in trouble, but could you have nodded off earlier and missed him?"

"I doubt it. I'd been on the phone with my brother."

"That late?"

"He lives in California."

"Did Luther Cransford seem to be driving all right?"

"Yeah. The car wasn't weaving or nothing. I figured he might have been visiting family or something. I gave him a friendly wave and thought no more about it." Abbott paused. "I guess you could check his car for damages."

"Well, under the circumstances I hate to trouble him. It's been a tough time. I figure he's been through enough. From your description it doesn't sound like he's our culprit."

"That's decent of you," Abbott said. "I saw the picture in the paper of him tusslin' with those Indians. The man deserves a little slack."

"Then let's keep this conversation between us. I wouldn't want him thinking you reported him."

"I didn't," he said with alarm.

"That's right. But people can get the wrong idea. Thanks for your help, Mr. Abbott." I disconnected, confident the guard wouldn't say anything unless we needed his testimony to press charges.

"Sounds like Luther lied to us," Wakefield said. "You want to go back and confront him?"

"No. Let's see what the ME has to say first. Did you note the name of the firm where Luther's son works?"

"Yes. Wilder and Hamilton."

"I want to check out when Darren Cransford came into work today. Do you think you can find a way to do that without raising suspicions?"

Wakefield thought a moment. "I could ask if he was there and say I was a friend who wanted to make sure he made it back to DC safely."

"Why wouldn't you have his cell number?"

"Good point. How about I'm offering condolences from the department?"

"Two days late?"

"Well, damn it, Barry. It's your idea. Why don't you call and say you're following up from the funeral home as part of your customer service?"

"What time is it?"

He looked at the clock on the dashboard. "Ten thirty. Why?"

"I want to remember when you had a good idea in case it never happens again."

Wakefield laughed. "Barry, working with you makes all my ideas sound good."

When I returned to Eurleen's grave, the lab techs had finished and were packing up their equipment and envelopes of soil samples. Panther's body had been removed. ME Howard Tuppler and Tommy Lee stood about ten yards down the slope in close conversation. The sheriff waved for me to join them.

"Everything OK?" he asked.

"Yes."

"Good. Fill me in later. Howard's got some preliminary findings you need to know."

The medical examiner caressed his goatee as he organized his thoughts.

"Just the highlights, Howard," Tommy Lee said. "The details can come in the written report."

Tuppler shrugged. "All right. Then here are the Cliff's Notes. Jimmy Panther was killed by a single bullet just behind the left ear. Probably a twenty-two, maybe a twenty-five. I expect the autopsy will find the slug as there is no exit wound. Bad part about a shot to the head with those lighter calibers is the bullet probably ricocheted inside the skull like a damn pinball machine."

My mind jumped forward. "With no exit wound, can you determine where he was shot?"

He nodded. "We're fairly certain he was killed at the grave. Blood on the ground was consistent with the wound and the flow pattern across his clothing. Traces of gunpowder and particle residue should have adhered to the dirt. I expect the lab tests will confirm their presence. I estimate the time of death between midnight and two this morning."

"Any sign of a struggle?" I asked.

Tuppler gave a quick glance at Tommy Lee and I knew I'd hit upon a key question.

"Yes and no," the medical examiner said. "There were no overt signs of a beating. No visible scratches or extensive bruising. But there were abrasions around both wrists."

"He was bound?"

"Yes. And he struggled to free himself. My guess is someone used PlastiCuffs and didn't care how tightly they were applied."

PlastiCuffs were lighter and cheaper than metal handcuffs, but could be easily overtightened if an arresting officer wasn't careful. They were disposable and eliminated the need for cleaning whereas metal cuffs could spread disease if not properly sanitized between uses. PlastiCuffs were not part of our standard gear at the Sheriff's Department, but I'd used them in Charlotte when we were dealing with mass demonstrations that could result in multiple arrests.

I turned back to the grave. "Did you find PlastiCuffs beside the body?"

"No," Tuppler said. "They must have been cut off and taken by the killer."

"Why?"

"I have no idea."

"I do," Tommy Lee said. "Panther was captured by his killer or killers somewhere else and brought to this site for his execution."

"OK," I agreed. "But that still doesn't explain why the cuffs are missing."

"It does if we're meant to think Panther drove here himself and was discovered at the grave. We should start pursuing that hypothesis until evidence or the good doctor here proves differently."

"You'll get top priority." With that promise, Tuppler left to join his techs.

"Let's walk a little farther," Tommy Lee said. "Bring me up to speed on Luther."

I recounted our visit and Luther's reactions that appeared to be both genuine shock at Panther's death and deceit as to his own activities.

"The guard's testimony doesn't help," Tommy Lee said. "And we don't know when Luther left his house."

"You think he lured Panther to the cemetery?"

Tommy Lee stopped walking. "I'll be damned if I know what to think. If Panther drove himself to Heaven's Gate Gardens and Luther ambushed him, why the PlastiCuffs? On the other hand, if Luther abducted him, someone else had to drive Panther's truck because Luther needed his car to return home." Tommy Lee sat on a marble bench close to the wooded edge of the cemetery. "I've been on my feet for nearly two hours. My knees aren't what they used to be."

"I hear after the mind, knees are the second thing to go."

"Smartass. At least I had a mind once. And I've still got enough sense to know we should back away from Luther for the moment. Check any friends close enough to have been accomplices. Hell, even the mayor, although I can't see Sammy Whitlock having the stomach for murder. Then we need to focus on the movements of Jimmy Panther."

"Have you contacted the Cherokee Police Department?"

"Yes. I gave them enough details so they could notify next of kin." Tommy Lee stood. "Let's get back to the department, get things working there, and then we'll head for the reservation." He scanned the headstones dotting the grassy hillside. "Our answers are with the living, not the dead."

As soon as we walked into the Sheriff's Department, Deputy Reece Hutchins came running across the bullpen to intercept Tommy Lee. "The mayor's been by twice looking for you."

"Did you tell him I was at a crime scene?"

"Yes. He knew about Panther. Luther called him."

"Figures." Tommy Lee stepped around Reece. "Let's talk in my office."

The sheriff flipped on his Mr. Coffee without bothering to check if either grounds or water were ready. Marge, our chief dispatcher, always prepped the machine when she beat Tommy Lee into the department. He plopped behind his desk and the old metal swivel chair squealed in protest as he leaned back. Reece and I sat in two chairs across from him.

Tommy Lee laced his fingers behind his head. "So, Sammy came running in here right after Luther called him?"

"No," Reece said. "Not the first time. He came in waving an envelope."

The chair squealed louder as Tommy Lee rocked forward. "What envelope?"

"One that came to his office last Friday. He was out because of Eurleen's death."

"All the owners," I said.

"What are you talking about?" Reece asked.

"What was in the envelope?" Tommy Lee asked.

"A broken feather and a note to stay away from Bell Ridge." Reece looked at me. "Owners? Did Luther and Archie get envelopes?"

"Yes," I said. "None signed and no return address."

"Does the mayor still have his?" Tommy Lee asked Reece.

"No, I logged it into the evidence room."

Tommy Lee turned to me. "What about Luther's?"

"I've got it as well as Archie's."

"Good," Tommy Lee said. "Give them to Reece."

"You want me to log them in?" Reece asked.

"Yes. Then I want you to take them to the FBI field office in Asheville."

Reece's eyes expanded to the size of baseballs. "The FBI?"

"Yeah. They're going to be involved sooner or later. We have a dead Cherokee who might have been abducted from the reservation. If it's kidnapping and murder, we're looking at crimes across lines of sovereignty beyond simple state boundaries. I want to be preemptive in establishing our lead role. We have the murder, but the FBI has the best lab resources in the world. I'll call Special Agent Lindsay Boyce to let her know you're coming."

Reece nodded vigorously. An assignment with the FBI ranked at the top of his bucket list. I saw not only the wisdom of letting Reece be a glorified errand boy, but also the advantage of contacting Lindsay Boyce. She was Tommy Lee's niece and she idolized her uncle. She'd watch his back if the feds tried to throw their weight around.

"How about Luther's children?" Tommy Lee asked.

"I'm checking on Darren. Wakefield's tracking Sandra."

"I've heard Luther brag on both of them," Reece said. "You'd think the boy was the kingpin of Washington DC and his sister's some big executive in an Atlanta dental equipment company."

Tommy Lee waved us away. "Let's get to work, gentlemen."

Reece hesitated. "Will you call the mayor?"

"Yes," Tommy Lee said. "Why'd he come back the second time?"

"Because Luther called him." Reece looked at me and I saw a rare expression of sympathy. "He said Luther complained that Barry had harassed him about his whereabouts last night."

Tommy Lee smiled. "If Luther thinks Barry harassed him, he'll love it when I knock on his door."

I swung by Deputy Wakefield's desk on my way to my own. "Any luck with Luther's daughter?"

He looked up from his computer screen. "Yeah. Sandra works for a company called G. A. Bridges in Atlanta. I called their headquarters and they said she was in a sales meeting. It started at eight and goes through lunch. That matches what Luther said, so I didn't leave a message." He glanced back at the monitor. "Now I'm checking with neighboring sheriff and police departments in case Luther was involved in any traffic stops."

"Good. I'll put on my best funeral director voice for my call to Darren's firm."

Wilder and Hamilton's website listed key staff and contact numbers. Darren Cransford's name wasn't one of them, but Luther had said he was a junior member. I called the general number.

"Wilder and Hamilton." The woman's voice was pleasant and, more importantly, she was alive. Not the recorded start of a list of impenetrable menu options to navigate before speaking with a human being.

"Good morning. I'd like to speak with Darren Cransford, please."

For a few seconds, the line went silent. "Did Mr. Cransford handle your account?"

The "did" leaped out of the sentence. I rethought my play.

"Yes. Has Darren been transferred elsewhere?"

"I'm sorry. Mr. Cransford is no longer with the firm. If you'll give me the name of your company, I'll connect you with someone who can help you."

I hung up.

Chapter Six

There is no easy way to get to Cherokee, North Carolina. The roads leading in and out of the reservation, or Qualla Boundary as it's officially known, frequently become clogged with tourist traffic. The Boundary borders multiple counties and is gateway to the Great Smoky Mountains National Park, the most visited in the entire fifty-eight-park system. I read that more than nine million people visit the Smoky Mountains each year, over twice the number that view the runner-up, a little national park called the Grand Canyon.

But on a Monday in late September, the roads were clear as Tommy Lee drove the patrol car into the town of Cherokee. The approach was itself a journey back in time. The ramshackle buildings lining the street sported signs hawking tee shirts, moccasins, inflatable rafts and tubes for the river, Indian trinkets, and local gemstones. Mom-and-pop motels were scattered among the national chains.

"I haven't been here since I was a kid and it looks the same," I said. "Like Myrtle Beach without the ocean."

Tommy Lee braked for a stoplight and a herd of Harleys crossed the intersection in front of us.

"But with the same bikers," I added.

"There's a difference or two," Tommy Lee said. "I'm confident that as a trained detective you'll notice them."

He turned right and within a few blocks I saw twin towers rising above the mishmash of shops and gas stations. Behind them lay a complex of glass, stone, and brick that appeared to cover acres. Beside an entrance road, the sign HARRAH'S CHEROKEE CASINO & HOTEL rose several stories above the ground. Cars and buses lined up turning into the parking lot.

"Man," I said, "this is a far cry from tribal bingo."

"Las Vegas comes to the Smokies."

Tommy Lee turned right again and I leaned forward to catch a closer glimpse of the posh casino. "You ever been inside?"

"No. I have enough trouble holding onto what little money I do have."

"Do they have live games or just video?"

"They've got the works: blackjack, craps, roulette, poker. But I doubt if you'll find James Bond in a tuxedo at the baccarat table. Here Double O Seven going undercover would mean shorts and flip-flops."

We left the casino behind and drove into the center of town. On the right, I saw Oconaluftee Islands Park, a strip of land in the Oconaluftee River reachable by a wooden footbridge from the bank. Families with children too young to attend school were wading in the shallow current. A few picnickers enjoyed late lunches at scattered tables. I imagined that in the summer the park would be swarming with tourists both in and out of the water.

About a hundred yards farther, a large oval sign read "Museum of the Cherokee Indian." Behind it a well-designed building conveyed a sense of respect for the culture exhibited within its walls.

"Impressive," I said. "I don't remember this being here when I was a kid."

"It wasn't," Tommy Lee said. "The heritage of the tribe has benefited from the influx of casino money. And increased tourism means increased opportunities to tell the real Cherokee story, not just sell rubber tomahawks and cheap jewelry." He turned left and then made a U-turn in the museum's parking lot. "I got talking and missed the road to the police station."

A mammoth carving of an Indian head bordered the entrance to the museum. Imagine a tall totem pole but with only one image, a long rugged face with a single feather pointing from a headband to the sky. Tears were permanently sculpted in the corner of the eyes, never to roll any farther down the high cheekbones.

"That's quite a statue," I said.

"Sequoyah," Tommy Lee said.

"The tree?"

He laughed. "Tree and subject. The carving was made on a single redwood log that was a gift from the Georgia-Pacific Company. That's Sequoia the wood. Sequoyah the man was the Cherokee who invented the alphabet for their language so they could match the writing advantage of the European settlers."

"Why not just learn English?"

"Because the Cherokee are a proud people and losing their language would have killed their culture. Sequoyah is a heroic figure, a genius really, and they claim he's the only individual in known history to single-handedly create a written language."

"I see the word *Indian* everywhere. I thought that was politically incorrect."

Tommy Lee turned onto the main road and backtracked a block. "There's pushback on the label Native American. A feeling that once again they're being lumped into a category created by others and diluting their unique identity."

"So, if I try to be politically correct I'll offend them?"

"Barry, I'm confident you'll find a way to be offensive no matter what you say."

If the casino revenues were pouring money into the tribe, the flow was bypassing the facilities of the police department. The small single-story building sat on a ridge above the river and town. The metal front door could have used a fresh coat of paint, but impressing visitors wasn't its purpose. Restricting access seemed to be the primary function.

A sign instructed us to press the intercom button to announce our intentions. One didn't just walk into the station.

"May I help you?" A woman's voice vibrated through a tinny speaker.

"Sheriff Tommy Lee Wadkins and Deputy Barry Clayton to see Detective Sergeant Hector Romero."

"Romero?" I whispered.

"Marriage on and off the reservation has created the same variety of surnames you'll find in any American community. I've worked with Hector before. He's a good man."

The door buzzed and Tommy Lee yanked it open.

We entered a short hall that resembled an airlock. On the left, a woman sat behind a glass partition that looked more like a movie ticket booth than a receptionist's office. A clipboard with a sign-in sheet lay on a ledge. A coiled tether insured no one abducted the attached ballpoint pen.

"Write your name and the time, please," the woman said. "I'll let him know you're here."

Tommy Lee signed for both of us while the receptionist picked up the phone and spoke to someone.

"He'll be out in a moment," she announced. "Make yourselves comfortable."

Making ourselves comfortable meant sitting in the two battleship-gray steel chairs pushed against the far wall of the cramped space. Neither Tommy Lee nor I took advantage of such luxury.

We couldn't have waited more than a minute before the inner door opened only to be filled by a man of roughly the same size and proportions. Jet black hair topped a square head. His chest was long and broad, adding more to his height than his legs, which were each as thick as my waist. If a black bear were ever transformed into a human, the end result stood in front of us.

Bright white teeth flashed in the wide bronze face. "Well, if it isn't Rooster Cogburn and his one-man posse."

My mind jumped to the original film, *True Grit*, and John Wayne playing the cantankerous one-eyed U.S. marshal. The comparison held a degree of truth.

"That's why I feel so at home in Indian country," Tommy Lee said. He stepped forward and shook the Cherokee's hand. Both men turned to me. "This is my deputy and lead investigator,

Barry Clayton. Barry, meet Hector Romero, the modern edition of Sequoyah."

Romero laughed as his hand swallowed mine. "He's kissing up to me, which means the poor Indian is gonna get screwed again."

"Save it," Tommy Lee said. "You know the whole reason for my being here is to make you look good."

"Rooster, with a face like yours, you make everybody look good." He slapped Tommy Lee on the back. "Come to my office and we'll sort things out."

We followed him down a narrow hallway with doors on either side. This wasn't a bullpen layout like our department, but a warren of small offices. Several policemen passed in the opposite direction and Hector had to turn sideways before they could walk by.

At the far end, he entered a room not much bigger than a barn stall. The decor of battleship-gray was carried out by a steel desk, a swivel chair, and two mates to the ones we'd been offered in the waiting area. Tommy Lee and I sat without an invitation.

Hector closed the door and squeezed past us to drop his bulk behind his desk. "So, how did Jimmy Panther manage to get himself shot in your county?"

"Probably by managing to be abducted from the reservation," Tommy Lee said.

The Cherokee rocked forward in his chair. "What? This isn't confined to white man's land?"

White man's land? Indian country? Maybe I was in a John Wayne movie after all.

"We don't know for certain," Tommy Lee said. "Preliminary indications at the scene suggest Panther was bound with Plasti-Cuffs, but they had been removed from his body. His truck was there. If he were caught and cuffed on site, why bother to cut him free either before or after shooting him?"

"To make it look like he drove there," Romero said.

Tommy Lee gave an appreciative nod. "That's what I think."

Romero smacked his palm on his desk. "Damn. And here I

thought you were making a courtesy call to give me information I could share with the family."

"Did you talk to them this morning?" Tommy Lee asked.

"Yep. Soon as we got the word." He looked at me. "Well, if the homicide occurred in the cemetery, then you're still the lead investigator."

"Yes," I said. "The evidence is definitive. Panther died on Eurleen's grave."

Romero's dark eyebrows merged together. "Who?"

"The woman whose burial Panther disrupted."

"Better give me the whole story."

I briefed him on everything that transpired from the unearthing of the Cherokee remains to the discovery of Panther's body. I stopped short of telling him about my interview with Luther Cransford or that his son was no longer employed where Luther said he was.

"What about suspects?" Romero asked, pushing into the area I'd avoided.

Tommy Lee jumped in. "We're investigating those angered by the demonstration. But I'm bothered by where Panther was shot. If he was in the cemetery already, then did someone lure him there?"

Romero rubbed his square jaw while he thought a moment. "Maybe he was and then bound until someone else arrived. Someone who wanted to witness the execution or even pull the trigger."

The Cherokee raised an interesting possibility that undercut our abduction premise.

But, as soon as he voiced it, he waved his hand in dismissal. "As much as I'd like to think otherwise, the abduction fits better."

"How?" Tommy Lee asked.

"Jimmy's family was surprised he would go into the cemetery at night. Any cemetery where there had been recent burials."

"Was he superstitious?" I asked.

"Inasmuch as one person's spiritual beliefs might be viewed as superstitions by another. His grandmother said Jimmy had become more than a preserver of a bygone culture. She said he'd adopted the old ways, and that one of them was the belief that souls might linger for a time. Night held too much of the unseen, both in this world and the world of the spirits."

"So, he especially wouldn't have gone to the grave of a woman who had died within the past week," Tommy Lee said.

"That's the way I see it," Romero agreed. "If you're pursuing this abduction possibility, have you brought in the FBI and state police?"

"Not officially," Tommy Lee said. "I wanted to speak to you first."

"Not officially? How do you do something unofficially with the FBI?"

Tommy Lee laughed. "My niece heads the office in Asheville. Lindsay Boyce."

"Get out of here. Lindsay's your niece? Finally someone with brains in your bloodline."

"I know. Hard to believe. She said she'll come into the case when she's needed."

"And in the meantime?" Romero asked.

Tommy Lee looked to me. The case was my case.

"I'd like to retrace Panther's movements yesterday," I said. "He might have gone to the cemetery before dark."

"Sure," Romero said. "But he ate supper with his grandmother and sister and didn't leave for home till nearly nine. It would have been after dark even if he drove straight to the cemetery."

"Then his grandmother and sister might have been the last to see him alive. Do you think they're up to speaking with me?"

"They will be, if I go with you." Hector Romero rose from his chair and grabbed his duty belt from a hook on the wall behind him. "The family will probably have kinfolk and friends around. I'll go in first and tell them we need to speak in private. People will understand. They want us to find out what happened. But we'll take my car. No sense broadcasting your presence."

"Would they be resentful?" I asked.

"No. But you have to understand we Cherokee are a big family, and we can be tight-lipped when it comes to outsiders.

Jimmy's grandmother and sister might suggest others we should talk to, and I don't want them clamming up if they think you're poking into their business without my blessing."

"You know what we need to know," Tommy Lee said. "We'll play it however you think best."

"Good. I'm not saying they won't be cooperative, but we could be peeling an onion and uncovering layers of this story we don't even know exist."

I stood. "You mean Jimmy Panther had enemies other than those he might have made at the burial protest?"

Hector Romero's face tightened. "Jimmy was an extremist who saw the Cherokee culture as being under attack from within and without. He came down hard against development and any perceived violation of Cherokee heritage. In other words, Jimmy was an obstacle and an obstruction to the powerful. He and a growing number of followers stood on one side. Money, and lots of it, stood on the other. You tell me. Do you know a better way to make enemies?"

Chapter Seven

Detective Sergeant Hector Romero drove his patrol car down a narrow gravel road bordering a bold stream. We were heading into one of the coves of the Great Smoky Mountains so sheltered that it only emerged from shadows a few hours a day when the sun climbed high enough to clear the ridges.

I'd grown up in the Appalachians, but the Smokies were a range unto themselves. The mountains were squeezed together like deep wrinkles on a prune. Botanists claimed the diversity of plants was unequaled by any other site of temperate climate in the world. With elevations ranging from under a thousand feet to over six thousand six hundred, the latitude equivalent was like driving from Georgia to Canada.

The Great Smokies are among the oldest mountains in the world, and during the Ice Age became the refuge of wildlife escaping the glaciers. They are a zoologist's dream.

They also separate humans into enclaves of hollers and coves—isolated from one another. The farther we followed the road, the fewer the mailboxes along the shoulder.

"Does Panther's grandmother live in the national park?" I asked. We had to be getting close to the edge of the Cherokee Qualla Boundary.

"No," Romero said. "But her farm's adjacent to it."

"Farm?" I looked at the steep ridges. "She must plow using a mule with short legs on one side."

Romero laughed. "She's on in-between land. A bowl that's neither reservation nor national park. Land she actually owns and isn't part of the Cherokee's federal trust."

As he spoke, the stream on our right branched away and the narrow wedge of flat land between the ridges widened into a small valley. The scruffy vegetation became green pasture and, behind barbed wire, several cows stared at us as they chewed their cud.

"What's the grandmother's name?" I asked.

"Emma Byrd," Romero said. "That's Byrd with a *y*. She's Jimmy's maternal grandmother. Jimmy's mother died about ten years ago of breast cancer. His father deserted the family shortly after Jimmy's sister Skye was born, a good twenty years ago. Emma's pretty much raised both of them."

The farmhouse sat on a shelf of land above the flood zone of the mountain stream. The gentlest slope of the surrounding ridge was behind the weathered structure, providing protection against excessive runoff during a torrential downpour.

The gravel road stopped at the base, leaving the final approach as a rutted dirt lane that rose to the front yard. There was no garage or discernible driveway. Several vehicles were parked haphazardly near the sagging porch.

Romero swung his patrol car around the right side where a rusted heating oil tank hugged a paint-chipped wall. He rolled down the windows before killing the engine. "Wait here," he said.

The Cherokee left us, Tommy Lee in the front passenger seat and me behind the partition separating prisoners and officers. Instead of heading toward the porch, Romero lumbered to the rear and climbed makeshift cinder block steps to the back door.

"Why's he doing that?" I asked.

"Because he's smart. Friends are bringing in food so one or two people will be coming in and out of the kitchen. Hector will ask someone to let the grandmother know he's there without having to make a grand entrance. Then, together, they can decide how and where to answer our questions."

I turned in the backseat for a better view of the vehicles in the yard. I expected Romero might ask visitors to leave, but after five minutes, no one had emerged from the house.

Tommy Lee opened his door. "There he is. Let's go."

Through the front windshield, I saw Romero help an elderly woman down the cinder block steps from the back door. She was thin as a cat-o-nine-tails reed with flowing white hair that reached her waist. Her brown shapeless dress stopped a few inches above her tan moccasins. Romero summoned us with a wave of his broad hand.

"How do you want to play this?" I asked Tommy Lee.

"Let Hector set it up. Then just ask your questions and go with the flow. She's lost her grandson, and you've talked to more grieving families than Hector and me combined."

As we neared, the Cherokee woman cocked her head and her dark eyes scrutinized us.

Romero cleared his throat. "Emma, this is Sheriff Wadkins and his investigating officer, Deputy Barry Clayton. They're doing everything they can to find who killed Jimmy."

"We're very sorry, Miss Byrd," Tommy Lee said. "And we appreciate any help you can give us."

"Let's walk." Her words came out as a whisper on a single breath. Without waiting for us to follow, she started up the slope away from the farmhouse.

Romero looked at us and shrugged. He fell in step behind her.

We entered the woods on a well-worn path that arced to the right in a gradual ascent above the stream. We hiked in silence, like one of Tommy Lee's Vietnam patrols, with the war veteran bringing up the rear. After a quarter mile or so, the trail leveled onto a natural terrace created by the underlying rock formation. Two dwellings perched near the edge. One was a single-story rectangle with bark-covered walls and a thatched roof that extended about six feet beyond the front to form a porch. The second was a conical structure of clay that looked more like a beehive than a house.

Emma Byrd stopped in front of them.

"Jimmy lived here?" Romero asked.

"Yes," the old woman replied. She pointed with a slender hand to the more traditional building. "Here when it's warm." She gestured to the circular one. "And in the asi when it's cold."

Asi. I wasn't familiar with the term and made a mental note to remember it.

"Come. We can sit in the shade." Emma Byrd walked to a split-log bench that ran along the front wall to the right of the door. Two plastic chairs faced it. She and Romero sat on the bench. Tommy Lee and I took the chairs.

"This is good," she said. "Better to talk about Jimmy here than in my house."

"I agree," Romero said. "May my friends ask you some questions?"

Her thin lips formed a wry smile. "Isn't that why we climbed here?"

Romero nodded, and then turned to me.

I leaned forward, striving to show sincerity without escalating the encounter into an interrogation. "We're trying to retrace Jimmy's activities yesterday. See if there was anything unusual that might explain what brought him to the cemetery."

"Nothing would have brought him to that cemetery." Emma Byrd looked at Romero. "Not at night."

"Did you see him yesterday?" I asked.

"Twice. Breakfast and dinner." She bit her lower lip in an attempt to stave off her rising grief. She gazed down the trail. "Jimmy could smell my cooking no matter which way the wind blew."

"Did he seem particularly troubled at either meal?"

"Troubled? You mean was Jimmy upset?"

"Yes. Or behaving differently."

The old woman stared up at the porch's roof. Her fingers drummed against the bench. Romero, Tommy Lee, and I sat waiting, listening to the arrhythmic tapping. Two minutes passed.

"He was happy." She whispered the words to the air above me.

"Happy?"

Her dark eyes focused on me. "Yes. At breakfast and supper."

"And normally he was unhappy?"

She shook her head and the long white hair rippled like a windblown cape. "Happy in the sense of contented. Unhappy in the sense of agitated, obsessed with his fight against termination."

"Preservation, not termination," I said.

Emma Byrd glanced at Romero. "Did he hear that from you?"

The policeman shook his head.

"Jimmy spoke the words to me," Tommy Lee said. "At the site of the remains we unearthed in Laurel County."

"And when he blocked Eurleen Cransford's funeral procession," I added. "What's it mean?"

Emma's lips tightened as if holding back a flood of words. Then, in a even cadence, she said, "Kill the Indian and save the man." She looked at Romero and tears trickled along the crevices of her cheeks. "But they killed the Indian and the man."

Romero put his arm around the old woman and took a deep breath. "It's OK, Miss Emma. I'll explain it." He turned to Tommy Lee and me. "Most in the white world don't know termination was the code word for the government's policy of driving out all vestiges of Indian heritage. The goal was forced assimilation and the abolishment of reservations. In short, civilize the native people that white society viewed as savages.

"Schools were built where Indian children were forbidden to speak their native tongue or practice traditional customs. In a generation or two, the Indian within would be eradicated, and what was left would be an individual swallowed up in mainstream culture."

"Kill the Indian and save the man," I repeated. "I thought that was from the late 1800s."

"It was," Romero said. "But the policy officially flourished from the 1940s through the 1960s when the government dissolved recognition of numerous tribes and gave states the responsibility to govern the former reservation lands."

"Were the Cherokee terminated?" I asked.

"No. Terminations were done on a tribe-by-tribe basis and had to move through Congress and court challenges. A backlash built, the American Indian Movement coalesced around the common interests, and the documented effects of termination on education and health care proved devastating, the exact opposite of what was promised."

"The termination policy was terminated," I said.

Romero pulled his arm away from Emma, and she wiped her eyes on her sleeve.

"Yes," Romero said. "Thanks to Richard Nixon."

"Tricky Dick?" Tommy Lee scowled. "What was in it for him?"

Romero shrugged. "I guess he had enough Vietnam War protesters on his hands without adding Indians to the list. And the states didn't want responsibility for the tribes, especially with no federal funds. So, Nixon changed the policy from termination to self-determination."

The history lesson still didn't give me the answer to my question. "Then why would Jimmy say preservation?"

Emma Byrd pointed a finger at me. "Because self-determination is leading us to our self-termination. Jimmy fought not only against forces without but also forces within. Whether it was your cemetery or a tribal council meeting, Jimmy made no distinction. He saw no shades of gray when it came to preserving and protecting the spiritual core of the Cherokee people."

"And yet, yesterday, he was happy," I said. "Contented. Why?"

"I don't know," Emma Byrd said. "And if I'd asked, the very question could have broken his mood. It was enough that he was happy."

And less than twelve hours later, he was dead. I thought about the information Romero shared at the police station. "Miss Byrd, we understand that your grandson went home after eating supper with you."

"Yes. He left a little before nine. Skye stayed longer."

"Your granddaughter, Jimmy's sister?"

"Yes."

"Anyone else?"

"No. Sometimes Eddie Wolfe comes with Skye. He's her boyfriend, but last night he was working second shift."

"Where?"

"Some box factory near Murphy."

"That would be about forty-five minutes away," Romero said.

"OK," I said. "Miss Byrd, it looks like there's no road up here. Where did Jimmy keep his truck?"

"Down at my house. He parked it off to the side."

"And he didn't drive off after supper?"

She shook her head. "I saw his flashlight from the kitchen window. He was going up the trail."

"Did you hear his truck start later that night?"

"No, sir."

I wondered how good was the old woman's hearing. I turned away from her and looked down the trail. "Would you have?" I asked softly.

She laughed, and I knew she'd seen through my little test.

"Yes. Unless he rolled off before turning on the engine."

"Rolled off?"

"My house is up on a hill. He parks on the slope so the truck can coast down to the gravel road. Then the sound is masked by the stream."

"Why does he do that?"

"Jimmy knows—" Her breath caught for an instant. "Jimmy knew I'm a light sleeper. He always rolled off after ten."

"And when he came home?"

"He'd leave the truck at the bottom of the hill. I'm an early riser so I'd usually see it the next morning. Only this morning it wasn't there."

"Emmama!" The cry came from the trail.

I turned in my chair and saw a young woman bounding up the path like a deer. When she drew closer, I recognized her as the woman who came with Jimmy and the other man the morning Howard Tuppler examined the Cherokee remains. She stopped at the corner post of the porch roof, holding onto the bark-covered pole for support while she caught her breath.

Emma stood. "What is it, child?"

"They said Hector Romero turned you over to some off-reservation policemen." She stepped forward, pointing her finger at the Cherokee detective. "What'd you do? Wait till you saw me leave and then sneak up the holler?"

Romero got to his feet. "Calm down, Skye. These men are investigating Jimmy's death."

The woman looked at Tommy Lee and me. "The same men who warned Jimmy off that cemetery? The foxes are investigating the henhouse."

Tommy Lee and I rose together. The scar on his cheek twitched as his jaw tensed.

"We informed you and your brother of the law," he said. "We protected those remains. Now we're exercising the same efforts to find who killed your brother."

Emma Byrd stepped in front of her granddaughter. "I asked them to come up here. It's where I want to talk about Jimmy."

Skye Panther's stony face crumbled. She reached out, pulled her grandmother to her, and then pressed her face against the old woman's thin neck. The muffled sobs pushed us back and we gave them space.

For what must have been five minutes, Emma comforted her granddaughter. *Emmama*. It dawned on me the name was a child's contraction of Emma and mama. The woman must have been more mother than grandmother to Jimmy and Skye.

When the two did break apart, Emma clutched the young woman's hand. "We need to help them. Otherwise we're helping whoever murdered Jimmy."

Skye's lower lip trembled, but she nodded. She pulled loose and wiped the tears from her cheeks.

Emma walked to the front corner of the makeshift house where a rock about the size of a cantaloupe rested next to the wall. She flipped it over and retrieved a rusty key. "I'll bring out another chair."

"I'll get it," chorused three male voices.

"All of you might as well come in," Emma said. "I reckon you need to see where Jimmy lived. I haven't been inside since we got the news. So many people have been by."

With Skye close behind her, Emma lifted the padlock and inserted the key. The plank door squealed on dry hinges and we followed her inside. The room was dimly lit by only the open door and four small square windows, one on each wall. The floor was packed clay. Although Jimmy had built his own shelter, his handcraft didn't extend to the interior furnishings.

A few lawn chairs were scattered around a circular metal table. Eight lanterns hung from wrought-iron arms spaced two to a wall. A ninth lantern sat on a low stool positioned beside an army cot in the back right corner. A patchwork quilt was neatly folded at its foot, and a few magazines and books were visible on a tarp beneath it.

In the other rear corner was a waist-high, dingy metal cabinet that could have been salvaged from some kitchen in the 1950s. It must have held dry goods and other supplies. A double-burner Coleman stove sat on top.

There was no sink or bathroom. I figured Jimmy had an outhouse about fifty feet in the rear and that he brought his drinking water up from the stream.

Pine boards and cinder blocks created shelves that reached the sill of the windows in each side wall. One section held folded clothes, another contained an assortment of hand tools like screwdrivers, hammers, and a bucksaw. One lay empty, surplus shelves offering space in a room of no more than three hundred square feet.

Skye stumbled in front of me, as if the dirt floor had an unseen hole. I caught her arm, but she wrenched it away.

"Emmama! They're gone." She staggered toward the empty shelves and ran both hands over the smooth wood of the top one. "Someone stole Jimmy's collection." She wheeled around to face Detective Sergeant Romero. "My brother's Cherokee artifacts were right there. You find who stole them and you'll find his murderer."

Chapter Eight

"Don't touch anything." Detective Sergeant Romero gently moved Skye away from the empty shelves. "There might be fingerprints. We should all go outside."

Tommy Lee and I exchanged a glance. The robbery was clearly beyond our jurisdiction, but according to Romero we were also off the reservation.

The Cherokee policeman ushered the women through the door and gestured for them to sit.

He turned to Tommy Lee. "Technically, we're in Swain County. I should call Sheriff Lott, but then we'll potentially have five agencies involved. You, me, the state boys, the FBI, and Swain County. Might as well invite the CIA and Homeland Security."

"No," Emma Byrd insisted. "No more outsiders. You and these gentlemen are all I want to deal with."

I looked to Tommy Lee. He was the one to speak for our department.

"Why don't we see if there are any signs of a break-in," he said. "Then we'll know for sure we're dealing with a robbery."

"Of course we're dealing with a robbery," Skye snapped. "Jimmy's been collecting those artifacts since he was a kid. He wouldn't have given them away."

"Let Detective Romero and me do our check," Tommy Lee said. "Then we'll talk about the next step. Barry will wait with you."

Tommy Lee and Romero disappeared around the corner of the building. I sat in one of the plastic chairs, not sure why I'd been left to babysit.

"Emmama, was anybody up here yesterday?" Skye asked.

I understood Tommy Lee's wisdom. I was left to listen, to make sure a story wasn't concocted if the women had something to hide.

"Not unless they came while we were at church. I took some clean clothes up for Jimmy that morning. Surely I would have noticed the empty shelves."

"Did Jimmy go to church?" I asked.

"Jimmy wasn't a churchgoer," Emma said. "But he was spiritual in the Cherokee way. He was still here when we left. Skye was kind enough to drive me."

"Was he here when you returned?"

"No. His truck was gone. I didn't see him till supper."

"Do you know where your brother went?" I asked Skye.

"No. He just told us he had business to tend to."

"For his job?"

"Probably. There was a game yesterday afternoon."

"Game?"

"Ball-play."

She must have read the blank expression on my face. "Indian ball."

"Oh, like lacrosse," I said.

Skye scowled. "Yeah, just like preppy, intercollegiate lacrosse."

Emma took pity on my ignorance. "Ball-play was a very important part of Cherokee life, involving the honor of the entire town. Preparations for a game lasted for days and were highly ritualistic."

"Jimmy was playing?"

"He would have loved to." Emma smiled. "In the old way. No, it was for the youth only. Jimmy worked at the Cherokee Boys Club. It's an integral part of the school system and not just for boys. But, that's its heritage and no one feels inclined to change the name. Jimmy drove an activity bus during the week. He also taught youth classes on Cherokee life and trained students to work at Oconaluftee Village."

I knew Oconaluftee Village was the cultural attraction that created an authentic and populated Cherokee town from the era of when white settlers first arrived. Living history, like Williamsburg. "And so ball-play was one of the things he taught?"

"Yes," Emma said. "Not just how to play, but also the rituals involved."

"And how to craft the sticks and the balls," Skye added. She looked at me with less hostility. "Jimmy's prized possession was a ball-play stick that's been in our family for nearly two hundred years." She glanced at the closed door. "It was part of his collection."

"You should itemize what you remember," I said. "We can put out a notice to museum dealers and other potential buyers."

Emma patted her granddaughter's leg. "We can do that. What I don't understand is if somebody robbed Jimmy here, how did he wind up in the cemetery?"

"I don't know, Miss Byrd. Maybe after he was killed, the perpetrators knew his house would be vulnerable. But at this point, we can only speculate. It's premature to draw conclusions."

Tommy Lee and Romero emerged from the side of the house.

"We checked all the windows," the detective said.

"Were they locked?" I asked.

"Yes. No broken glass, no marks of a crowbar." Romero walked to the front door and eyed the padlock and clasp. He pulled a handkerchief from his back pocket and tilted the lock up to see the key slot. "No scratches. This wasn't picked. Who knew about the key under the rock?"

"Anybody who came up here with Jimmy," Emma said. "He never carried the key. He would have opened the lock in front of whoever was with him."

Romero glanced at Tommy Lee and shook his head. The suspect pool was hopelessly large.

"Why bother with a lock at all?" I asked.

"We've had hikers wander onto the property," Emma said. "And fly fishermen sometimes come downstream from the national forest. The lock discourages people from thinking this is some kind of ranger outpost."

"And you heard no vehicle during the night?" I asked.

"No," Emma said. "And I didn't particularly sleep well."

I turned to Skye. "What time did you leave last night?"

"Around ten."

"You didn't see any vehicle on the way out?"

"No. Just those parked along the roadside by the houses. No one between here and the nearest neighbor."

"And you went straight home?"

She flushed. "Yes, of course."

Skye was lying and I had a good idea why. Some questions could wait till we weren't in front of her grandmother.

"Who is the man who came with you and your brother that first day at the cemetery?"

"Eddie. Eddie Wolfe. He's a friend to both of us."

"Your grandmother said he's your boyfriend."

She shot her grandmother a questioning look. "Yeah. It's no secret."

I wasn't certain but I estimated Skye to be in her early twenties and from the driver's license in Jimmy Panther's wallet, I knew he'd been twenty-nine. Sometimes boyfriends and big brothers don't get along.

"Eddie had to work last night?" I asked.

"Yes. Second shift."

"On a Sunday?"

"He works at Cherokee Boxes. Every three months they pull apart the corrugating machines for cleaning and maintenance. It happens over the weekend so as not to disrupt production."

"Did you see him when he got off?"

"Oh, God, no. He's a mess of ink and grease."

"You talk to him?"

Skye stiffened. "Why are you so interested in Eddie?"

"He was Jimmy's friend. Maybe he heard from Jimmy before going into work."

"Eddie was with me in the afternoon. We were hanging out at his place. He left for work a little before three."

"Have you seen him today?"

"Yes. He came by as soon as he heard about Jimmy." She looked at her grandmother. "He wanted to stay but Emmama said there was no sense in him missing work."

Emma nodded in agreement. "Nothing he could do."

I looked up at Romero. "Would you set up a time for me to talk to him?"

"Yeah. Any angle in particular?"

"I want to know why Jimmy was happy."

"Happy?" Skye asked.

"Your grandmother said he seemed more content than usual. Do you agree?"

Skye thought about the question. "I don't know. I guess so. He was no longer upset about the cemetery, if that's what you mean. He thought he'd made his point, and when that man attacked him, he received a lot of sympathy both inside and outside."

I stood. "My thanks to both of you. And I'm very sorry we're meeting under these conditions." I helped Emma up from the bench.

Romero stepped back to clear the way. "I'd like to dust for prints on the shelves. No need for y'all to wait here. I know you've got company to tend to. I'll get my kit from the car." He took Emma by the arm and started down the trail.

I stepped in front of Skye, blocking her path. "One word in private, please." I nodded for Tommy Lee to go on.

Skye took a step back, startled by my action.

"I want to apologize. I shouldn't have asked you about your personal relationships in front of your grandmother."

"She knows Eddie and I go out."

"I understand. It's just when I asked if you went straight home last night, you hesitated. I thought maybe you stopped someplace else. Someplace you didn't want to mention."

Skye's eyes narrowed. "What I do is my business."

"What I do is everything I can to find who murdered your brother. And when someone's not being honest with me, I ask why. Nothing is too trivial or too personal."

She exhaled slowly and looked over my shoulder. I turned to see Emma, Romero, and Tommy Lee disappear into the woods.

"All right," she said. "I swung by Eddie's first."

"I thought he was working."

"Sometimes the maintenance weekend finishes early. Eddie's trailer's in a dead zone for cell coverage, and he keeps his phone in a locker when he's on the job. When he didn't answer, he could have been either place. But he wasn't home."

"So you left?"

"I have a key. I waited about an hour and then went straight to my apartment. When Eddie saw me today, he said they didn't clock out till midnight."

I stepped aside and we started walking together.

"Any particular reason you went by so late?" I asked.

"To apologize. We had a silly argument yesterday afternoon."

"Anything to do with Jimmy?"

"Everything to do with Jimmy. Eddie was worried the demonstration at the cemetery had backfired. The man was burying his wife. I said Jimmy wasn't afraid to put it all on the line. Eddie took it as a criticism. That he was less committed to our people."

"And you wanted to apologize for that accusation?"

She stopped at the edge of the woods. "No. Because I never made that accusation. I wanted to tell him he might have been right about the cemetery. It was too much."

Her candor surprised me. Perhaps because I'd been on the other side of that demonstration, she was saying what she thought I wanted to hear.

"What changed your mind?"

"Jimmy. Emmama told you he was happy. I saw something else last night. Smugness. I was afraid the confrontation on Saturday had gone too well and to his head. He called for a new beginning and new tougher tactics. He would reveal them when the time was right. The word 'we' vanished from his vocabulary, and I wanted to talk to Eddie about it."

"At supper last night, Jimmy didn't say where he was going afterwards?"

"No. He only made his little speech to me while Emmama was in the kitchen. Other than that, we had a very pleasant evening. I understand why Emmama thought he was happy."

I ran out of questions. Nothing Skye said seemed to offer any real leads.

"Thank you," I said. "If you think of anything else, please call me."

"Have you got a card?"

I pulled out my wallet and saw all I had were Clayton and Clayton business cards. I handed her one. "This is my cell."

She glanced at it, and then read it more closely. "The funeral home. How fitting."

Tommy Lee and I returned to Gainesboro a little after six. I checked for any messages that might have come through the department, but the only note was from the dispatcher saying State Senator Mack Collins would like to speak with me. The number wasn't a Raleigh area code, and so I figured it was his cell. I also figured he could wait until tomorrow.

I had three priorities for the case: follow up on why Darren Cransford no longer worked where his father said he worked, and therefore couldn't have been urgently returning to his job; push for the ME and forensic reports; and nail down time to interview Eddie Wolfe and perhaps Jimmy Panther's colleagues at the Cherokee Boys Club.

But my immediate priority was to check in with my wife. I had learned a good husband stays in touch, especially near meal times. I called her on speed-dial from the jeep.

"Where are you?" I asked.

"Just finishing rounds." Susan usually had several surgeries on Monday and always checked on her patients at the end of the day. "Where are you?"

"Leaving the department."

"Any progress?"

"It was a day of collecting information. I'll tell you when I see you."

"Are you headed home?"

I checked the dashboard clock. Six twenty. "I'm going to swing by the funeral home. I should be at the cabin about seven thirty, if that's all right."

"How does pizza and wine sound?"

"Superb."

"Good. I'll pick up a Supreme and have it ready with a salad. Don't be late."

"I wouldn't dare, Mrs. Clayton."

"Smart man, to use an oxymoron." She hung up.

The parking lot at the funeral home was empty except for a large, white Lincoln. I parked beside it and noticed a North Carolina State Senate license plate. The owner had to be Mack Collins, and I wondered if his call to me had been about a death in the family. He was married, but I couldn't remember his wife's name. Carol or Caroline?

He sat in the parlor with Uncle Wayne. A cup of coffee and plate of Mom's oatmeal cookies were on the side table by his chair.

"There he is." Uncle Wayne stood. "I told Mack you might be by. Barry, Mack was asking my advice on some legislation he's proposing. He wants to make funeral expenses tax deductible. I told him it's a great idea. High time too, don't you think?"

"Yeah," I agreed. I doubted Senator Collins called me at the Sheriff's Department to discuss tax policy, but I played along. "What can we do to help?"

"I'd even go to Raleigh," my uncle interjected. "Testify to one of those committees, like during Watergate. You know, what did I know? When did I know it?"

Collins rose from his chair. "I'll keep that in mind." He winked at me. "If I have to pull out the big guns." He shook my uncle's hand, sealing the high-stakes political strategy. "I've got another matter to discuss with Barry, but I left the paperwork in the car. Please thank Connie for her hospitality and I'll keep you posted on our progress." He turned to me. "Barry, have you got a few minutes?"

"Sure." I followed him to his car.

Instead of retrieving the alleged paperwork, Collins leaned against his trunk and folded his arms across his chest. He was a thin man with a long face and steely-gray hair. His eyes were cold-blue and close set. The dark shadow on his cheeks showed he had shaved early that morning, but his charcoal suit, white shirt, and muted red tie looked fresh. I wondered if he wore his business attire just to call on me.

He cleared his throat. "Barry, I didn't want to talk about it in front of your uncle, but I'm very upset over this Cherokee thing."

"I picked up your message and was going to call you when I got here," I said. "We're working the case as hard as we can."

Collins unlocked his arms and clasped his hands together. "I know. I'm not being critical. I'm just concerned because it looks like Luther has to be your prime suspect. We all witnessed what happened at Eurleen's funeral."

"Let me assure you we're not just focused on Luther. Jimmy Panther was an activist who might have angered other people. We're receiving terrific cooperation from the Cherokee tribal police."

Collins had a habit of working his thin lips in and out while he thought, a trait I noticed during our poker game but one that seemed to bear no relation to whether he held a good or bad hand.

His lips disappeared and reappeared several times, and then he nodded. "Good. I'm glad to hear it. I don't want this to become a contentious issue. I chair the committee on Indian affairs and an anti-Cherokee reaction could have statewide ramifications."

"Why would that happen?"

"There are people and companies who don't like the covenant we have with the reservation. They don't think it's fair that the Cherokee have exclusive gaming rights. Hell, the video poker people challenged the covenant all the way to the state supreme court. Fortunately, they lost. But, they're looking for any opportunity to overturn the legislation establishing that exclusivity. Pile on the Catawbas, and you've got a political mess."

"The Catawbas? Is that tribe even in North Carolina?"

My question fueled a rush of blood to Collins' face. He pushed himself off the Lincoln and started pacing back and forth. "Hell, no. Their reservation is in South Carolina. But they're petitioning to build a casino about thirty miles down I-85 from Charlotte by purchasing land and putting it into a federal trust like other reservation property. The governor's against it and the Cherokee are furious at the prospect of cannibalizing their revenues and disrupting their plans for a second casino."

"So, what are the Catawba tribe's chances?"

Collins stopped pacing and stepped close to me. "In politics, never say never. Two days ago, I would have told you slim at best. I can control my committee and wield influence with the state's Bureau of Indian Affairs, but there are significant private business interests that are all for it. We're talking a lot of money potentially pouring into relatively poor counties."

Collins pressed his index finger in my chest. "But, if the Catawba can do it, what's to stop another out-of-state tribe? I mean god damn it, Barry, what's to keep the Apache or the Sioux from showing up on our doorstep?"

"Why wouldn't the Catawba put this on their existing land?"

"Because South Carolina won't give them live gaming rights. The Cherokee casino has established the North Carolina precedent for Indian gaming. People want real dealers, real roulette wheels, and real poker. Our covenant with the Cherokee has worked great, and the state gets a share of the revenue. But now?" He threw up his hands. "They're going to kill the goose laying the golden eggs."

I understood the problem of how North Carolina could become an overbuilt haven of Indian gaming, but my murder case seemed irrelevant. "I don't get the connection to Luther and Panther?"

"Don't you see? If Luther's arrested, then people are going to draw up sides. There will be a lot of sympathy for a man whose mourning was turned into political theater. If Luther killed Panther in a turmoil of grief and rage, I predict a surge of support. Feelings that Jimmy Panther had it coming. Jimmy's supporters will turn him into a Cherokee martyr and that only ratchets up emotions. When people are pushed to extremes, they take extreme action. If this becomes a Cherokee versus Gainesboro issue, it could resonate all the way to Raleigh."

Collins shook his head slowly. "I don't want to see that happen. For Luther's sake. The guy's been my friend for nearly thirty years. He was one of the first people to welcome Corrine and me when we moved here from New Jersey to start our family. But I tell you, Barry, people are ready to exploit this whole tragic affair. None more so than his son Darren."

"Darren?"

"Yeah. He's helping the Catawba Indians pursue their casino. I got word because he claims to have access to me. I don't appreciate being used like that—by him or his Washington PR firm. Don't think he won't vilify the Cherokee if it serves his client."

I didn't know what to say. If what Collins said was true, it wrapped a new layer around Darren's involvement. Collins didn't know Darren no longer worked at the PR firm, and until I knew more, I wasn't about to tell him. Not while he was worked up in such an emotional state.

"Mack, you know Tommy Lee and I have to follow this wherever the evidence leads."

He put his hand on my shoulder. "I know. I'd just appreciate a heads-up if this is going to break bad for Luther. Don't mistake me. I'm sympathetic to Luther, but I feel a responsibility to do what's right for all the people in North Carolina." He stepped back, reached in his suit coat, and handed me a card. "Here are all my contact numbers in Raleigh, and my cell's on the back. I've got to go back to the legislature in the morning, but you call day or night."

He gave my shoulder a squeeze. "I owe you." He smiled. "Who knows? Maybe I can get your uncle in front of that committee."

I thought about my conversation with Collins the entire drive to my cabin. His political concerns had appeared tangential to my investigation until he mentioned Darren Cransford. Now dots could be connected that weren't coincidences but consequences. Mack Collins oversaw Indian and gaming legislation, Darren would know his father's friend from his childhood, and the Catawba Indian forces would be seeking any influence in Raleigh they could find. But how did that connect to Panther?

The discovery of the Cherokee burial site and Eurleen Cransford's death had been the catalysts, a convergence of events, each individually explainable and yet with no logical connection. Maybe there was no logical connection. They were a coincidence of timing, timing that someone saw as an opportunity for murder.

Susan's car was in its customary spot by the cabin porch. I saw a black Ford Escort with a Tennessee plate parked beside it. We had company, but I had no idea who.

I opened the front door and my yellow lab Democrat jumped up from his rug near the hearth and bounded for me. At the same time, a man sprang from the sofa, wineglass in hand.

"As I live and breathe, hasn't our funeral director gone and transformed himself into a right proper law officer."

I was stunned to see Kevin Malone, Boston police detective and Vietnam platoon mate of Tommy Lee. Although several years had passed since he was in Gainesboro to help solve a murder going back to that war, Kevin looked the same. His gray hair was a little thinner, but the impish Irish grin was as broad as ever.

"Kevin. What are you doing here?"

He raised the wineglass higher. "I've come to receive your gratitude, youngster. I know who killed Jimmy Panther."

Chapter Nine

I stood inside the front door, doubly shocked by Kevin's presence and his pronouncement.

"Well, come on in, lad. Susan's kind enough to invite me to stay for dinner." He sat down as if he were in his own den.

Susan came around the bar from the kitchen with a plate of cheese and crackers. "Hello, dear." Her sly smile told me she was amused by the situation. She set the appetizers on the coffee table. "You want a glass of Malbec?"

"Definitely."

Democrat gave up on getting a pat from me and trotted over to Kevin. He put his big head on the Irishman's knee and was rewarded with a scratch behind the ear.

"Can't believe he remembered me," Kevin said.

I broke my frozen stance and closed the door. "You're a hard man to forget."

He set his glass on the table and stood again, this time to give me a firm handshake. "I had a feeling our paths would cross again. Maybe Democrat did too." He returned to the sofa. "Tommy Lee said you're heading up this Indian killing."

I sat in a chair opposite him. "Did you see him?"

"No. Got him by phone as I was driving in. He said you and he spent the afternoon in Cherokee and he had to go to some civic meeting tonight."

My mind was racing. Kevin's car was obviously a rental, probably from the Asheville airport. So, he'd flown in from Boston.

How had he learned about the murder and gotten here so fast? And why? I could only think of one explanation. "Tommy Lee put you up to claiming you solved my case. What, are you here on vacation?"

Susan entered with my wine. "Dinner will be ready in about fifteen minutes."

Kevin patted the cushion beside him. "Sit down, Susan. I don't want you running around on my account."

She laughed. "I'm not. But it would be on your account before Barry's."

He grinned at me. "You've caught yourself a wicked one, son."

"You men talk," Susan said. "I'm going to walk Democrat up to the mailbox and we'll eat when I get back."

Democrat lifted his head at the sound of his name. He headed for the door.

When it closed behind Susan and the dog, Kevin's face turned rigid. "Francis Tyrell. He killed your Indian."

It didn't take a detective to deduce Kevin was dead serious. "Who's he?"

"A slick son of a bitch I wouldn't cross Newbury Street to piss on if he was on fire."

"And you flew in today because he's a suspect?"

Kevin eyed his wineglass. "This grape juice is nice, but do you happen to have anything stronger?"

"I have some Bushmills."

"Oh, be still my heart."

I went to the cabinet beside the fireplace and pulled out a fifth that had been a Christmas present several seasons ago. I'm not much of a drinker. "How do you want it?"

Kevin gulped down his wine and then pointed to the empty glass. "She can land right there."

I poured a couple of fingers and left the bottle on the table. He took a healthy swig, rolled it around his mouth, and then swallowed. "Ah. Aren't your Southern Baptists going to be shocked when they find God's got this on stock in heaven."

"Francis Tyrell," I prompted, pulling him back on topic. "What's the connection to Boston?"

He waved me to my chair. "Whitey Bulger. Know the name?"

"Who doesn't? We got coverage of the trial down here." Whitey Bulger was a notorious Boston mobster who had been on the run for years until he was finally nabbed in California and brought to trial for multiple murders. I didn't know the details, but I remembered the headlines and his alleged role as mastermind of the Winter Hill Gang, an Irish-American mob rooted in South Boston.

"And I guarantee you Francis Tyrell's name never appeared," Kevin said. "He was Whitey's society face."

"A lawyer?"

"No. A schmoozer. Like most sociopaths. I knew him as Frankie Tyrelli, a tough Italian kid surviving in an Irish neighborhood. He ran numbers in high school and Whitey tapped him as a sort of emissary to the New York families. You know, one of their own."

"Is he wanted for something?"

Kevin leaned forward. "I want him for three murders. Of course, I'm only short in one area." He swirled the Bushmills in his glass. "Evidence."

"So, he's a schmoozer and a hit man."

"I'm sure he smiles as he pulls the trigger. Over the last fifteen years, three potential witnesses against Whitey died of gunshot wounds to the head. Forensics leans toward a Walther P22."

"A ballistics match for all three?"

"No." Kevin took a drink, and then replenished his glass from the bottle. "Frankie's too smart for that. Yes, the slugs were recovered from the heads of the victims, but they weren't from the same gun. All were contact shots behind the ear. Scalp burns suggest a suppressor for two that happened in hotel rooms. The third victim was discovered in a construction site on Route 128 about ten miles out of Boston. That's where the high tech sector developed. The skin was singed enough to identify the barrel profile of a Walther."

"Over fifteen years," I said. "That's back when Whitey was still on the run."

"My theory is the victims either tried to fill his vacuum prematurely, or they had information they could trade for immunity from prosecution. Whitey didn't get where he did taking chances and leaving loose ends."

"Was Tyrell brought in for questioning?"

Kevin shook his head. "Not enough to tag him for the hits. The targets worked the drug side of Winter Hill's operations. A turf war runs off and on, especially after the Jamaicans moved in. The cases are still open, but most in the department think it was score-settling between the gangs. And good riddance."

"You don't?"

"The Walther P22 is a fine gun. Dependable, already threaded for a suppressor, and easy to conceal. Most of those Jamaican gangbangers pack Saturday Night Specials that are as likely to blow up in your hand as to fire properly. Frankie wouldn't be caught dead with crap like that."

"I'm not a gun expert but there are a lot of other quality semiautomatic pistols out there."

"True," Kevin conceded. "But a couple of months ago Frankie was stopped on a DUI. The officer found a Walther P22 in his glove compartment and Frankie was arrested for carrying a concealed weapon. Frankie claimed to have bought it in another state because he feared for his life." Kevin cocked his head. "Can you believe it, Barry? He said Whitey Bulger was coming after him because he had always cooperated with the authorities. This was when the trial was in full swing. Frankie cited the very murders I think he committed as the proof of the threats. And although Frankie was as innocent as a lamb, Whitey had it in for him."

"What happened?"

"An expensive lawyer, a thousand-dollar fine, and a suspended sentence. One week later a witness was found dead in a wooded area outside of Boston."

"Shot?"

"No. Poisoned."

The story rang a bell. "Cyanide, right? I thought they had someone for the crime and it was unrelated to Bulger."

"Of course they have someone for the crime. Conveniently served up with an outstanding debt motive. But I think there was another motive at play. Either off the witness or get a bullet to the head. Nothing's unrelated in Boston. I think Tyrell carried that Walther with him because he was going to take care of the witness testifying against Bulger. Then he got pulled on the DUI with the potential murder weapon, and he went to plan B to distance himself."

"So, you've been staking him out?"

Kevin nodded. "Whitey Bulger's trial was like turning over a rock. Lots of things crawled out, except in this case, they turned on each other and turned in each other. Frankie Tyrell's name started surfacing, and he might have been tying up his own loose ends as much as working for Bulger."

"And what does an Indian activist have to do with a Boston mobster?"

"You got me, pal. But, Frankie flies in on Friday and your boy's executed Sunday night."

"Then why would he kill Panther in that same manner? He'd have to know he risked drawing attention to himself."

Kevin held up his index finger. "One word. Arrogance. Tyrell is an arrogant son of a bitch, and like most arrogant crooks, he's not as smart as he thinks. Whitey was the brains and no one else came close."

"Where's Tyrell staying?"

"At the casino in Cherokee. Allegedly for a poker tournament running this week."

"Have you got enough for a search warrant of his room?"

"No. And I don't think the tribal police are anxious to hassle casino guests without compelling evidence. Frankie's probably dumped the gun. He wouldn't have chanced bringing it through airport security from Boston, so he either has an accomplice or he shipped it to some drop box near here."

I knew if Panther had been cuffed and driven to the cemetery, then whoever killed him had an accomplice. But if Panther had arrived at the cemetery only to be surprised by his assassin, then an accomplice wasn't necessary. That would make Kevin's case for Francis Tyrell weaker. How would an outsider know his way well enough to find the cemetery? And Tyrell arrived before Eurleen Cransford's funeral so Panther's actions at the interment couldn't have prompted his trip. What possible motive could he have?

Kevin must have read the skepticism on my face. He threw up his hands. "I know. You're looking at me like I'm nuts. Maybe I am. But I don't believe in coincidences and when a hit man comes to Cherokee and a Cherokee is murdered, I've got to take a sober look at it." He swallowed the last of his Bushmills and slid the glass away.

He wasn't exactly sober, but I could see that he was hell-bent on inserting himself in my case. I wondered what Tommy Lee thought of Kevin's theory.

"Why would Tyrell stay for a poker tournament?" I asked. "You think he'd be on the first plane out this morning."

"The only risks he takes are at the tables. If he came down for a job, he'd need a window of opportunity. Blowing in and out of town over the short interval of a murder does draw attention."

"Does he know you're tailing him?"

"I doubt it." Kevin shrugged. "But who knows. He's probably seen me testify against some of his fellow scumbags. I've tried to stay out of sight. Fortunately the casino is a big place."

"Were you on his plane?"

"No. We've got a trace on his credit card. He bought the tickets a week ago. I came down earlier Friday morning."

The date Tyrell booked his flight further diminished the prospects that he was connected to Luther Cransford and the cemetery. Kevin was overreaching. "Did you tail him Sunday night?"

"No. My damn bladder did me in. I went to the restroom and when I came back Tyrell had left the poker room."

"What time was this?"

"About nine thirty. I'm pretty sure he was winning, although I couldn't be sure from where I was watching. You know the casino?"

"No. I saw it from the outside for the first time today."

"Well, the poker room is on the second level so it's not real easy to see who's playing without going inside. Tyrell had been sitting with his back to the main door so I could cruise by now and then. Most of the time I nursed a drink and kept an eye on the entrance."

"Maybe there's a record of when he cashed out."

"When I lost him, I staked out the windows. I saw him cash out. Two a.m. But I'll be damned if I know where he was for four and a half hours."

The front door opened and Democrat trotted in, a yellow tennis ball proudly clenched between his teeth. He stopped by Kevin and dropped his treasure at the man's feet.

"He wants you to play." Susan closed the door with her free hand. The other held letters and a few catalogues. Only three months till Christmas and the deluge had started.

Kevin picked up the ball. Democrat sat on his haunches and swept the floor with his tail.

"No playing ball in the house," Susan said. "He thinks you don't know the rules and that he's going to pull one over on us."

"Is that right?" Kevin asked Democrat. "Are you a rule breaker?" The tail moved faster. "Can I take him out for a few minutes?"

"Sure," Susan said. "Barry can help set the table and we'll call you."

Kevin stood and Democrat scampered to the door, looking back to make certain he was being followed.

I followed Susan into the kitchen. She didn't look back because I'd better be following.

"So, what's up?" She asked the question as she handed me three dinner plates.

"Kevin says he's got a suspect for me. A mob hit man out of Boston."

"For Jimmy Panther?"

"Yeah. He's in Cherokee at the casino and Kevin doesn't know where he was Sunday night."

"His guy along with several hundred other people in the casino."

"I know. But I'm trying to have an open mind." I gave her the replay of the conversation while she sliced the pizza and tossed the salad.

"Can Kevin suggest a motive?" she asked.

"No. And there's not a lot I can do in the way of changing the direction of my investigation unless I get some evidence suggesting a link. I'll talk to Tommy Lee in the morning, but I doubt he'll think otherwise."

I carried the food to the table, refilled the wineglasses including Kevin's, and called him and Democrat to supper.

While the yellow lab gulped his food like it might disappear any second, Kevin picked up his glass before we sat. "I'd like to propose a toast."

Susan and I dutifully raised our wine.

"An Irish toast to the newlyweds. Here's to love, the only fire against which there is no insurance. And may the flower of love never be nipped by the frost of disappointment, nor shadow of grief fall among your family and friends. May you be poor in misfortune, rich in blessings, slow to make enemies and quick to make friends. And may you know nothing but happiness from this day forward." He swept his arm in an arc across the room. "May your home always be too small to hold all your friends. And may I always be one of them."

We clinked glasses.

"I'm sure you will be," Susan said.

We drank, still standing.

"Good," Kevin said. "Then I know you'll accept my gift. Tomorrow night you're my guests at Harrah's in Cherokee. I've made a reservation for dinner and booked you a room." He winked at me. "I'll even stake you to a couple of hands of poker."

I looked at Susan and she started laughing. We'd been had.

Chapter Ten

The next morning I went straight to Tommy Lee's office and summarized Kevin's proposal.

"I don't like it." The sheriff stood from his desk and paced in a small circle. "Especially getting Susan involved."

"What's going to happen? We sit in the poker room, play a few hands, and I watch Tyrell."

"Watch him do what?"

"I don't know. Maybe make contact with someone. Whoever killed Panther had an accomplice."

Tommy Lee dismissed my idea with a wave. "That won't happen in a poker game. I get the fact Kevin can't go near this guy and he wants someone to be his eyes and ears. But no offense, Barry, I've seen you play poker. Unless Kevin's providing you a big stake, you won't last twenty minutes. And I know Kevin. He's like a damn dog with a bone. He won't let go, and if he's got it in for Tyrell, he'll twist every coincidence or happenstance into proof of his case. I love the guy like a brother, but he can be a bull in a china shop."

"You told me he was Boston's Detective of the Year."

"Yeah. And he's broken some big investigations, but he's also been reprimanded for harassing suspects where there was insufficient evidence. Kevin sees things as black and white and justifies his actions accordingly. Shoot first, ask questions later."

Tommy Lee's last statement triggered a sobering memory. The first time I met Kevin he'd been on suspension pending an inquiry into a shooting, a crossfire in which Kevin had accidentally killed his partner. And there was Tommy Lee's accurate assessment of me as a poker player.

"How about Archie Donovan? He's the best player I know."

Tommy Lee's one eye widened in disbelief. "Did you hear what you said?"

I laughed. "Yeah, go ahead and have me committed. But he is a good poker player. And I don't want to disregard Kevin's view totally."

Tommy Lee returned to his desk chair. "We've got more promising leads."

"I know. I'm following up on the employment discrepancy of Darren Cransford. I also want to question Eddie Wolfe. Jimmy might have shared concerns with Eddie that he wouldn't tell his sister."

Tommy Lee nodded. "And you were going back to the reservation this afternoon and then stay over?"

"Susan doesn't have another surgery till Thursday and she's covered her rounds."

Tommy Lee drummed his fingers on his desk. "Oh, what the hell. Go ahead and humor Kevin. I'll cover your room. Kevin can stake Archie's expenses, but I'll be damned if I can see what Kevin hopes to accomplish."

"What's the word on the ME report?"

"Late today at the earliest. More likely tomorrow morning. I'll call if there's something unusual." Tommy Lee glanced at his watch. "Anything else?"

"Mack Collins came to see me yesterday evening."

"About Luther?"

"Yeah." I recapped the conversation with the state senator and the concern Panther's murder would become a weapon in the current political fight over casino legislation.

"I heard about the Catawba proposal," Tommy Lee said. "Sheriff Tomlinson in Cleveland County said the business community ponied up a considerable lobby fund to push through a covenant with the tribe. He's worried they're so enamored with the increased revenue that they're not accounting for increased costs. This so-called Catawba reservation annex doesn't have the support systems of the Cherokee's Qualla Boundary. It's just sixteen acres of land to hold the casino and hotel. Tomlinson's telling them they'd better be braced for a strain on basic services, road congestion, and law enforcement. He envisions the need to significantly expand his department."

"Money talks," I said.

"Yeah, but at the end of the day there's got to be more money than just what flows into private enterprise. Tomlinson's department isn't going to rake it in like some building or road contractor who'll make a killing and move on to the next deal. He'll need ongoing public funds and he knows it."

"Could Panther have been working against the Catawbas? Maybe he sees the casinos as a scourge across all the Native American tribes."

"Maybe. The Catawba PR connection to Darren Cransford certainly has me curious. Run that to ground, and stay close to Mack Collins. Find out who he sees applying the most pressure on this Catawba petition. It will be whoever has the most to gain, so follow the money."

"Follow the money." The gospel I'd heard preached by every law enforcement investigator I'd ever known.

"What about Luther?" I asked. "We've got that discrepancy between his account of where he was Sunday night and what the guard at the gatehouse said."

"Luther's not going anywhere. Let's see if we get some corroborating evidence that he went out. I'd like more than just Luther's word against the guard's." Tommy Lee turned to a stack of papers on his desk. "Now, go on. Get out of here."

I headed for the door.

"Barry."

I stopped. "What?"

"If Archie can't do it, let Susan play the hand. She's gotta be better than you."

"Thanks for your confidence."

I returned to my desk and pulled Kevin Malone's card from my wallet. He'd scribbled his cell on the back and told me to call any time. It was eight thirty in the morning and I didn't feel guilty if I woke him.

He answered on the first ring. "What?"

"It's Barry. Can you talk a minute?"

"Yeah. I'm just grabbing a cup of coffee and a bagel. Tyrell's eating a full breakfast far enough away that he won't see me."

"Is he alone?"

"So far. I expect he'll go up to the poker room from here."

"Listen. I'd like to propose a change for tonight."

"Hey, man, don't bail on me now." Kevin's urgent tone bordered on desperation. "I need you to be my eyes."

"Susan and I are still coming, but I don't think the poker cover will work for me."

"You know how to play, don't you?"

"Sure. If the goal is losing, and losing quickly. I've never been in a casino before and my inexperience would stand out like a pig in a dog show. But I've got a guy who's a good player and would probably fit right in."

"Yeah? Who's that?"

"Archie Donovan. He's part owner of the cemetery where Panther was killed. You met him when you were here before."

There was a long pause, and then he said, "He was with the mayor, right?"

"Yeah."

"He seems like a flake. They both do."

"They have their moments," I conceded. "But Archie's the best poker player I know. One other thing to consider is the chance someone might recognize me. If I'm called out as a deputy, it'll spook Tyrell for sure."

Again, the phone was silent for a few seconds. "OK. Then you can meet me at six."

"Where?"

"Better come to my room. You and Susan first. Have your

friend arrive at six thirty so we'll have a chance to talk ahead of time." Kevin gave me his room number.

"And if Archie can't do it, I'll give it my best shot."

"That's all I'm asking," he said. "I know you think it's a dead end, but I know Tyrell. If he was looking to gamble, he'd be in Vegas."

"You said it's a tournament."

"Yeah, but it doesn't officially start till tomorrow. There was really no need for Tyrell to come in last week. I'll get Archie Donovan signed up for Tyrell's table. I'm pretty sure that won't be a problem."

"OK. I'll call Archie now so you can sub my name if he can't do it."

"What are you doing the rest of the day?"

He asked the question in an offhanded manner, but I hesitated to give too many specifics to someone outside the department, even if he was Tommy Lee's friend.

"Some local follow up. We don't expect the full report from the ME until tomorrow. First, I need to track down Archie."

"Then don't let me keep you. See you tonight."

We hung up, and I was left with the feeling that Kevin hadn't told me everything.

Now that I had his blessing, my next challenge was enlisting Archie's aid without sending him into some fantasy of being an undercover agent. I was counting on his competitive streak to keep him focused on poker and nothing more. The beauty of the game was that carefully scrutinizing fellow players wouldn't be unusual. Archie could be hyperobservant as long as he kept his mouth shut.

His insurance office was on a cross street about two blocks from the Sheriff's Department. I decided against phoning him because Archie would start pummeling me with questions. Instead, the crisp fall morning offered the opportunity to walk. If Archie wasn't in, I'd at least get a little exercise.

DONOVAN INSURANCE AND INVESTMENTS was painted against the arc of a rainbow on the front window. Centered underneath, a leprechaun with a face bearing a striking resemblance to Archie's held out a pot of gold. On the door, office hours were listed as nine to five. I entered.

Joan Hitchcock sat behind a desk facing the entrance. She looked up from a stack of papers. "Good morning, Barry."

"Good morning. Is the wizard of Wall Street in yet?"

She laughed. "Come and gone."

"When do you expect him?"

"After his third cup of coffee and second plate of waffles. He ran up to the Cardinal Café. But he'd better be back soon with my egg sandwich." The scowl on her face told me she wasn't kidding.

Joan was probably in her early fifties. She had worked for Archie's father and Archie had given her a hefty raise when his father passed away. He understood Joan knew the business and the clients better than he did.

"Thanks," I said. "I'll try to catch him there."

"If you catch him, for God's sake don't hold him too long. I'm hungry."

The Cardinal Café was around the corner on Main Street. I was afraid Archie would be camped out at a table with his cronies, and I didn't have the time to wait till he was alone.

The café owner, Helen Todd, stood behind the cash register replacing a spool of receipt paper. "Hi, Barry, the rush is over. Sit wherever you want."

"I'm looking for Archie."

She tossed her head toward the rear of the restaurant. "Back booth. But don't delay him. He's taking an egg sandwich to Joan."

Clearly Joan had put out the word that Archie was on a mission.

"Is it ready?" I asked.

"No. The order goes in when Archie gets his third refill of coffee."

"Give me five minutes and if need be, I'll take it to her myself."

"OK. You've got five minutes with Archie. God help you."

He sat in the booth, his back to the main dining area, staring at the untouched waffle on the plate in front of him. If this was his second serving, I saw no sign there had been a first.

Archie had taken two butter patties, placed them as eyes, and then squirted a broad U of syrup beneath them to create a smiley face. He was focused on the waffle like he expected it to speak to him.

"Archie?" I whispered.

No response. I slid onto the booth bench opposite him. "Archie," I said louder.

He looked up and seemed momentarily bewildered to find himself sitting in a café. "Barry?"

"Archie, are you all right?"

He slid the plate aside. "I keep seeing that body on the grave. I can't get it out of my mind."

I looked at the smiley-faced waffle, Archie's bizarre attempt to purge the image of Jimmy Panther's bloody head.

"And to think Luther could have done such a thing," he said.

"We don't know that. Our investigation is just starting."

"You talked to Luther?"

I decided I needed to share something with Archie if I was going to ask for his help. "Luther says he was home Sunday night. He appeared genuinely shocked that Panther had been killed."

Archie shook his head. "Of course he'd say that. That's why I haven't called him. I can't bear to make him lie to me."

Archie's quick conviction of Luther surprised me. Yes, Luther's attack on Panther had been vicious, but it was prompted by his rage in the moment. Maybe it was a side of Luther Archie had never seen. He couldn't separate that sight from the executed body on Eurleen's grave. I should have known Archie's mind would fixate on the most melodramatic possibility.

"We're pursuing other leads," I said. "There's a chance Panther was abducted from the reservation."

"So what? Luther knows how to drive." He thought a second. "What if people think I'm an accomplice?"

"I'm sure you have an alibi."

"But I don't. Gloria and the girls are still in Weaverville. I was home alone."

"You're not a suspect, and you shouldn't worry about what other people think." I lowered my voice. "In fact, you might be able to help us with the investigation."

His eyes grew larger than the butter patties on the waffle. "Really? Like police work?"

I nodded solemnly. "You remember Kevin Malone, don't you?"

"That detective from Boston?"

"Yeah. He's trailing a man suspected of some killings in the Boston area. This guy came to Cherokee a few days before Panther died."

"A Boston hit man? In Gainesboro?" Instead of looking frightened, Archie seemed excited. Like the President had announced a campaign stop in our town.

"It's a real long shot that he's involved with anything local," I said. "He likes to play poker and there's a tournament at the casino this week. Odds are that's all there is to it."

Archie eyed me skeptically. "Poker? What's that have to do with a dead Cherokee? More importantly, what's that have to do with me?"

"Kevin wants to see if his suspect makes contact with anyone. You know, at the gaming table."

"This guy have a name?"

"Francis Tyrell. Kevin says Tyrell would recognize him so he's hoping you can get in the game and watch Tyrell. He asked me, but I told Kevin you're the best card player I know."

"What are the stakes in this game?"

"I don't know. Kevin's going to back you."

"Can I keep the winnings?"

"Come on, Archie, it's police money. And I'm sure he has a limit so don't lose it."

Archie grinned, his despondent mood cast aside. "Sure. I'll be glad to help. Certainly can't have you sitting in that game. You'd lose calling heads if you tossed a two-headed coin."

I left Archie devouring his waffle and I delivered Joan's egg sandwich on my walk back to the department.

My next priority was to find out why Darren Cransford had lied to his father about his employment. Since the PR firm was a dead end, I needed his home or cell number. Luther should have it, but he would wonder why I didn't reach his son at the office. I decided to approach Darren's sister Sandra.

Wakefield gave me her work number and I debated whether to announce myself as a deputy or the family's funeral director. I decided calling as Barry Clayton, town undertaker, would be less likely to stir up office gossip.

In a soft, southern accent, a woman answered, "G.A. Bridges." I asked to speak to Sandra Cransford and was immediately transferred to her assistant. I was surprised by an authoritative baritone voice announcing, "Sandra Cransford's office. How may I help you?"

"This is Barry Clayton of Clayton and Clayton Funeral Directors in Gainesboro, North Carolina. We served Ms. Cransford's family this past weekend and I have a few things I need to discuss with her."

"I'm sure she'd be happy to speak with you, Mr. Clayton. Let me check her schedule." He paused a moment, and then said, "She has a fifteen-minute window from four forty-five to five o'clock this afternoon. Will that work?"

"I'm sorry but it won't. This is an urgent personal matter that I'm sure she'll want to handle immediately. If she prefers to delay our conversation after I've informed her of the situation, then that's fine. However, I neither want to be responsible for keeping her in the dark nor do I want you to be in that same position."

I knew the man must have been a very efficient gatekeeper, but no one wants to make a solitary decision when it involves a death in the family of the boss.

"Hold, please," he said, and my ear was filled with elevator music.

After an orchestral version of "Da Ya Think I'm Sexy?" Sandra came on the line.

"Barry, what is it? Has something happened to my father?"

"Have you spoken with him since you returned to Atlanta?"

"Sunday night. To let him know I made it home safely. I should have called yesterday, but the day got away from me."

Her assistant probably couldn't work in a fifteen-minute window, I thought. "Jimmy Panther was killed Sunday night. His body was found on your mother's grave."

I heard her sharp intake of breath. I waited for her to speak.

"Nine thirty. That's when I spoke with Daddy. He said he was going to bed."

Sandra was jumping to the conclusion that her father was a suspect and she was trying to alibi him.

"On his cell?"

"The home phone. Surely you don't think he's responsible."

"No. But your father was pretty shaken when I told him. I wanted you to know."

"Thank you. I'll check in right away."

"And you're sure about the time on Sunday?"

"Yes. I'd just come in. I knew if I didn't call immediately I'd get bogged down preparing for a Monday morning breakfast meeting."

I jotted a note referencing Sandra's location during the estimated time of the murder, and that her call didn't alibi Luther. "One other thing. I tried to reach your brother, but his office said he no longer works there."

"He and the PR firm had a parting of the ways. Darren's working on his own now."

"Any reason your father didn't know?"

"Darren wanted to wait until he was more established. He didn't want Daddy to worry."

"This parting of the ways. Did it have anything to do with the Catawbas?"

Sandra was silent a moment. When she finally spoke, her tone was cold and guarded. "Barry, are you investigating my brother?"

I ignored her question. "Mack Collins said Darren was working for the Catawba tribe. There seems to be a lot of contention swirling around their casino proposal and I'm just trying to understand all the pieces."

"Then you'll have to talk to Darren or Senator Collins, but I don't see how any of this ties into the shooting of that Cherokee."

"At this point neither do I."

"But that doesn't mean you stop investigating, does it?"

"No."

She laughed, and the earlier tension in her voice disappeared. "Well, I'll help any way I can. Let me get you Darren's cell number. I have to read it off my own phone. With speed-dial, no one memorizes numbers anymore."

She gave me a Washington DC area code, and I wrote it down along with a few more notes on our conversation.

"Thank you for calling in person," she said. "I'm afraid Daddy's going to be a lost soul without Mom. I'll be coming to town more often. Maybe we can grab a cup of coffee."

"I'm a regular at the Cardinal Café."

"Then it's a deal. Thanks, Barry." She hung up.

I added one more item to my to-do list: Check the time of Sandra's call to Luther on Sunday night.

Chapter Eleven

"Darren didn't answer, so I left him a voicemail. If he hasn't called by mid-afternoon, I'll try again." I flipped my notepad closed and waited for Tommy Lee's reaction to my report.

We sat in a small conference room in the department where Tommy Lee could escape from his phone. He'd listened without interrupting while I summarized my conversation with Sandra Cransford.

"OK," he said. "I think I should run out to see Luther while you're in Cherokee."

"I can delay going to the reservation if we're ready to confront him."

"No. Let's stay with the plan. I'm Luther's generation. He might open up more to me one-on-one, especially if I tell him his car was reported returning well after midnight on Monday morning. He won't have to face you with his lie."

"Are you going to say anything about Darren?"

Tommy Lee shook his head. "We need more information. Did Sandra say how the PR firm learned Darren was moonlighting for the Catawbas?"

"I didn't think to ask. Should I call her?"

"No. It's probably better to get that information straight from Darren. Let him know you learned about it from Sandra but you haven't told his father."

"Are you trying to create friction between brother and sister?"

"I'm looking for a wedge between father and son. If Luther and Darren are involved together, we need something to pry apart their story. I'm going to get authorization to obtain their phone records. We'll see if they match what Luther tells me."

"And what Darren tells me," I added. "Can you get the tracking of the cell towers to recreate his location Sunday and yesterday?"

"Good point," Tommy Lee said. "That will take longer but will verify their truthfulness. Check with me as soon as you talk to Darren."

With our immediate plans confirmed, we set out on our separate assignments. I reached Detective Sergeant Romero who informed me Eddie Wolfe would meet us at the Cherokee police station at two. Susan dropped Democrat off with Mom and we headed for the reservation.

"My God. This room is the size of a football field." Susan stepped onto the ground floor of Harrah's where rows and rows of video gaming machines filled the space.

The sheer scale overwhelmed us. I stood with an overnight bag in each hand and my mouth agape. Susan walked ahead, and then turned around. "Come on, Barry. You look like a rube who just jumped off a truckload of cabbages."

Trying to project the nonchalant air of a seasoned gambler, I followed her into the cavernous realm of lights and luck. There were no "one-armed bandits" like I'd envisioned the slot machines would be. Instead, people pushed buttons and their winnings and losses were adjusted against their running balance with each play. The screens contained colorful icons, combinations of playing cards, and other moving graphics that gave me no clue either as to what was the game or how to win it. Maybe I should climb back up on a truckload of cabbages and stick with Friday night poker at the mayor's house.

Then the sea of machines transitioned into live gaming tables. At least now I recognized roulette and blackjack. A number of players gathered at tables identified as three-card poker. I'd never heard of the game, but figured the fewer the cards, the fewer the ways I could lose.

We found our way to the hotel registration desk and realized we'd taken the long route through the casino when we could have simply pulled up to the hotel entrance. The woman at the front desk was Asian. I took a quick look at our surroundings and noticed very few of the staff were Cherokee.

She asked if we were first-time guests, and when we answered we were, she suggested we acquire Total Rewards cards that would activate the gaming machines and create an account. We also qualified for a five-dollar credit so we could play with house money. In my case, the house money would never leave the house.

Although it was only one o'clock, we were able to check in early. Our room was on the fourth floor. Kevin Malone was on the sixth. I wondered if either room had been booked in close proximity to Francis Tyrell's. That would have required the assistance of the hotel management, and I didn't know if Kevin had announced his presence as an officer of the law. If I had to make that wager, I'd say no. And I doubted he'd checked in with the Cherokee police.

Susan slid the electronic keycard into the slot and opened the door. "Nice," she said. "Spacious too, but not so alluring that a serious visitor would forego the action in the casino."

The room was big enough that the king-size bed left space for a conversation area including a small leather sofa and two chairs. A wide window overlooked a view of the forest where leaves displayed a rich palette of reds and yellows.

"Do you want to hang out here while I see Romero?"

Susan set her valise at the foot of the bed. "No. I want to explore. Why don't I drop you at the police station and you can call me when you're finished?"

"OK." I started unbuttoning my shirt.

Susan looked at the suitcase by my feet. "Are you changing into your uniform? What if Tyrell sees you and remembers you?"

"Who says I'm getting dressed? Since we've got forty minutes and we're at a casino, I thought maybe I'd get lucky."

Susan leaned across the jeep's console and kissed me. "I could grow to like this casino life," she said. "So, don't spend all your energy investigating."

I returned the kiss. "Then don't wander out of cell coverage or your sugar daddy won't be able to call you."

I climbed out of the passenger's seat and watched Susan drive down the hill toward the village. If Eddie Wolfe's interview was short, we could be back at the hotel with plenty of time before our six o'clock meeting with Kevin. Nurturing that hope, I buzzed the door of the police station.

The receptionist behind the sign-in window recognized me. "Detective Romero asked for you to wait." She punched an intercom button and spoke too softly for me to hear. Then she motioned me to take one of the steel chairs. "He'll be right out."

I opted to stand and in less than thirty seconds, Hector Romero's bulky frame squeezed through the door. His leather jacket was the first thing I noticed after his smile. Evidently we were going somewhere.

"You undercover?" he asked, noting I wasn't in uniform.

"I figure you're intimidating enough for both of us."

Romero laughed a deep rumble that sounded more like a landslide. He pumped my hand. "I can see you hold your own against Rooster Cogburn."

"Tommy Lee sends his regards and asks that you keep me out of trouble."

"Now where's the fun in that?" His face turned serious in answer to his own question. "I've taken the liberty of changing our schedule. We've got a missing thirteen-year-old boy who lives close to Eddie Wolfe. I've got to interview the parents and thought we would save time if we bundled the two together. I hope you don't mind."

My vision of Susan and the king-size bed vanished. "No. I just need to call my wife. She dropped me off and was going to pick me up. We're having dinner at Harrah's."

"No problem. I can bring you to the casino when we finish."

Being seen getting out of a patrol car wasn't an ideal way to stay undercover, but the odds were probably good Tyrell wouldn't spot me.

"OK. I'll give her a call."

I hit speed-dial as we walked around the station. Susan's voicemail picked up and I left a brief message.

When we were heading out of the village, I asked, "What's the story with the boy? How long's he been gone?"

"Swifty was last seen yesterday morning."

"Swifty?"

"Daniel Swift. Everyone calls him Swifty. And the kid's really a fast runner so the nickname fits two ways."

"Has he run off before?"

"Not that his parents reported. He's a good kid. Active in the Cherokee Boys Club. Never been in trouble that I know of."

"The Cherokee Boys Club is where Jimmy Panther worked."

Romero considered the connection. "Yeah. But most of the tribal kids are involved there in one way or another. Swifty excelled at sports so he's on every team."

"Who are we seeing first?"

"Eddie Wolfe. He's working a four-to-midnight shift at the box factory. I don't know how long you'll need with him, but we could go as late as three thirty before he leaves for work."

"That should be plenty of time. And I don't want to hold up your meeting with the boy's parents."

"Thanks. But I'll be surprised if Swifty hasn't returned home by the time we get there."

Again, we wound up deep in a mountain cove, but still on the reservation. A strip of terraced land held about ten mobile homes. Some were singles, others double-wides. A few had window boxes with late-blooming marigolds and painted latticework around the foundation while the rest looked liked they'd been hauled into place and left without any landscaping improvement.

"Are these all rentals?" I asked.

"Some. Some are occupied by owners. No one possesses land

on the reservation because it's all a federal trust, but there's a housing shortage, what with outsiders moving here to work in the casino."

"My wife and I walked through it earlier. I didn't see many Cherokee there."

"A lot of us like outside work. When you grew up in the mountains, standing behind a roulette wheel's not particularly appealing. And then there's the per capita."

"That's the casino's profit sharing?" I asked.

"Yes. Twice a year one half of net gaming income is distributed to about fourteen thousand tribe members. Payments average over seven thousand dollars per person a year. Not a ton of money, but it provides a jolt to our economy every June and December. Banks have to bring in extra tellers and lots of cash." Romero pulled in front of one of the trailers and parked beside a shiny red Camaro. He turned toward me. "We go on alert because it's the perfect time to knock off one of the branches whose vaults are overflowing the day or two before payout. If you want to moonlight, you could pick up security work during per capita week."

"Thanks, but Tommy Lee keeps me busy enough." I unsnapped my seatbelt. "Still, seven thousand is way below the poverty level."

Romero pointed to the Camaro. "Eddie Wolfe's in his late twenties. I bet he bought that car out of his coming-of-age trust."

"What's that?"

"When I said all tribe members get per capita, I meant everybody. Even minors. Some of the kids coming out now have trust funds of over one hundred fifty thousand dollars. They qualify to collect at age eighteen if they've graduated from high school and have taken a money management class. Or they get the money at age twenty one with no strings attached. Not all of them make good choices with their nest egg."

"Eddie Wolfe's employed," I said.

Romero opened his door. "And so am I. Let's get to work."

Stairs of treated lumber led up to a front door located in the middle of the single-wide trailer. It opened before we could reach the steps and Eddie Wolfe stepped out on the small landing.

During our previous encounters, I'd not paid him much attention. Panther had been the focal point on both occasions and Eddie had blurred into the background. I guessed he was younger than Jimmy, probably around Skye's age. His hair hung to the collar of a green flannel shirt, and his black jeans rode low on his scrawny hips. A pair of black ankle boots were laced over the ends of his pant legs, and I suspected their rounded steel toes were part of a mandatory safety wardrobe for his job.

"May we come in?" Romero asked.

Eddie stared at me, clearly surprised by my arrival. "What's he doing here?"

"Deputy Clayton's heading the investigation."

"I know. Skye told me, but I thought I was just talking with you."

I stepped forward. "Detective Sergeant Romero will be present during our whole conversation, but unless you don't want to find who killed your friend, you have no reason not to talk to me."

Eddie Wolfe wiped his hands on his thighs. "No one wants to catch that son of a bitch more than me. Come in."

I followed Romero into the mobile home. A waist-high counter divided the center space into a living room and a rudimentary kitchen. A MacBook Pro laptop sat on the counter and two stools were tucked beneath it. The screen saver was a series of Indian artifacts drifting across the display in random motion.

The living room had just enough space for a sofa and a recliner. On the far wall hung what must have been a fifty-inch flat screen TV. The frozen image of some video war game showed we'd interrupted Eddie in the middle of a fantasy battle.

"Take a seat. I'll get an extra chair for me." He retrieved one of the stools and placed it between the sofa and recliner. The taller height brought Eddie to the eye level of Romero seated on the sofa, but would have left me looking up at him.

"I'm good to stand," I said. "I've been in the car for hours."

"Suit yourself." He perched on the stool and looked at me.

Although he tried to appear calm, I saw the glisten of sweat on his upper lip. He rocked back and forth, waiting for me to begin. I stared at him until he glanced down at his hands.

"Well, you going to ask me something?" he mumbled.

"Like what?" From the corner of my eye, I saw Romero's broad forehead wrinkle. He probably thought I had to be the all-time worst interrogator.

"Hey, man, you came to talk to me."

"I came to listen," I said. "What do you want to tell me?"

"I didn't have anything to do with Jimmy's death."

"Because?"

"Because I was at work."

"Not because he was your friend?"

Eddie flushed. "Of course, he was my friend. What kind of question is that?"

"A pretty simple one. How long did you know Eddie?"

"All my life."

"So, you were friends all your life, even though he was older?"

"We got closer over the last year. Before then, I knew who he was. You know, to speak to."

"And over the last year, is that when you started dating his sister?"

He sat up and crossed his arms over his chest. "Yes, so what?"

"So, nothing." I looked around the room. "I mean nothing at all shows you have anything in common with Jimmy other than his sister."

For a few seconds, no one said anything. The absence of any item with Cherokee cultural connections in Eddie's home made my point loud and clear.

Eddie spun on the stool to face Romero. "You've seen me at the rallies. I've been right by Jimmy's side. Just because I haven't turned my place into a museum doesn't mean I'm not commit-ted to the cause."

"What cause is that?" I asked.

"Returning to the core of our heritage. The energy of the sacred fire. The struggle to be in harmony with nature."

"I see. Like your fire-engine red Camaro and the struggle to win the battle of the Xbox."

"You wouldn't understand," he snapped. "The truth is I have to live in both worlds. I've got a job and responsibilities."

I remembered what Romero told me. "Does one of your worlds include the per capita?"

His face darkened. "I use that money to fund our activities."

"How did Jimmy use his per capita?"

Eddie looked at the floor. "He wouldn't take it."

I decided to ease off a notch before I turned him into a hostile witness. "You weren't just a yes-man then? You had your own opinions?"

Eddie squared his shoulders. "I did. Jimmy knew where I stood."

"Like the protest at the funeral?"

"I warned Jimmy that was a mistake. We'd done enough to put you on notice with our first visit, and you were handling the remains by the book. But Jimmy wanted the publicity, especially since the dead woman was the wife of one of the owners."

"But you went along," I said.

"I went for Skye. I was worried about her if things got out of hand. And they did."

"When was the last time you saw Jimmy?"

"Sunday afternoon at the Boys Club. He was preparing for the ball-play game. I ran by on my way to work. It was about three."

"How did he seem?"

"Fine. He was focused on getting the boys organized."

"He didn't say anything about going to the cemetery that night?"

Eddie hopped from the stool. "Ain't no way he went to the cemetery. Those bastards caught him, took him there, and killed him."

"Who are those bastards?"

Eddie started pacing the small space along the kitchen counter. "Isn't it obvious? The Cransford family. Maybe they had help from their friends."

"The whole family? Son and daughter too?"

Eddie stopped in mid-stride. "I don't know the family. They could all be murdering lunatics."

"Skye and her grandmother said Jimmy walked home after Sunday supper," I said. "Skye said his truck was still there when she left at ten. Do you find it believable that the Cransfords would have abducted Jimmy from his home? And that his grandmother wouldn't have heard anything?"

Eddie slid back on the stool and glanced at Romero. "I don't see how that would be possible. The old woman has ears like a deer."

Romero smiled. "True enough. So I'm assuming Jimmy went out later. Where?"

Eddie slapped his hand on his thigh. "I tell you I don't know. He never said anything to me. We staged the protest and that was the end of it."

"You know his collection of Cherokee artifacts is missing," I said.

"Yes. Skye told me."

"And he didn't say anything about that Sunday afternoon?"

"No. But like I said, we only talked a few minutes."

I looked down at my notepad as if reviewing a list of questions. "Aside from the incident at the cemetery, has Jimmy led other protests?"

"Yes. We've demonstrated at tribal council meetings."

"Against anything in particular?"

"Mostly casino issues. There was a strong debate over whether to build the second. As far as Jimmy was concerned, one was one too many. At least the first casino brought visitors to the museum, Oconaluftee Village, and the outdoor drama. Jimmy said the second will bring nothing but gamblers from Atlanta and undercut support for our cultural attractions. It's on the outskirts of the reservation near Murphy and no one will bother driving into the village."

"Do you agree with him?"

"Yes. A second casino is all about making money, pure and simple."

"And it means more per capita."

"I suppose so."

I scribbled "per capita increase for everyone" on my pad. "Did Jimmy's stance draw a lot of opposition in the tribe?"

"Tribal politics is a full-body contact sport. Everyone knows it's the way it's played. We lost the vote on the second casino and we're moving on. I can't see anyone in the tribe killing him."

"Moving on to what?"

Eddie Wolfe shrugged. "We hadn't decided."

"Or Jimmy hadn't told you his decision."

The young Indian glared at me. "Then he didn't tell anyone else. Face it, Deputy Clayton, your only suspect is the crazy man who attacked Jimmy at the cemetery. Don't try to throw this killing back on the Cherokee."

I smiled and softly said, "I'm just asking questions, Eddie. One final one. What did Jimmy think about the Catawba tribe's efforts to build a casino across the state line in North Carolina?"

The question seemed to take Eddie by surprise. "What's that have to do with anything?"

"You tell me. Was he for it or against it?"

"Jimmy was for it. He thought the competition would make our expansion a risky undertaking, and the banks might reconsider the construction loans to the tribe."

"And if a Cherokee and a vocal band of his followers demonstrated in Raleigh for the Catawba to be allowed the same gaming rights in our state?"

Eddie Wolfe and Detective Romero both looked at me with raised eyebrows.

"It would certainly muddy the legislative waters," Romero said.

"I don't know about legislative waters," Eddie said, "but it would piss off a lot of people." Then he added, "Just the kind of thing Jimmy loved to do."

Chapter Twelve

I asked Eddie Wolfe for his cell number in case I had follow-up questions. As we left, Romero said, "I'm going to see the Swifts. Did you know Swifty is missing?"

Eddie leaned against the metal door jamb. "Yes. Dot came by earlier asking if I'd seen him. I hope the boy just wandered too far and got caught out after dark. He's a smart kid. He knows how to live in the wild."

"When did you see him last?" Romero asked.

"At Sunday's ball-play. Not to speak to. He was warming up for the game."

"Any place in particular he might hike?" Romero asked.

"You'll have to ask his friends."

"Were Swifty and Jimmy close?" I asked.

"I reckon," Eddie said. "Jimmy was his coach and his bus driver."

"What are you thinking?" Romero asked me.

"Danny Swift disappeared yesterday, the day everyone learned of Panther's death."

Romero nodded. "The kid's run off to grieve."

"I bet you're right," Eddie agreed. "If you need a search party, call me. I'll clock out and help." He stepped back inside and closed the door.

I turned to Romero. "I'll wait in the car while you talk with the parents."

"What are you going to do? Just sit and twiddle your thumbs? There's no cell coverage." He jerked his head toward Eddie's trailer. "And that was a good question about Swifty's relationship with Jimmy."

"All right. If you want an extra set of ears."

I followed Romero up the gravel road past three mobile homes to the last one in the row. It was also the one with the neatest landscaping. A flagstone walk outlined with white pebbles arced from the driveway through beds of blue pansies. Gray latticework around the base of the mobile home provided the backdrop for a row of wild azalea bushes. The steps and landing to the front door had been stained a dark oak color in contrast to Eddie Wolfe's unpainted lumber.

"They own their place?" I asked Romero.

"Yes. And the home next door that they rent out. David works as a surveyor's assistant. In the summer, Dot works at Oconaluftee Village. She demonstrates how Cherokees make pottery. During the school year, she teaches elementary reading. Swifty's their only child."

"I guess you'd be worried sick regardless of how many children you had."

"True." Romero sighed. "But Swifty was a difficult delivery. Dot can't have any more children."

At some point in the near future, Susan and I would like to have kids. The prospect that we couldn't would be a shock and a disappointment. "That's too bad. Let's hope Swifty's already home."

"Yeah." Romero pointed to the yellow Toyota Corolla in the driveway. "That's Dot's car. David has an old van. Maybe he's gone to pick the boy up."

I stayed in the yard while Romero climbed the steps and rapped on the glass storm door. Within a few minutes, Romero stepped aside to reveal a slender woman in wheat jeans and a purple tunic. Her jet black hair was pulled back in a single braid that fell over the front of her right shoulder to below her breasts. I estimated her age to be close to my own. Thirty-five at the most.

"Any word?" Romero asked.

She didn't speak. Just shook her head spilling fresh tears down her cheeks.

Romero gestured to me. "This is Deputy Barry Clayton. He and I are investigating Jimmy Panther's death. We talked to Eddie Wolfe. Is it OK if he comes in with me?"

She shrugged and pushed open the storm door. I crossed the threshold and gave her my warmest smile.

"Would you like some coffee?" She spoke so softly I had trouble hearing her.

"None for me," Romero said.

"No, thank you," I said.

The layout of the room was similar to Eddie Wolfe's trailer, but where he had stark walls and a wide-screen TV, the Swifts' home seemed to contain only things made by craftsmen. The furniture was constructed of wood and cane, and the upholstery looked like the cushions were covered in handwoven tapestry. Shelves along the walls held pottery of all shapes and sizes. Plates, vases, cups, urns. I remembered Romero said Dot worked summers at Oconaluftee Village demonstrating Cherokee crafts.

"Your home is lovely, Mrs. Swift," I said. "Did you make all these pieces?"

"Most of them. David and Danny worked on the furniture." She swept her right hand in an arc. "Please. Have a seat."

Romero sat on the sofa and the wood creaked under his weight. He smiled. "Sturdy stuff."

I took a cane-back rocker and Dot sat on the edge of a hard-back chair.

"David's not here," she said. "He's gone to the Oconaluftee Village to see Robbie Ledford."

"What's Robbie doing there?" Romero asked.

"He works after school burning canoes."

I sat quietly, not understanding the conversation.

"Swifty working there too?"

"Yes. Danny demonstrates the blowgun for the tourists."

I noted how Dot didn't refer to her son by his nickname. Most mothers never accepted a nickname conferred upon their children by those outside the family.

"Barry, Robbie's a boy Swifty's age," Romero explained. "Since the village stays open in October through leaf season, some of the kids have part-time jobs after school. They play roles in the portrayal of a 1760 Cherokee settlement." He turned to Dot. "Did Robbie say he knew where Swifty went?"

"No. They all heard about Jimmy at school and Danny left at lunch. No one's seen him since."

"Why did your husband go to the village if you already learned this from Robbie?"

"David wanted to see Robbie face-to-face. He thinks Robbie must know more than he's telling, and he wants to look him in the eye."

"Kids will protect each other," Romero agreed. He looked at me, inviting a comment.

"Mrs. Swift, did your son have a bicycle at school?"

"No. The bus picked him up at the end of the road."

"So, he left school on foot."

"I suppose so."

"Are any of his friends old enough to drive?"

"Not that I know of. Danny mainly hangs out with boys his own age. Mostly members of his ball-play team."

"Is there any place at the Cherokee Boys Club he might be hiding?"

Dot Swift leaned forward in her chair. "We drove by after Danny didn't come to the village to work. No one had seen him."

"I'll swing by again," Romero promised. "Maybe he's holed up in a storeroom or something."

I didn't know what relevance the boy's disappearance had to my case other than Jimmy Panther's murder could have triggered it. Still, I wanted to help if I could.

"Do you have a photograph of your son?" I asked.

She rose from the chair and went to a bookshelf at the end of the room. She took down a rectangular piece of pottery that was a picture frame. The eight-by-ten featured a grinning Cherokee boy standing in front of a roughly cut open field. He held a wooden stick with a circular webbed pocket at one end. A beaded headband pulled his black hair off his high forehead. He stood shirtless, the ball-play stick angled across his chest.

In the field behind him, other boys were frozen in mid stride as they ran—some with shirts, some without.

"Nice looking kid," I said. "How old's the photo?"

"About a month. He was playing a team from one of the other towns. Danny had a great game."

"Did your son ever take part in any of Jimmy's protests?"

"No," she said emphatically. "While David and I agree with some of what Jimmy is fighting for, we didn't go along with his confrontational tactics. Jimmy never let the kids get involved."

"How did your son feel about Jimmy?"

"Danny idolized him," Dot said. "Second only to his father. Sometimes I think David was a little jealous."

It sounded like Swifty didn't need a father figure, but as an only child, he might take to Jimmy as a big brother. "Is it fair to say he would be very upset by Jimmy's murder?"

"Devastated." Again, the tears flowed. "But not as devastated as I will be if something's happened to him."

Romero looked pained by the woman's distress. "We'll find him, Dot. Don't you worry. And I'll talk to Robbie myself." He stood. "Anything else?" he asked me. His tone told me my answer should be no.

"One other thing if it's not a bother. Could I see your son's room?"

Tommy Lee had told me always check the bedroom of a runaway. Sometimes there could be clues through magazine clippings or saved pictures as to the child's destination.

"Yes," Dot said. "But he didn't leave a note or take any of his things. He didn't know Jimmy had died when he left for school yesterday."

"It's a good idea, Dot," Romero said. "We might learn something."

She led us down a short hall to a bedroom at one end of the mobile home. A single bed with a plain brown blanket was underneath a window overlooking the front yard. Over a dresser on the opposite wall hung twin ball-play sticks crossed like blunt spears. A desk with a goose-necked lamp sat under a smaller window in the trailer's end wall. Three books were stacked on the desk. I picked up the top one. *Harry Potter and the Goblet of Fire*. Not unusual reading for Swifty's age. Below it was *The Hunger Games*, also popular with teenagers and shot in the western North Carolina mountains. The third book wasn't in the bedroom of many readers of any age. *Ultimate Guide to Wilderness Living*.

"Is your son reading this for a group activity?"

"No. It's his own interest. Danny likes nothing better than being in the forest."

I flipped through the pages but no notes or bookmarks fell out. "So, he's read it?"

"That and at least ten others," Dot said.

The boy could probably outlast a Special Forces patrol, I thought. Unless he's been injured, he'll come in when he wants. I looked around the room again. No toys, no video games. I dropped to my knees and looked under the bed.

"He doesn't keep anything under there," Dot said.

I pulled out a ball-play stick.

"I don't know where that came from," Dot said. "Maybe he was making it."

To my uneducated eye, the wood looked older than the sticks above the dresser. The webbing or whatever they called it at the end was worn and broken.

"Let me see that," Romero said.

I sat on the floor and raised the stick to the giant towering over me. He moved the shaft laterally in front of his eyes.

"I've seen this before. It belongs to Jimmy Panther."

I scrambled to my feet. "Would Jimmy have given it to him?"

"Maybe." Romero gave a slight shake of his head, cuing me to let it go. He turned to Dot. "Mind if I keep this? I'll ask Emma for a positive identification."

"OK. But I know my boy didn't steal it."

"I'm sure he didn't," Romero said. "And I'll show it to Robbie. Maybe he'll know why your son has it."

"It wasn't there Saturday," Dot said. "I dusted under the bed."

"Probably has nothing to do with anything else. But we'll go straight to the village. You have a landline, don't you?"

"Yes." Dot went to her son's desk and wrote the number on a sheet of paper. "Please call if you learn anything."

"You'll be the first to know," Romero assured her.

We said good-bye and walked down the gravel road to the patrol car. Eddie Wolfe was heading to his Camaro when he turned at the sound of our footsteps. He eyed the ball-play stick.

"Is that Swifty's?"

"No." Romero stopped in front of Eddie. "It's definitely not Swifty's."

Eddie's eyes widened as he studied the stick. "That's Jimmy's. Is Swifty back? Did he bring it with him?"

Romero walked over to the patrol car and tossed the ball-play stick across the backseat. "Swifty's still missing. We found the stick under his bed. Any idea why he'd have it?"

Eddie stared at the patrol car. "No," he finally said.

Romero slammed the back door and signaled me to get in the car.

"You don't think Swifty's the one who stole Jimmy's collection?" Eddie asked.

"Not for a second." Romero got in and started the engine.

As we pulled away, I looked back. Eddie stood frozen by the Camaro, watching our departure.

"Is that the ball-play stick Skye mentioned?" I asked. "The one that's been in the family so long?"

"Yes. I don't know how many greats in front of grandfather, but one of them fashioned it before the Trail of Tears. That's pre-1838."

I knew the Trail of Tears had been the forced relocation of the Cherokee to Oklahoma so that Georgia could claim part of their land, the land on which gold had been discovered. President Andrew Jackson defied the U.S. Supreme Court and let the ethnic cleansing occur. Over thirteen thousand Cherokee were driven from their ancestral homeland in the winter of 1838 without proper clothing, food, or shelter. Between four and six thousand died along the forced march. It was a shameful blot on our history and national character.

"Why are you so sure Swifty didn't take Jimmy's artifact collection?" I asked.

"Because he would have had to have stolen it after Sunday night. Jimmy would have sent out a hue and cry if he'd found it missing. If Swifty didn't learn of Jimmy's death till noon yesterday, he couldn't have made it to Jimmy's on foot before we got there. By then the collection was already gone."

"So, what are you thinking?"

"That the ball-play stick might pry loose Robbie Ledford's tongue if he knows anything. How's your time?"

I checked my watch. Three thirty. "I'm OK. I need to meet my wife no later than five."

"Then let's see where this ancient stick leads us."

Chapter Thirteen

When we hit the main road, my phone became an earthquake of vibrations, signaling that multiple calls had gone to voicemail while I was out of coverage.

Romero smiled. "Either you're very popular or you've got the noisiest belly I've ever heard."

I scrolled through the list of messages. Two were from the Sheriff's Department, one from Susan, and one from the number I recognized as belonging to Darren Cransford. "I'd better check these."

I played Darren's first. "Deputy Clayton, sorry to miss your call. It's crazy here in the office. I'll try to connect with you later." I didn't know which office was crazy because he certainly didn't work at the one in DC. I decided not to get into a conversation over the phone with Darren in front of Romero. Instead I texted that I would call him at five.

Susan left a message that she was back at the hotel and she would see me when she saw me.

The calls from the Sheriff's Department were from Tommy Lee and both shorter than Susan's and Darren's combined. "Talked to Luther," was one; "ME Report," was the other. I punched callback.

"Where are you?" he asked.

"Riding with Romero."

"Rooster!" the detective sergeant interrupted. "I'm taking good care of your boy."

"Tell him it's not you I'm worried about," Tommy Lee said.

I relayed the message and got a volcanic laugh in return.

"Luther broke down when I talked to him," Tommy Lee said. "He admitted lying about where he was Sunday night, but not because he had anything to do with Panther's death. He said he just felt smothered in the house, couldn't go into the kitchen where Eurleen died, and he needed to get out."

"Where?"

"Up on the Blue Ridge Parkway. An overlook where he and Eurleen had their first picnic before they were married."

"In the middle of the night? You believe him?"

"I want to. But I can't without proof. Wakefield's headed up there now looking for any forensic evidence to support Luther's claim."

"Why did he lie?" I asked.

"He says he didn't want to appear foolish in front of you and Wakefield. Then when you told him about Panther's murder, he knew his actions would look suspicious. He only told me because we had the testimony of the guard at the gatehouse."

"Did he change his story about when his children left?"

"No. Did you get a hold of Darren?"

"I missed his call. I'm calling him back at five. What about the ME?"

I heard Tommy Lee shuffle some papers.

"Nothing that reverses anything he viewed at the scene. Markings on the wrists are consistent with standard PlastiCuffs. Entry wound is consistent with a twenty-two and the slug ricocheted inside the skull. Markings can provide a ballistics match but I doubt we'll find them in the system. Time of death still holds between midnight and two."

I heard a page flip.

"There is one interesting item Tuppler uncovered back at the morgue. He found an arrowhead lodged in the waist of Panther's jeans."

"Someone shot him with an arrow?"

Romero yanked his eyes from the road and gave me a curious stare.

"No," Tommy Lee said. "It was trapped under his belt. Tuppler said it looked like Panther had been dragged through soft dirt. There was also a lot of dirt under his fingernails and on his clothing."

"Eurleen's grave was fresh," I said.

"That's what I thought. But Tuppler found high traces of mica that's not present in the soil in that section of the cemetery."

"Lends credence to your theory that Panther was killed elsewhere."

"Yep. And we have that single arrowhead but I don't know what to make of it."

"Maybe Panther caught whoever stole his collection and they fought. Could explain the dirt and the arrowhead getting trapped in his jeans."

"And then they kill him on Eurleen's grave? Why would they do that? There are lots of ravines where they could have dumped the body."

I thought for a moment. Tommy Lee was right. It was more logical that Panther would have been killed in a confrontation with a thief than captured, cuffed, and executed. "If it wasn't Luther, then someone knew enough about what happened at the cemetery to try and frame him."

"That's the way I read it," Tommy Lee agreed. "Where are you and Romero headed now?"

"Oconaluftee Village."

"How's that tie into Panther?"

"Indirectly. I'll brief you later."

"And you're still on with Kevin and Archie?"

"That would be a ten-four," I said.

"Barry, just make sure Kevin doesn't get you into something that's more than you bargained for. His instincts are great, but his self-restraint is nonexistent. And whether Tyrell's connected to our case or not, remember he's a cold-blooded killer."

My mind didn't jump to Kevin or Archie, but to Susan. "Don't worry. I will."

Romero bypassed Oconaluftee Village's stone ticket stand. A guide was just starting with a small group of tourists. He wore a white tunic and red pants with a braided belt cinched over the tunic around his waist. A claw necklace hung midway down his chest. He spoke in an incomprehensible language I assumed was Cherokee. The visitors appeared confused and some laughed nervously.

The guide saw Romero and waved. The detective said something in Cherokee and got a short burst of syllables in response. Then he grinned and spoke to his group. "What I've been saying is Welcome to Oconaluftee Village and the year 1760. What you're witnessing is…"

"Come on," Romero said. "He's with the weapons."

We walked past Indian women in native garb doing beadwork, others throwing river clay for pottery, a man striking flint to fashion arrowheads, and more women weaving baskets.

"What are they using?" I asked Romero.

"River cane and white oak. Each woman likes to develop her own patterns."

"When you spoke Cherokee, were you asking about Robbie Ledford?"

"Yes. He's back at the blowgun demonstration."

"I thought he made canoes." I remembered Robbie's job in the village because three canoes in various stages of completion lay on our left. An older Cherokee with streaks of gray running through his hair tended a small fire burning in the center of one.

"He usually does," Romero said. "Not the actual fire, but he scrapes out the charred wood after it's extinguished. You burn a small section, scrape the burnt remains, and then burn again. We don't want Robbie being a role model for kids going home and burning out a log to make their own canoes. Our lawyers wouldn't like it."

"So, you turn him loose with a blowgun?"

Romero laughed. "Let's call it a demonstration of a father teaching a son to hunt. And hollowed-out river cane is harder to come by than a pack of matches."

Ahead, a small group broke into applause.

"Robbie must have hit the target," Romero said. "But he's not the shot Swifty is."

The applause died and the visitors moved on, leaving a tall man of about thirty beside a boy holding a river cane pole twice his height. The man's hair was buzz-cut like Jimmy Panther's. His tunic was the same style as the first guide's, but red with a white-and-red beaded belt.

The boy was pudgy. His round face was framed by black hair touching his shoulders. The smile generated by the applause vanished when he saw Detective Sergeant Romero.

"How are you, John?" Romero asked.

The man nodded. "Fine. It's kinda slow."

"Tuesdays usually are. I need to talk to Robbie a few minutes."

John glanced first at the boy beside him and then at me. Romero didn't bother with an introduction.

"Robbie seems popular this afternoon," John said.

"Oh, yeah? Anybody besides David Swift?"

Both John and Robbie seemed surprised Romero knew Swifty's father had been there.

"No," John conceded. "Just David."

"Good. The next group won't be here for a few minutes. Why don't you take a break?"

"Sure. Whatever you say." John ambled off toward the village entrance.

Robbie looked at me with a combination of suspicion and fear.

"Let's walk behind the housing exhibit," Romero said. "No sense standing out here and ruining the time period."

"Who's he?" The kid's eyes never left me.

"Deputy Clayton from Laurel County," Romero answered. "He's helping find who murdered Jimmy. You want to help him, don't you?"

Robbie swallowed and looked down at the ground. The nod was barely perceptible.

"I thought so." Romero nudged Robbie along with a hand to his shoulder like a big mother bear steering her cub.

I followed as we arced around various demonstrations till we stopped behind a clay-walled structure with a thatched roof. There were no rear windows so we were unseen by the tour groups.

"Now it's important that you tell us the truth," Romero said. "If you do that, you won't get in trouble."

Again, the faintest of nods.

"When did you see Swifty last?" Romero asked.

"Yesterday. Lunch at school."

"Did he seem upset?"

"Yes."

"Because he heard about Jimmy?"

The kid looked up at us, his eyes wide. "That really set him off."

I didn't wait for Romero to ask the question begged by the boy's answer. I stepped closer. "So, he was upset before then?"

Robbie flushed. He knew he'd revealed more than he intended.

"Come on, son," Romero prompted. "You're not doing Swifty any good by holding back."

"Don't tell Mr. Swift," the boy pleaded. "I only told him Swifty left school at lunch and I didn't know where he was going. That was the truth."

"Only part of the truth," Romero admonished. "What's the whole story?"

Robbie looked over his shoulder as if someone might be sneaking up to eavesdrop. Then his high, whiny voice fell to a whisper. "Jimmy caught Swifty looking in the back of his truck."

"When was this?"

"Sunday. At ball-play. Swifty told me the bed of the pickup was covered with a tarp. Usually it was open. He peeked under it."

"What did he see?" Romero asked.

"Old Indian stuff."

Romero shot me a piercing glance. We both sensed the investigation was about to take a significant turn. I nodded for him to continue.

"What kind of stuff?"

"Boxes and boxes filled with arrowheads, flint tools, some broken pottery. You know, stuff like they have in the museum."

"Jimmy's collection?"

"That's what Swifty said. He'd seen it before. He was surprised that Jimmy got mad at him."

"For finding it in the truck?"

The boy licked his lips. He was obviously afraid we didn't believe him. "I guess. Swifty said Jimmy told him not to tell anyone. That he was thinking about donating it to the national Indian museum in Washington. He didn't want anyone in the tribe to know."

"That doesn't seem like something he'd need to keep a secret," Romero said. "The collection was his."

"Swifty thought the same thing. He didn't believe Jimmy and he told Jimmy so. Jimmy said sometimes you have to do something bad in order for something else that's good to happen."

"Did Jimmy tell him what those things were?"

Robbie's dark eyes locked on Romero. "No. But that's why Swifty was upset. And because of what Jimmy gave him for keeping quiet."

"The ball-play stick," Romero said. "It was in the truck and he gave it to Swifty."

Robbie's mouth fell open. "You found it? You found Swifty?"

"No. But we found the stick under his bed. He hasn't been home for it." Romero leaned against the wall of the dwelling and relaxed. "You're doing good, Robbie. We're almost done."

The kid swayed from side to side. "I need to get back to work."

"In a minute. First tell me when you heard this story from Swifty."

"Yesterday morning before school. Then when we learned what happened to Jimmy, Swifty said the bad thing must have caused it. And now the good thing that meant so much to

Jimmy wasn't going to happen. Swifty said he would find out what that was. And he left school. He made me promise not to say anything."

"And you haven't heard from him since?"

Tears flowed down the round face. "No. Do you think Swifty's dead too?"

"No." Romero laid his hand on the boy's shoulder. "And we'll find him. But not a word of this to anyone. Promise?"

Robbie wiped his eyes on his sleeve. "Yes, sir."

"Then run on. And if you think of anything else, you call me."

The boy scooted around the corner of the house. When the footsteps faded, Romero asked, "What do you think?"

"I think he's telling the truth as far as what Swifty told him. But what it means could be completely different from the way the boys interpreted it."

"Maybe Jimmy told Swifty more than Swifty told Robbie," Romero said.

"Like what the bad thing was that would make something good happen?"

"Yeah." Romero started walking back to the car. "We can assume Jimmy's collection wasn't stolen. At least not from his home."

"And it explains how the arrowhead came to be under his belt."

"That could have happened carrying them to or from his truck," Romero said.

Or if his killers dragged him across the arrowheads, I thought. "How much would the items be worth?"

"Not enough for a man's life."

"And yet Jimmy gave the kid the ball-play stick, his most prized possession, for his silence," I said. "That doesn't add up."

"And Swifty ran away without taking it. Where did he go and why?"

I swept my eyes across the panorama of the Oconaluftee Village and its replication of the culture driven nearly to extinction. "Preservation, not termination." Jimmy Panther's words rang in my head. If he were still speaking to me, what was he saying to a thirteen-year-old kid who idolized him? And how did a collection of artifacts in the bed of a pickup tie into an execution in a cemetery?

I grabbed Romero by the arm, halting the big man's stride. "Would the discovery of artifacts have the same effect as discovering an Indian burial site?"

"You mean was Jimmy going back to salt a wider area of your cemetery?"

"Yes. Both Skye and Eddie Wolfe said he was growing more confrontational. Could he effectively have shut the cemetery down?"

Romero's lips tucked into a fine line as he thought about my question. "Your cemetery's not public property, is it?"

"No. It's privately held."

"Then it would clearly need to be categorized as a burial site and not simply an archaeological find. The Archaeological Resources and Protection Act is federal law enacted to protect irreplaceable archaeological resources on federal, public, and Indian lands. That's what we most commonly enforce when we come across artifact hunters on the Qualla Boundary. But off reservation, human remains would trigger the more extensive actions regardless of who owned the property."

"Would Jimmy go so far as to exhume bones from a known site to perpetrate a hoax?"

"I find that hard to believe," Romero said. "He'd be desecrating one site for the sake of another. A site we're not even sure is more than a single grave."

"Doing something bad so that something else good would happen," I said, quoting what Panther supposedly told Swifty. "It describes that scenario perfectly."

"Yes. But it runs counter to everything I knew about Jimmy. You're talking about disturbing the dead. He wouldn't have taken that action lightly. And his grandmother said he was happy. That doesn't square with grave robbing. He should have been troubled."

"When we pressed her, his grandmother said contented, not happy," I corrected. "I've helped enough terminally ill people make their funeral plans to witness an unexplainable peace come over them once everything is set."

Romero stared at me. "You're saying Jimmy knew he was going to be killed?"

"No. I'm saying he was content to let his plan play out. Whatever that plan was, he was ready to activate it." Skye's word came to me. Not contented. Smugness. "Jimmy must have been confident of its success."

"And instead he wound up dead on a fresh grave."

"With evidence he was killed elsewhere, and a missing collection of artifacts and possible human remains that could have salted the scene of his most recent protest."

"Can you have it both ways?" Romero asked. "That his target was the cemetery and yet he was killed someplace else?"

The detective sergeant had put his finger on the dilemma. The cemetery made Luther my main suspect. The possible abduction introduced other motives from within the reservation. Motives that might have caused a thirteen-year-old boy to go into hiding, or worse, try to find answers on his own.

And there was Kevin Malone and his Boston hit man. I had no idea how they figured into things, only that Kevin's tactics depended upon Archie Donovan, and that made me very nervous.

Chapter Fourteen

Romero dropped me off at the casino around four thirty. I went straight to the hotel room and swiped my keycard through the electronic lock. The steady sound of streaming water came from the shower and I knew Susan had started getting ready for our big night at the gaming tables. I cracked the bathroom door enough to let steam pour out.

"Got room in there for a good-looking guy to soap up with you?"

"Yes," she shouted. "But my husband will be back soon."

"Very funny." I closed the door and sat on the leather love seat by the window. I needed to call Darren Cransford, but I figured I should check in with Tommy Lee first. He was still at the department.

"What's up?" he asked.

"I spoke with Eddie Wolfe. He claims not to know anything, but he did say Panther was supportive of the Catawba casino efforts. Eddie wouldn't put it past him to stage some kind of public demonstration, maybe at the legislature in Raleigh."

"Was something planned?"

"Not that Eddie knew of."

"I thought Panther and Eddie were tight," Tommy Lee said.

"Yeah, but according to Skye and Eddie, Panther was taking their cause in a more confrontational direction. He might not have confided in them. And there's a new development. Hector

Romero asked me to accompany him on an interview regarding a runaway thirteen-year-old boy." I recapped the conversation with Dot Swift and the Oconaluftee Village interview with Robbie Ledford.

When I finished, there was silence on the other end of the phone. I didn't press Tommy Lee for a response. I knew he was thinking.

The water cut off in the shower. Susan opened the bathroom door. She was barely covered by a plush towel with a second one wrapped around her wet hair. "You need to get in here?"

I pointed to the phone at my ear and mouthed, "Tommy Lee."

"Too bad." She spun around, whipping off the body towel a split-second before disappearing behind the bathroom door.

"Bad," Tommy Lee echoed. "And then good."

"What?" I thought Tommy Lee had heard Susan's tease.

"That phrase the kid said. Something bad had to happen for something good to happen. That doesn't sound like a picket line in Raleigh."

"No. But it could be salting the cemetery with his Cherokee artifacts."

"Barry, it's nice to feel our town's important, but that cemetery isn't a cause worth sacrificing what everyone says was so valuable to Jimmy Panther. And if Kevin's right, although I'm hard pressed to see how he could be, Francis Tyrell didn't come down to Cherokee to take out a guy who embarrassed Archie, Luther, and Mayor Whitlock. Believe me, it didn't happen."

"But something was worth it," I said.

"I agree. And you've opened up an interesting possibility. Especially since Luther's alibi seems more probable."

I stood from the sofa. Tommy Lee had new information. "What did you learn?"

"Luther told us he had a couple of Miller Lites up at the Blue Ridge Parkway overlook Sunday night. Wakefield found the bottles."

"Could Luther have planted them later?"

"Maybe. He would have had to do it before I talked to him because I sent Wakefield up there as soon as Luther told me. Luther wouldn't have had time to stage the scene afterwards. Given the way you said he reacted to the news of Panther's death and the site supposedly being the spot for his first picnic with Eurleen, I find his actions credible. When you lose someone close, you take comfort in shared familiar places."

I thought of Emma Byrd taking Romero and me to Panther's lodgings because she wanted to feel close to her grandson. Then I thought of a grieving thirteen-year-old. "My God, Tommy Lee. I think you've hit on something. Danny Swift might be doing the same thing."

"Can you check it out?"

"Not now. I've got to meet Kevin at six. But I'll phone Romero."

Tommy Lee grunted. "I wish we hadn't agreed to this stupid poker thing. If you're right, I'd rather you talk to the boy with Romero."

"Do you want me to hold off?"

"No. If the boy's there, he needs to be found. We don't want the parents worrying a second night."

"I mean do you want me to hold off on the poker game? I can't believe anything's going down at the table."

"Nothing's going down. But I don't think that's the intent."

Tommy Lee wasn't making sense. "You think Kevin's just hassling the guy?" I asked.

"Archie's got his eyes on Tyrell, you'll have your eyes on Archie and Tyrell, and no one will be watching Kevin."

"Watching him do what?"

"Anything he has to, Barry. Don't forget it." Tommy Lee hung up.

I tried to reach Detective Sergeant Romero at the Cherokee police station but was told he'd left for the day. I followed up with his cell, but that went straight to voicemail. I left him the suggestion that Swifty could be at Panther's and asked him to call me. Then I retrieved Darren Cransford's number from the phone log, took out my notepad, and moved to the small desk opposite the bed. I remembered Tommy Lee's goal to drive a wedge between the stories of father and son. But with Luther a less likely suspect, Darren Cransford now merited a different approach.

"Hello?" He sounded tentative, like he'd never answered a phone before.

"Darren, it's Barry Clayton."

"Yes, Mr. Clayton. Is anything wrong?"

Darren and I were about the same age and he'd called me Barry up till now. The new formality put distance between us, and I didn't know whether it was a defensive move or continued anger at the debacle in the cemetery. I decided to forge ahead aggressively.

"Yes, Darren. Something's very wrong, especially for Jimmy Panther. He was found dead yesterday morning in the cemetery."

"I know. My sister told me. Do you suspect my father?"

"What has he told you?"

"I haven't spoken with him."

That response surprised me. "You're kidding? A man is murdered on your mother's grave and you don't talk to your father?"

"I knew any discussion would only upset him."

"Did your sister agree with your decision?" I asked.

"She did. She spoke with him and he assured her he had nothing to do with it. I thought it was better to leave it at that."

I jotted down that Darren claimed no contact with Luther after the murder. "And I guess things were crazy at your office."

"You know it. I had to catch up on a lot of work after mother's funeral."

"Now which office would that be? You're no longer employed by Wilder and Hamilton."

Silence.

"Where did you go Sunday night when you told your father you had to get back to DC?"

"Did you tell him?" Darren whispered the question.

"No. If he knows, it's because he called them or your sister told him."

"Sandra wouldn't say anything."

"And why's that?"

"She wouldn't want to create a rift between my father and Mack Collins."

"What's Mack Collins got to do with any of this?"

"He's the one who got me fired. Called my boss and complained I was lobbying for the Catawbas."

Darren's disjointed answers suddenly made sense. Sandra told me her brother had taken on the Catawba tribe as a client using his family connection to State Senator Collins. But Mack Collins wasn't in favor of the Catawba casino proposal. His loyalty was to western North Carolina and to preventing the negative economic impact a rival casino would create. Darren had to be the dullest knife in the drawer if he hadn't seen that conflict.

"Had Mack asked you directly not to represent the Catawbas?" I asked.

"Yes, but I thought that was just for show. I knew he had aspirations for statewide office, maybe even governor, and bringing jobs and growth to another part of the state would play in his favor."

"So, he called your firm and told them you were moonlighting. When was this?"

"Two weeks ago. Since then I've been working full time for the Catawba tribe and a group of businessmen in Kings Mountain."

"Where did you go Sunday? And don't lie because we can backtrack your phone."

"I went to Kings Mountain. We had a meeting that night."

"Can anyone verify it?"

"Verify it?" His voice rose to an indignant shout. "Barry, you think I'm lying to you?"

"You've already lied about your job, so don't get high and mighty on me. Who was at the meeting and why was it so important?"

"OK, OK. Chandler Gibson is president of the chamber of commerce. He'll tell you I got to his office a little before seven.

And this is ironic as hell because we were meeting about Jimmy Panther."

I wrote "Panther and Kings Mountain" on my pad. "Because of the funeral?" I asked.

"Because the Indian freaked me out. He knew we were burying my mother and still he sent that broken feather and picketed the cemetery. He proved to me he was a loose cannon and I wanted no part of him."

I thought back to our ride in the family car and how Darren told his father not to get upset over the warning letter and that they didn't know for sure who sent it. Now I understood he was protecting Jimmy Panther, his ally.

"You enlisted his help, didn't you?"

"Yes," Darren admitted. "Panther contacted someone in the Catawba tribe and the information was passed to me. I thought he could be an effective spokesmen with the legislature or any rallies we might hold. But he started speaking out on his own, and giving us orders."

"What kind of orders?"

"To be ready to press an advantage he was creating. Something that would affect the dynamics of the whole debate. A game-changer, he called it."

"What was it?"

"I don't know. He wouldn't say. And then he got sidetracked with the Indian remains in the cemetery, and everything went to hell as far as I was concerned."

"Did your friends in Kings Mountain feel the same way?"

"Yes. They're respected members of their community. They don't want to be embarrassed."

"Were they angry?"

"You mean angry enough to kill him? No way. We voted to drop any association with him and pretend we'd never known him."

Darren's story sounded plausible, but I would need to check it out.

"Where are you now?" I asked.

"In Cherokee. With Panther out of the picture, I thought I'd see if someone else might be a more restrained and reasoned voice of support."

I decided not to tell him I was on the reservation as well. "Are you talking about others in Panther's protest movement?"

"Yes. Too soon to see his sister, but I understand her boyfriend might be a possibility. Eddie Wolfe's his name."

"OK. Then I'll be back in touch. Be careful."

"About what?"

"About your life. Somebody saw Panther as a threat and unless you know a lot more than you're telling, the waters are too murky to know what lies beneath them. Watch your step."

"You too," he replied, in a voice as cold as a frozen mountain stream.

I sat at the desk for a few minutes, thinking over what I'd learned so far. The events and interviews pointed to a very specific act that Panther planned. I could only speculate at its impact, but conservatively I estimated we were talking about millions of dollars, not counting what projected increases in per capita payments might flow into the tribe. And Panther wasn't breaking the law; he was triggering it.

"You off the phone?" Susan stood in the bathroom doorway. She must have changed in the small hallway while I'd been engrossed in my conversation with Darren.

"At least till after we see Kevin."

She walked to the bed and sat on the edge. Her black dress was simple in its elegance. The tight waist showed off her figure. The thin shoulder straps left plenty of space for the necklace of jade and opal gracing her neck. Her auburn hair hung loose to her shoulders, its soft sheen overshadowing the subtle highlights of the silver encasing the semiprecious gems.

"You set a high bar, Doctor Clayton. If James Bond is in the casino tonight, he's going to look more than twice."

She smiled and patted the necklace. "You like it? I bought it this afternoon."

"I like it. But you could wear a string of popcorn and still look beautiful."

"And how's my James Bond? Do you have a few minutes before you get ready to tell me about your day?"

I checked my watch. Five twenty. All I needed was fifteen minutes for a quick shower and change of clothes. "Definitely. And then you can tell me if I'm crazy."

I summarized what happened after she left me at the police station. Telling the events helped reinforce the theory percolating in my mind. And Susan's sharper intellect would be the perfect sounding board.

Fifteen minutes later I finished with Darren's warning to watch my step.

"He knows more than he's telling," Susan said.

"I think so. But I'm not sure of his motive. I don't think he had anything to do with Panther's death, so who is he protecting?"

"Maybe he's afraid of someone," she suggested.

"Mack Collins is the only one he ran up against. That got him fired and so there's not much more Mack can do to him. Despite Darren's actions, Mack professes to be close to Luther and upset that he could be charged as a suspect."

"But we're talking about the casino, not the cemetery, being at the heart of the case."

"Yes. The arrowhead and the dirt lead in that direction." I stood from the desk and paced between the bed and window. "We uncovered artifacts and Cherokee remains at the cemetery, spurring Panther to draw attention to the protection of Indian relics. He pursued his efforts, going for maximum press coverage. He further gained an opportunity with Eurleen Cransford's death."

"Do you think you missed foul play?"

"No. She wasn't in good health. I think her death and the discovery of the burial site presented Panther with an opportunity to enhance a plan he already had in place."

"And this is where the arrowhead and dirt come into the spotlight?"

I nodded. "Exactly. Panther wasn't going to salt the cemetery.

He was going to salt the construction site of the new Cherokee casino. Romero told me artifacts at an archaeological find on Indian land are protected by federal law. Construction would have been shut down until the exact nature of the discovery had been determined. No telling how extensively Panther would have spread his items, and you know he would have been there to see them uncovered and make sure the world heard about it."

"You think the discovery at the cemetery gave him the idea?"

"No. I think his plan was already underway, and someone found out about it. That would explain why Frankie Tyrell came to Cherokee before we discovered the relics at the cemetery. Panther read Melissa's article and jumped at the chance to begin his protest early. That press momentum would have carried over to the salted casino site, creating an even bigger story."

"Have you got a soil match?" Susan asked.

"No. We haven't requested one yet. I don't know the exact location, but we'll get samples tomorrow."

"You think someone caught him in the act?"

"Yes. Or knew ahead of time he was going to be there. Swifty might not be the only one who saw the artifacts in the pickup. And Swifty might know who that other person could be."

"Do you think the kid's in danger?"

"Only if someone thinks he's got incriminating information." My mind flashed to Dot Swift holding the picture of her son. "Whether Swifty actually does or not isn't the point."

"And your suspect list?"

"Just ballooned to anyone who stands to lose a lot of money. With a new casino, that's everything from construction to the contract for gaming machines, or a fellow Cherokee whose per capita could potentially double for life."

"How many's that?" Susan asked.

"Around fourteen thousand tribal members."

"How many could hire a hit man?"

I toasted her with an imaginary glass. "That, my dear, might be the determining factor. And our friend Kevin Malone may have the key to our case after all."

Chapter Fifteen

"You look absolutely stunning." Kevin Malone held open the door to his hotel room and seemed enraptured by Susan's appearance.

"Thank you," Susan replied as she slipped by him.

He turned to follow her, leaving me to catch the door for myself. "No, I mean it. Absolutely stunning. If you're in the poker room, then no one will be looking at their cards. Especially Frankie. He has an eye for the ladies."

"Then I suggest we keep Susan out of the poker room."

Kevin pivoted and grinned. "Oh, hi, Barry. You look acceptable."

I wore a tan sport coat, white open-neck shirt, and charcoal slacks. I knew I was a little overdressed, but I was the escort for the Queen of the Poker Room.

Kevin indicated we should sit down in the conversation area between the bed and window. Like our room, there was a small love seat and matching chair. A folder lay in the seat of the chair. Kevin picked it up and sat down. Susan and I took the love seat. We watched Kevin open the folder and flip through the thin stack of papers. He extracted a photograph and passed it to me.

The eight-by-ten showed a middle-aged man in a finely tailored charcoal suit. The picture caught him stepping into a limousine with his head turned toward the camera as if the photographer had called his name. Behind the car I could make out the corner of a bar and the letter O with an apostrophe after it. The remainder of the word was blocked by a delivery van traveling in the opposite direction. The sign could have read anything from O'Brien's to O'Shaughnessy's.

I studied the man closer. He didn't have the feral features I'd expect of a hired assassin. His face was oval, swarthy, and framed by tight black curls. His nose had a slight twist like it had been broken and not properly set. In a strange way, it gave a rugged look to an otherwise plain face. Although he was bent to enter the rear seat, I estimated his height to be six feet or six-one. He appeared fit. I remembered Kevin calling him Whitey Bulger's society face, and I could see him comfortably wearing an Armani suit or brass knuckles. Maybe both at the same time.

"Is this Tyrell?" I asked, and gave the photo to Susan.

"Yes," Kevin said. "The picture was shot about a year ago when we were tailing him during the discovery phase of the trial. When the DA's witness list went to the defense, we checked in on Bulger's known muscle."

"Like the story you told me about Tyrell and the Walther P22."

"Correct." Kevin pulled a second photo from his folder. "I took this earlier today. I didn't have proper paper to print it on and it's a little blurry because I shot it through the lobby window when Tyrell went out for a smoke."

Tyrell was framed from the waist up in a three-quarter profile. He cupped a cigarette, protecting it from a breeze. He wore an aqua-blue shirt unbuttoned at the neck. The rolled-back sleeves exposed hairy forearms more muscular than one would have thought from the first photo. Tyrell seemed to be staring intently at something out of frame.

"What's he looking at?" I asked.

"Nothing," Kevin said. "He was just thinking. Smoked two cigarettes back-to-back and then went up to his room."

"You tail him?" I asked.

"Not to his room. I don't want him to see me. That's why you, Susan, and Archie have to be my eyes tonight."

I returned the pictures to Kevin. "What makes you think something's going to happen?"

"Because when the tournament starts tomorrow, access to the poker room is restricted. Tyrell won't be moving in and out as freely, and spectators keep their distance. Have your phones handy, but out of sight, and text me if you see anything unusual."

"What are you going to be doing?" I asked.

"Drinking in a dark corner of one of the bars." He laughed. "Don't worry. It will be a wee one. Or two, if your man Archie's as good a player as you say he is."

I pointed to the folder. "You going to show him those photos?"

"The last one, so he knows who he's dealing with. The other one looks a little too much like a cliché mobster and his driver. Besides, my uncle owns O'Malley's, the bar in the background, and I don't want to spread around a picture of his fine establishment with a six-foot-high dog turd standing in front of it."

"If Tyrell did execute Panther, who do you think hired him?" I asked.

Kevin shrugged. "That's where your investigation comes in. I'm giving what I think are the means."

"But there must be some link back to Boston."

"Isn't organized crime deep in the casino business?" Susan asked.

Kevin set the folder on the floor by his chair, got up, and went to the minibar. "If you're going to make me think, then I need a drink. What will you have? I'm afraid the only Irish in stock is Tullamore Dew, but it's a fine Irish product and triple distilled."

Susan and I declined. Kevin opened a minibottle and emptied the liquor into a hotel glass.

He raised it to us. "May God hold us in his hand. And not squeeze his fist too tight." He wrapped his own hand carefully around the glass and returned to his chair. "The casino business is business, my dear. Now it's highly regulated and traded on the stock exchange. That's not to say certain favors and reciprocal expectations don't exist. But you'll find that in any business."

He took a sip of whiskey and smacked his lips. "I don't think the money for the hit came from Boston. Something else is going on here. So far, I haven't seen anyone meet with Tyrell, but if it happens tonight, don't be surprised if it's a local face because I think your Indian was a local problem."

Kevin's assessment didn't contradict anything my investigation had uncovered. I decided it was time to be more forthcoming and I gave him a summary of where the case stood. I knew I held his interest because he neither interrupted nor took a drink during my report. When I concluded, he reached down for the glass and drained it in one swallow. He looked out the window as if searching for something in the surrounding hills.

When he finally spoke, he kept his eyes focused on the view. "How well do you know this Darren Cransford?"

"Not real well," I said. "We were in grade school together and then his father sent him north to boarding school."

Kevin shifted in his chair and stared at me. "Boarding school? How many mountain people send their kids to boarding school?"

"A few. Luther was a successful businessman. A real estate developer when times were flush. Mack Collins' children went to prep school, and I guess Luther thought if it was good enough for his friend's kids, it was good enough for his own. I've not seen Darren or his sister Sandra much other than when they're home for holidays."

"But the families must have kept up if Darren thought he could influence Mack Collins for the Catawbas."

"Luther and Mack are tight," I agreed. "That's why Mack's so worried Luther's our prime suspect. Where are you going with this?"

"The B word. It's my first thought because the landscape of Irish history is littered with it."

The only B word that came to my mind was bitch, and I could think of no reason Kevin would be reticent to say it. "Sorry, I'm not following you."

"Betrayal. What's the best way for a movement to fail, from Judas and Christ to the Cherokee Trail of Tears I've been reading about? It's to put your trust in the wrong people. What if Darren Cransford wasn't really working for the Catawba tribe but was loyal to this state senator who's against their casino? If Panther had a plan, Darren Cransford would be in a position to sabotage it."

"But Darren's the one who told me Panther was planning a game-changer. Why would he even raise the possibility?"

"Don't underestimate man's capacity for deceit," Kevin said. "The best way for Darren to shift attention away from himself is to feed you plausible explanations leading you to believe he's trying to help."

"But killing Panther on his own mother's grave?"

Kevin shrugged. "Certainly puts him at the rear of the suspect line, which is where he'd want to be."

"You're saying because he's the least likely culprit, he's the prime culprit. Using that logic, Susan and I are more likely candidates."

"He's here in Cherokee, isn't he? He knew about the broken feathers, the fight at the cemetery, and his alibi with the businessmen is only as good as the length of the meeting and the travel time back here. How long would that be?"

"Darren said he had his meeting at seven in Kings Mountain. If it lasted two or even three hours, he could be back at the cemetery by eleven thirty or midnight at the latest."

Kevin nodded. "Well within the time frame of Panther's death."

I looked at Susan. She nodded her agreement with what Kevin said.

"All right," I said. "Darren's still on the list. Tommy Lee's pulling his phone records and reconstructing any location info we can. But that still doesn't give us a connection to Tyrell."

"I know," Kevin said. "And maybe our luck will change tonight. Keep an eye out for Cransford. Does he know Archie Donovan?"

"Yes. But he also knows Archie likes to play poker, so if Susan and I see him first, we'll try to fade into the woodwork. Archie by himself shouldn't raise suspicion."

A knock came from the door.

"That's him now," I said.

"Let him in." Kevin opened his folder and pulled out the single photo of Tyrell at the casino. He slipped everything else under the bed.

Archie flashed a big smile as he entered the room. "Everything's set. I'm ready to do this."

Kevin offered his hand. "Good to see you again, Mr. Donovan."

"Likewise. And call me Archie. I'm glad to help. I don't want to screw it up." He looked to Susan. "Wow, you look great." Then he tugged at the sleeves of his blue blazer. "Do I look all right? I wasn't sure how I should dress."

Archie wore an open-neck white dress shirt under the standard blazer. His khaki pants were sharply pressed and his tassel loafers were buffed to a soft shine. He wasn't wearing socks. Time travel back fifteen years and he could have been heading for a frat party.

"You look fine," Susan said.

"Come in and sit down," Kevin said. "The main thing is for you to be comfortable." He indicated that Archie should take the vacant chair while he sat on the edge of the bed.

Susan and I returned to the love seat.

"I thought I should have layers," Archie explained. "In case you need me to wear a wire." He patted his chest. "This sport coat has a deep inside pocket."

"Good thinking, but that won't be necessary. Just play your best poker. Tyrell's very competitive. If he sees you're the man to beat, I'm betting he'll hang in there."

"How much seed money will I have?"

"Two thousand. Can you make it last?"

"I guess I'd better. Is this guy packing heat?"

Packing heat and wearing a wire. Archie had been watching too much TV.

Kevin laughed. "As long as you don't cheat or accuse him of cheating, you'll be safe." Then he frowned. "You're not carrying, are you?"

"No. Not even an extra ace up my sleeve."

Kevin handed Archie the photograph. "Here he is. I've made arrangements for you to be in the game at seven thirty. Don't seem overly interested in him. Just let things develop naturally."

Archie studied the picture. "A smoker. He does live dangerously. I wonder if he'll have to take a break."

"If he does, Barry and Susan will be positioned to watch him. You just keep him in the game. Note if he makes eye contact with anyone in particular in the poker room. I'll debrief you when it's over."

"How will I know when to cash out?" Archie asked.

Kevin looked at me. "Barry will come in and give you a nod. Then you can call it quits."

"What if I'm winning?"

"Then quit immediately. I can explain more money being returned to the department better than less."

Archie took a final look at the photograph. "Sounds simple enough."

"Good. Why don't you grab a bite to eat? It could be a long night. We'll meet back here when it's over."

Kevin and Archie stood and shook hands a second time. I walked Archie to the door.

I was feeling pretty good about the way he was playing it. That was until he whispered, "Don't worry, Barry. I've got this." When Archie tells you not to worry, it's time to worry.

Susan and I spent the next thirty minutes wandering the casino. I tried my luck at video blackjack and actually won a few hands. The problem was that the electronic cards were dealt so fast that the very process of calling for a hit or stand became addictive and I was racing through the hands. Susan sat at a machine beside me and I noticed she took the time to study each play with a more discerning eye. She was also up forty dollars.

"You want to quit while you're ahead?" I asked.

"You want me to quit while I can still cover your losses?"

"Maybe that's not such a bad idea. Let's each get a glass of wine and watch some of the action at the live tables. Then we can migrate to a position outside the poker room."

I went to the nearest bar and bought two glasses of pinot grigio. "What would you like to see?" I asked Susan.

"Since we've been playing video blackjack, I'd like to watch how it works with a dealer." She tipped her glass to me. "Maybe I'll build up the nerve to try a few hands."

Signs above the tables indicated the various games. We walked past a crowd encircling a roulette wheel. The clatter of the ball built an air of excited anticipation as eager faces followed the bouncing marble until it rested in a slot. Double zero. A united chorus of groans rose from the table.

"Easy come, easy go," I said.

"There's the blackjack tables." Susan pushed her wineglass ahead like a baton. "Oh, my God, it can't be."

I found the nearest blackjack sign and then looked beneath it. Two men sat side by side on stools directly across from the dealer. One looked like a rotund potato that had fallen out of a giant grocery bag. It was Mayor Sammy Whitlock in a brown polyester leisure suit that must have been the fashion hit for fifteen minutes in 1975.

The other man was long and lean with his baggy black trousers hitched up halfway to his armpits. He wore a western-style shirt and a string tie, evidently his idea of a cardsharp's wardrobe. A pair of sunglasses rested on top of his curly white hair.

I stepped quickly ahead of Susan and hurried to the table. I leaned in and whispered to the taller man, "Just what the hell do you think you're doing?"

Uncle Wayne turned around and glared at me. "Ssshh," he hissed through gritted teeth. "We're undercover."

Chapter Sixteen

I looked at the mayor. He stared straight ahead, refusing to acknowledge my presence.

"You two have to get out of here immediately," I said.

"Is there a problem, sir?" The dealer spoke to Uncle Wayne with the hint he could make the problem go away.

"No." Uncle Wayne flipped up his facedown card. "Blackjack."

The dealer slid over a stack of chips and I noticed my uncle sat with a small fortune in front of him.

"Sammy, would you hold my seat for me?" Uncle Wayne asked the mayor. "Is that all right, young man?" he asked the dealer.

"Yes, sir. Take your time."

"Oh, this won't take long at all." Uncle Wayne slid off the stool and dropped the sunglasses over his eyes. He must have thought he looked cool. He looked blind. "Come on."

He led Susan and me away from the congestion of the tables to a spot under the wide stairway to the second level. "Sammy and I are helping Archie help Luther."

"Archie had no business bringing you into this," I argued.

"All we're doing is watching some guy Archie's playing poker with. The guy doesn't know us from Adam." He looked around the casino. "Look at all the old people. Sammy and I blend in better than you and Susan."

As he spoke, a busload of seniors came through the door. My uncle had a point.

"That's all," I insisted. "Just watch."

"If the guy gets up to go to the john or grab a smoke, we'll shadow him."

"No. Definitely not."

Uncle Wayne drew his old frame up to full height so he was looking down at me. "What's the difference between watching him play cards and watching him walk to the bathroom?"

"You have to be in motion."

"Me and hundreds of other people. Sammy and I will spread out. The guy's not going to think either one of us is Joe Friday."

"Who?"

"You know. From *Dragnet*. Just the facts, ma'am."

I had no idea what he was talking about.

"Never mind. Before your time."

My knee-jerk reaction to losing an argument was to latch onto any possible problem. "But you don't know what the guy looks like."

Uncle Wayne waved the objection aside. "Archie's got that figured out. First time the guy ups a bet, Archie's going to tug his earlobe."

"And you think he won't notice that?"

"Of course not. Archie's tugging his own earlobe."

I heard Susan's unsuccessful attempt to smother a laugh. I knew I'd lost.

"I've got to get back to the table," Uncle Wayne said.

"How many of those chips are your money?" I asked. "I don't want you losing your shirt."

"Thirty dollars."

"Thirty dollars? There must be three hundred dollars worth of chips at your seat."

Uncle Wayne shook his head in disbelief. "Well, ain't that the point? When I was stationed in Korea, I doubled my pay playing blackjack and sent it to your mother each month. I may be old, but I still know how to hold my own in a place like this. Might be fancy, but the cards still come out one at a time. Now, if you'll excuse me." He flipped the sunglasses up on his head and walked away.

"Maybe you've got the wrong guy in the poker room," Susan said.

"Maybe we need to come back here with my uncle and our lifesavings."

Susan hooked my arm with her own. "It's almost seven thirty. We'd better get in place."

"Yes, my queen."

We ascended the curving staircase, arm in arm, with our wineglasses in our free hands. We were halfway to the top when my left elbow was knocked to the side, sloshing pinot grigio down my pants and splattering the back of the aqua-blue shirt of the man pushing by me.

Frankie Tyrell scowled over his shoulder without so much as an "excuse me" or "I'm sorry," and then bolted up the remaining stairs.

"I don't know if he's a killer," Susan whispered, "but he's a first-class jerk."

"I hope Archie cleans him out," I said.

The poker room was crowded and it took several minutes for me to spot Archie at one of the back tables. Monitors placed around the room listed names of players waiting for positions to open, and I guessed Tyrell had been in a hurry to take his seat before he was bumped. I saw him in his wine-splattered shirt sitting directly across from Archie. There were ten players in all.

"Where are the dealers?" Susan asked.

"These are electronic poker tables. Everything is handled by a computer. Players use a shielded monitor to view their cards and place bets. You buy in and add funds to your account through the cashier." I pointed to a window in one corner. "They only bring in live dealers for the big national tournaments."

Susan walked to one of the tables nearer the door. She watched a couple of hands and then returned. "They're playing a different kind of poker than I learned."

"Yes. They don't take their clothes off."

She gave me a sharp elbow in the ribs. "You're one to talk,

Mr. Wet Pants. You should go change before people think you're incontinent."

I did feel sticky. And cold. "Let me watch them get started, then I'll run up to the room." I angled my position so that I could see a side view of Archie and Tyrell. Both men concentrated on the center of the table where the community cards were displayed.

"You probably learned stud and draw poker." I told Susan. "This is called Texas Hold'em. Each player gets two cards face down on his personal screen. The Hole cards. Cup your hands around them and the corners fold back for viewing. There's a round of betting. Then three cards called the Flop are dealt face-up in the center, and there's another round of bets. A fourth card named the Turn is dealt followed by bets, and finally a fifth card, the River, comes up. After a final round of betting, those five community cards are played in common and the player who makes the best five-card poker hand combining his cards with the community cards wins the pot."

I saw Archie's eyes trace the progress of the betting as he studied each opponent's face in turn. Tyrell did exactly the same. Each man sought any facial or body tells that would prove an advantage over the course of play. When the sweep of Archie's gaze landed on Tyrell, he tugged his left ear. I glanced back at the door and saw Uncle Wayne and the mayor. My uncle displayed no reaction to Archie's gesture, but Mayor Whitlock gave an OK sign that was as subtle as a cannon blast. Uncle Wayne quickly retreated, leaving the erstwhile undercover, overly dramatic His Honor to scurry after him. I hoped they would find discreet viewing positions along the mezzanine outside the poker room.

I took a few minutes to study the other players at Archie's table. Although I thought Kevin's theory that Tyrell might connect with someone during the game was not only a long shot but extremely risky on his part, I memorized the eight faces in case one of them met Tyrell afterwards. All were men; all were white. Four seemed to know each other. Probably poker buddies who were on a guys' retreat. They sat beside each other arcing the table from Tyrell to Archie. From their ages, I took them for retirees who could hang out overnight at the casino in the middle of the week without worrying about a treacherous drive home through the curvy mountain roads.

On the other side of Tyrell sat a player in his mid-twenties. He looked nervous and unsure of himself. An older man on his right frequently whispered to him. I took them to be father and son. Perhaps dad was teaching the game as part of the family heritage.

The two remaining players to Archie's left weren't so much serious gamblers as serious drinkers. The game hadn't gone five minutes before they signaled for another round. They made exaggerated gestures when they folded and I expected their card acumen to fall as their alcohol level rose.

I decided to risk sneaking a photo that I could send Kevin. I whispered my plan to Susan and used her as a shield while I readied my phone for the picture. I made sure the flash was off and then slid from behind Susan, holding the phone against my dark suit. I snapped a few shots and then checked them. The light level was sufficient so I repeated the maneuver from two other positions to get at least a decent profile of each player. I sent the three best photos to Kevin.

From the tone of the table conversation, I gathered that Archie and Tyrell were the more consistent winners. Occasionally one of the others would win a big hand, but that seemed to be in spite of their playing ability. Tyrell and Archie watched each other closely, each apparently realizing the other was the strongest competition.

"Is Archie doing OK?" Susan asked.

"As far as I can tell. The other players are providing a flow of chips to keep him in the game with Tyrell. The two of them seem evenly matched." I tugged my sticky pants off my thighs. "This is a good time for me to change if you're comfortable staying alone."

"With Uncle Wayne and Mayor Whitlock as backup? Don't give it a second thought."

I left the poker room and stayed on the second floor, following the signs to the hotel tower elevators. A large senior tour group must have been checking in below because each time the elevators opened, the interior looked like an AARP sardine can. After four unsuccessful attempts, I opted to take the stairs. Our room was only two flights up and I would avoid being remembered as the stinking wino who jammed himself into the herd of gambling grandparents.

I pulled the door open to the fourth floor and started to step into the corridor. To my surprise, Kevin Malone was bent over the electronic lock of one of the rooms a few doors down. He was between me and my room so I couldn't walk by without being seen. I immediately ducked back.

I cracked the stairwell door enough to peer out. Kevin held some black box about the size of a cell phone. Short wires curled from it to the edge of a card inserted into the slot of the lock. Kevin was watching the elevators farther down the hall. He hadn't heard or seen me.

The latch clicked. He pushed open the door and pulled his mysterious device free. I had no doubt he'd somehow generated the security code and was breaking into Frankie Tyrell's hotel room.

I waited a few minutes to make sure he wasn't immediately coming out and then I tiptoed down the hall to my room. I fell back on the bed, my mind racing. Had Tommy Lee suspected Kevin would try something like this? Why else would he have pointed out no one would be watching Kevin? We were to be Kevin's alarm system in case Tyrell left the poker room. This whole alleged stakeout was nothing but an opportunity for Kevin to execute a warrantless search without fear of being surprised.

But what should I do? If I called Tommy Lee, I'd be forcing him to confront his friend, set Kevin up for disciplinary action, and maybe enable a guilty Frankie Tyrell to get off. Kevin knew he couldn't use anything he discovered in the room. Maybe he was looking to confirm his suspicions and then press for a warrant when he was certain a search would yield incriminating evidence. A more ominous possibility struck me. What if Kevin was planting evidence?

My phone rang and I thought Susan must be alerting me that Tyrell had left the game. I snatched it from my belt and read a number, not a name. "Yes?" I answered.

"Barry, it's Hector."

Detective Sergeant Romero. He and the Cherokee Police Department would be brought in if I reported Kevin.

"You got my message?" I asked.

"Yes. I didn't call you back because I went straight up to Emma Byrd's place."

"Had she seen Swifty?"

"No. But Eddie Wolfe had been out there."

"He didn't say anything to us about it."

"That's because he hadn't gone yet. He went right after he left us. When he saw Jimmy's ball-play stick, he must have thought Swifty had been up there and maybe gone back."

"Did you talk to him?"

"No. He'd left."

"Did you go up to Jimmy's?"

"Yes. I didn't see anything different from when we were there yesterday."

"You checked both the summer and winter lodges?"

"Yes. The asi looked like it hadn't been disturbed in months. Emma said Jimmy usually moved into it about the first of October."

"Just a week away," I said. "The nights are getting cold enough that I'd want a fire if I were out in the open."

"Or staying in the asi," Romero added. "I asked Emma to keep an eye out and let me know if she saw, heard, or smelled anything."

"Is she OK? I mean with someone possibly trespassing on Jimmy's property?"

"She's worried about Swifty. She knows he was close to her grandson. She's hoping he'll show up."

"All right. What next?"

"Assuming Swifty doesn't come home tonight, we need to talk to Eddie Wolfe tomorrow morning."

"We?" I asked.

"Yes. I find it curious that Eddie didn't suggest to us that Swifty might be at Jimmy's. And even more curious that he told Emma to let him know first if she saw Swifty before notifying anyone else. That would link Swifty and Eddie in a way that sounds like Eddie wants to interject himself into your case."

I agreed. "He either wants to know what Swifty knows, or make sure their stories match. Either way strikes me as having underlying motives."

"That's what I think," Romero said. "Emma said she'll call me first." He paused a second. "Can you stay over in Cherokee? I can put you up if you need a bunk."

I hadn't told the detective that Susan and I'd be spending the night because I didn't want to explain the now-tainted surveillance of Tyrell. "Thanks. Susan and I decided to make an evening of it so we got a room."

"Good. Can you be ready for an eight o'clock pickup?"

"Yes. I'll be waiting where you dropped me this afternoon."

I hung up. Suddenly my murder case had too many moving parts. A missing boy, a friend of the murder victim wanting to control access to that boy, a mobster hit man, a PR man who might be sabotaging his own client, and a potentially rogue cop making up his own rules for his own version of justice.

Burying people sure was a lot easier than uncovering who killed them.

I changed into another pair of dark slacks, rolled up the sleeves of my dress shirt and ditched the sport coat. When I left the room, I didn't look back down the hall but walked straight to the elevator.

Susan waved to me from a cocktail table standing just outside the poker room. She was still nursing her wine.

"Anybody try to pick you up?" I asked.

"No. But I'm taking that as a sign that everyone must have seen my dashing escort and realized competition was hopeless."

"Just keep telling me that."

She studied me a second. "What's wrong? You look upset."

"I'll tell you later." I looked around the mezzanine. "Any sighting of our fearsome twosome?"

"No. Either they're masters of disguise or your uncle returned to the blackjack table and will need an armed escort when he leaves."

"How about Archie?"

"Doing well, as far as I can tell. The father-son duo dropped out and a man and woman took their place."

"Husband and wife?"

"I doubt it. They're too lovey-dovey."

"We're husband and wife and we're lovey-dovey."

"Would you want me nibbling your ear at a poker table?"

"No. But let's take a pass through the room so I can get another photo for Kevin. I don't want to fall victim to the old ear-nibble ruse."

She laughed. "Of course, a variation of Archie's earlobe tug. Why didn't I think of that?"

"Because you're not a highly trained, professional law enforcement officer."

Susan sauntered away, and then looked back over her shoulder. "Well, come on, Barney Fife. The sooner we do this, the sooner you can show me your handcuffs."

A passing elderly woman, whose hearing must have been keener than Susan expected, whipped her walker around. "If you don't want him, honey, send him my way and I'll put the cuffs on him."

Susan blushed and I felt my face grow warm.

The woman looked at each of us and laughed. "Just as I thought. All bluffs and no cuffs." She set off again, and I'd swear there was a little more bounce in her step.

Susan and I made a leisurely circle of the poker room before moving to a position to study the new participants. As Susan described, the couple sat close together and held hands. I pegged the woman at mid-thirties and the man in his late twenties. He looked ex-military to me in a tight-fitting pullover sweater with part of a neck tattoo peeking over the rolled collar.

The blonde-from-a-bottle also had a store-bought tan, but she didn't appear to be a brainless floozy. She eyed the other players carefully, noting their checks and raises, and I wondered who had picked up whom. She could have been the one with the money simply enjoying a little time with a temporary boy toy. I took their picture.

Susan and I headed for the door so I could upload the new photo to Kevin in less crowded circumstances, when Kevin walked in. He looked right through us, in keeping with the way I'd expect him to behave.

But for someone who had expressed concern that Tyrell might recognize him, Kevin looped around the room so that he could approach his quarry head on. I had a better view of Archie and I saw his eyes widen for a second as Kevin circled behind him. Then Archie focused on the exposed cards in the middle of the table.

I moved quickly to a spot where I could see Tyrell's face. He glanced up as his eye caught the motion of someone getting too close to the players across from him. Then his poker face broke into undisguised shock as Kevin stepped between Archie and the man sitting on his right.

Kevin said nothing. He smiled, raised his left hand to his forehead, and formed a capital L with his thumb and index finger. Loser. Then he pointed his index finger at Tyrell, letting the upturned thumb become an imaginary hammer on a pistol. He pulled the trigger. Still smiling, he walked away.

"Hey, who are you calling a loser?" The blonde turned in her seat, shouting the question to Kevin's back.

Kevin disappeared down the stairway.

I heard Archie ask, "What was that all about?" A normal question, given the scene.

Tyrell's face had gone red. All he said was, "Let's play cards."

But Kevin's theatrics had clearly shaken him, and his poker skills deserted him. After losing several hands, he abruptly got up without so much as a word to the others, and left the room.

A new player took his place, and ten minutes later, I gave Archie the signal to cash out.

Chapter Seventeen

"What the hell was that all about?" I didn't wait for the door to Kevin Malone's room to close behind me. I wanted an answer and I wanted it right then.

Kevin walked to the far side by the window, turned to face Susan and me, and threw up his hands. "I know. I know. Change of tactics. I decided to poke the bear and see what reaction we get."

"And what did you learn?"

Kevin shrugged. "That remains to be seen. But you, Susan, and Archie are in the clear. If he makes a move, it will be against me."

A soft rap came from the door. Kevin went to the bed, pulled a pistol from under the pillow, and waved for Susan and me to get in the bathroom. He wanted us out of the line of sight, or possibly the line of fire. I put Susan behind me and peeked around the bathroom door jamb. My weapon was packed in my suitcase.

The knock came a second time. Kevin stood at the side of the door, well clear of the peep hole. Using it would have given Tyrell a gift shot to Kevin's head.

"Who is it?" Kevin asked.

"Archie Donovan. Is Barry with you?"

Kevin snapped the door open and yanked a startled Archie inside.

"You should have called first." Kevin threw the deadbolt.

Archie gave Susan and me a quizzical look as we stepped from the bathroom. "What's going on? Is Tyrell after me?"

"No," Kevin said. "But he might keep an eye on this room now that he knows I'm here."

"Why'd you do that?" Archie asked.

"To rattle his tree and see what falls out. How'd you do in the game?"

Archie shook his head and reached in his pocket. "There's a problem."

"Did you lose the money?" Kevin asked.

"No. I won." He handed Kevin an envelope. "Four thousand dollars. The casino withheld twenty-five percent for federal taxes. I had to fill out a form. How are you going to get that money?"

Kevin laughed and patted Archie on the back. "I won't. Use it toward your own tax bill. You did great. How much of the four grand came from Tyrell?"

"About fifteen hundred. He lost it after you showed up."

"Even better. Let's have a drink." Kevin headed for the minibar.

"None for me." I wanted a clear head because I planned to confront Kevin later, just the two of us.

"Me either," Susan said.

"I'll have a Scotch," Archie said.

"One Scotch coming up. I'm afraid the ice has melted. There's a machine at the end of the hall."

"Neat's fine." Archie looked back at the door. "Maybe we should stay out of the hall for a while."

Kevin poured the two drinks, keeping his the Irish whiskey. He clinked glasses with Archie. "Job well done. Did you see anything unusual happen at the table?"

Kevin was playing his ruse through to the end. He never expected anything to happen.

"Not at the table," Archie said.

Both Kevin and I picked up on Archie's answer.

"Did something happen elsewhere?" I asked.

"I don't know if it means anything, but your uncle saw Tyrell get into an argument with Mack Collins after he left the poker room."

"What?" Kevin stepped away from Archie and looked to me for an explanation.

"Where was this?" I asked.

"At the foot of the stairs. Wayne was posted near one of the roulette wheels."

"Posted!" Kevin's ruddy face turned crimson. "Barry, you brought your uncle into this?"

"I did not. Archie cooked this up all by himself. I learned about it right before he went into the game."

"I thought we needed backup," Archie said.

I was afraid blood might spurt from Kevin's ears.

Archie seemed unfazed. "You said you couldn't be seen. Barry and Susan were working as a team in the room because Tyrell wouldn't recognize them. But what if somebody else recognized them? Someone who was supposed to come to the room. Panther was killed in my cemetery and somebody local has to be involved. You don't know the locals. Wayne and Mayor Whitlock do."

"The mayor? You brought the god damned mayor?"

"Yeah. Everybody knows he likes to play cards."

"Arguing is getting us nowhere," I said. "What's done is done. Tell us about Mack Collins."

"That's your state senator?" Kevin asked. "The one you said was in the middle of this Cherokee Catawba casino rivalry?"

"Yes. He can make or break the Catawba's request for a North Carolina casino."

Kevin cooled down. "Then tell me about this argument."

"Not much to tell," Archie said. "You ought to talk to Wayne directly. He said Mack was angry. That Tyrell pushed the senator out of the way and went outside."

"Did Mack follow him?" I asked.

"No. He headed for the hotel lobby. Wayne thought it would be better not to be seen. Mack would want to know what he was doing here."

"What do you make of it?" Kevin asked me.

"Tyrell pushed me going up the stairs to the poker room. Maybe he did the same to Mack."

"He's a rude bastard," Kevin said. "Is Mack Collins hotheaded?"

"He's used to getting his way," I said.

"Where's Wayne now?" Kevin asked.

"He and the mayor checked into the Days Inn across the street," Archie said. "Too late for them to drive back to Gainesboro tonight."

Kevin gulped down his drink. "Let's go see them. I want to know exactly what happened."

Archie stared at his untasted glass of Scotch and then set it on the desk. "I'll go find out their room numbers. Want to meet in the Days Inn lobby?"

"OK," Kevin agreed. "And we shouldn't all leave together. I'll arrive last and alone."

Archie slipped out the door.

"What do you think?" Kevin asked me.

"Could just be a coincidence, but we need to explore it. Yesterday Mack Collins told me he was going to Raleigh and tonight he shows up here at the opposite end of the state."

"Is he a dirty politician?"

"No scandal I know of."

"He's been an active and respected citizen," Susan said. "I think he's been elected five or six times."

"Is he a lawyer?" Kevin asked.

"He owns a construction company."

Kevin mulled that over a few minutes. "I expect a new casino would create some lucrative opportunities for a construction company."

"Yes," I agreed. "Either or both new casinos would. You want me to check it out?"

"If you can do it quietly. We don't want to spook him if there's a connection and we don't want to piss him off if there's not."

I looked at Susan. "Let's go to our room and I'll make a call." I checked my watch. "It's nearly ten. Let's meet at ten after. That will give Archie a little more time to round up my uncle and the mayor."

"All right." Kevin shook his head.

"What?" I asked.

"I hate to admit it but Archie was right. We needed more eyes that would recognize local faces."

"For God's sake don't tell him. He'll be injecting himself into every investigation I do from now on."

"Sometimes good ideas come from unlikely sources," Kevin said.

And sometimes those sources should be off limits, I thought. Like illegally breaking into a suspect's room.

When we were alone in the elevator, Susan asked, "What's your plan?"

"I'm starting with Melissa Bigham. She has the newspaper's resources and the archives on any stories involving Mack. Most importantly, I can trust her discretion."

"You want me at the Days Inn meeting?"

"Would you be insulted if I said no?"

She laughed. "Would you be insulted if I told you to stay out of my operating room?"

"Thanks. I need to move forward as a deputy, not a trophy husband."

"I expect you to be both. So don't stay out all night."

Once in our room, Susan kicked off her shoes and curled up in the love seat with one of those magazines featuring tourist attractions. I sat on the far edge of the bed and speed-dialed Melissa Bigham.

"What's up, Barry?" She sounded like she was up. At least I didn't wake her.

"Are you at home?"

"Who are you? My mom?"

"I just wondered if you had access to a computer."

She groaned. "What now? Did you lose Internet service at the cabin?"

"I'm in Cherokee."

"Oh?" Melissa suddenly seemed interested. "The Panther murder?"

"Yes."

"I'm at work. Jonah's at a publishers' conference in Austin and he left me in charge of putting the paper to bed."

I knew that meant looming deadlines after a long day. "Sorry. I guess it's not a good time."

"It's fine," she exclaimed. "I was just packing up. What do you need?"

"This might be nothing, but I want you to see if you can find a connection between a Francis Tyrell of Boston and Mack Collins."

"Collins? How's he figure in this?"

I paused, collecting my thoughts. I had to make sure Melissa didn't go into reporter hyperdrive. "I don't know if he does at all, so play this slow and easy. I've been told he got into an argument with Tyrell at the casino, and Tyrell is a person of interest in our case."

"Because?"

There was no way to understate it. "Because Tyrell is suspected of being a hit man for Whitey Bulger and his Boston mob."

"Jesus." The word rushed out in a single hiss.

"Melissa, I don't have a shred of evidence, just a coincidence of timing. I want to know if there was any record of Collins and Tyrell intersecting at some point in the past. Or any issues regarding Collins' exercise of political power and personal gain regarding the Cherokee casino or other construction for that matter."

"I understand. Leave no footprints."

"If you can avoid it. Are you good with our usual arrangement?"

"Yes."

Our usual arrangement meant she got the first interview and extensive background once the case was solved. For a reporter, breaking the story was as good as it got.

"Great," I said. "Call me whenever you have something."

"Barry, any hint as to how Boston can be connected to Cherokee?"

"Not a clue. That's why I'm counting on you." I hung up.

"Is the barracuda on the prowl?" Susan asked.

"Yes. And very hungry."

We met in Mayor Whitlock's room because His Honor had already changed for bed. He sat in his orange Clemson warm-up suit in the only chair, leaving Uncle Wayne, Archie, and me to share the edge of the king-size bed.

Kevin remained standing, clearly viewing the scene as his meeting. "Wayne, walk me through exactly what you saw. Nothing is too trivial."

"Well, I was standing at the railing on the mezzanine, drinking a soda and watching people lose their money on the roulette wheel. Then out of the corner of my eye I saw that man from the poker room. The one Archie gave us the high sign on. He was looking around, and not looking too happy. I figured Archie must have got the best of him."

I expected Archie to jump in with some boastful claim, but he said nothing.

"Then he spotted someone on the lower level and beelined it down the stairs."

"Could you tell who it was?"

"Not at first," Uncle Wayne said. "He just started pushing people and following somebody with his eyes. I looked where he was looking and saw Mack Collins. Mack was walking real casual, in no hurry. The poker player yelled something."

"Mack's name?"

"Nah. More like 'wait up' or 'hold up.' Anyway, Mack looked up the staircase and his face turned red as a vine-ripe tomato. He headed for the man and both of them looked mad as smoked-out hornets. I thought there was going to be a fight, but they just got up in each other's face. Mack said, 'Who brought you down here?' and the man said, 'Who brought the law down here, you stupid son of a bitch?' Then Mack looked around, like he remembered he was in public. He said, 'You better get out of here and don't let me see your face again.' Poker Man said, 'I ain't done nothing, old man. Get the hell out of my way.' And he pushed Mack and walked toward the exit."

"What did Mack do next?" Kevin asked.

"He watched him go, and then straightened his suit coat and headed toward the hotel lobby."

"So, he was clearly surprised, but he definitely knew Tyrell."

"Tyrell?" Uncle Wayne asked.

"Yes," Kevin said. "That's the poker player's name."

"He never said it, but he definitely knew him."

Kevin looked across the broad bed to Mayor Whitlock. "Did you see any of this?"

"No. I ran into Luther at the bar and we started talking."

"What?" I jumped from the bed. "Luther's here?"

"Yeah," Mayor Whitlock said. "And I think it's good for him to get out of that house. He's with his daughter from Atlanta. Sandra thought it would do him good." Whitlock waved his hand. "Don't worry, Barry. I didn't say anything about us watching that fellow. I told him I was feeling the same way. Eurleen was my sister and I needed to get away too."

"What about Darren?" I asked. "Did you see him?"

"No. Darren's in DC."

I knew he wasn't, but I didn't know if Sandra hadn't yet told Luther the truth about Mack costing Darren his job, or if Luther knew and was embarrassed to tell his brother-in-law. What I did know was that Luther, Darren, Mack, and Frankie Tyrell were all at the casino.

"I told Luther I'd meet him for breakfast," Mayor Whitlock said. "Is that all right?"

I looked to Kevin.

"Yeah. That's fine," Kevin said. "Wayne, you can join them if you want. Then I suggest you both head back to Gainesboro. Archie, you might want to leave before daylight. Tyrell's unpredictable and if he happened to see you with me, he might figure you set him up."

Archie paled. "Set him up for what?"

"Doesn't matter. If he gets that thought in his head, he'll expect you to tell him. And he can be very persuasive."

Archie got to his feet. His hands were shaking. "Then I may as well run on. I can be home by midnight."

"I think that's wise," Kevin said. "You did a good job."

Archie managed a smile. "Thanks. See you all later." He was out the door with the final syllable.

"Anything else?" Kevin asked me.

"One thing." I stared at the mayor. "It should go without saying, but neither of you is to mention what happened tonight. Not Archie's poker game. Not Mack's run-in with Tyrell. Understand?"

The mayor's head bobbed.

"Say it out loud. Kevin's my witness and if you don't keep this among us, he can charge you with obstruction of justice." I added that threat knowing Mayor Whitlock was impressed with anyone from a big city, whether Kevin had jurisdiction or not.

In unison, my uncle and the mayor said, "I promise."

"One last thing. Uncle Wayne, how much did you win at blackjack?"

He cracked a sly grin. "Just south of five hundred dollars."

"Then you can buy breakfast for Luther and the mayor tomorrow. That will give you something to talk about."

"Good idea," the mayor said.

I realized the buffet line would take a major hit in the morning.

When Kevin and I stepped into the hall, I said, "There are a few things I still need to go over with you before I report to Tommy Lee."

"OK. Why don't we hit the casino bar and grab a nightcap."

"No. I want this private."

Kevin cocked his head and eyed me curiously. "You think Tyrell could overhear us?"

"Who knows where he is now that you don't have the rest of us doing your surveillance work for you."

Kevin colored just at the base of his neck, but enough to show I'd hit a nerve. I walked away and we didn't speak until we entered his hotel room.

Kevin went straight to the desk and picked up Archie's glass of Scotch. "No sense wasting it. Now what's the burr under your saddle?"

"Seeing you break into Frankie Tyrell's room."

The Scotch stopped a few millimeters shy of his lips. He glared at me over the rim of the glass. "Were you following me?"

"No. I spilled wine on my pants and returned to the room to change. I came up the stairwell and saw you with your electronic gizmo."

"Why didn't you say anything?"

"I didn't know what to say. It wasn't the kind of conversation to have in a hotel hallway."

He sighed and set the drink back on the desk. "All right. Sit down. Let's talk."

This time he took the love seat and left me the desk chair.

"First. I'm not officially here."

"You're not working the case?"

"I'm working the investigation. Boston PD is interested in Tyrell and his connection to unsolved murders for Whitey Bulger. But there was no budget to send me down here. I'm on my own nickel."

"Do they know it?"

"My lieutenant probably suspects what I'm up to."

"What are you up to?"

Kevin frowned with impatience. "Exactly what I told you. When we saw Tyrell's travel plans with no known reason why he'd suddenly come to the Cherokee reservation, I listened to my instincts. Something wasn't right."

"Were his phones tapped?"

"The ones we know about. Burners are so easy to get and dispose of. I was suspicious because none of his conversations mentioned anything about his trip."

"So that poker money—"

"Was my own stake," Kevin interrupted.

"And that stunt of breaking into his hotel room?"

Kevin leaned forward with his elbows on his knees. "Look, Barry, I didn't plant anything in his room. I wanted to see if he might still have a weapon matching what killed the Indian. If he did, I would have worked through channels to push for a legitimate search. But I didn't want to alert Tyrell if there was nothing to find."

"Did you find a weapon?" I asked.

"No."

"Then if you didn't want to alert him with a search warrant, why the hell parade in front of him in the poker room?"

"To call him out. Get inside his head and let him know he's got a shadow sticking to him like glue and see if he runs to whoever contracted him."

"I've got to tell you it sounds like you're on a personal crusade."

Kevin got up and reached under the bed for the file he'd shown me earlier. He took out a photo and handed me the shot of Tyrell getting into the car in front of the bar.

"O'Malley's," he said. "Not too far from where I live. Not too far from where my brother and his family lived. Eight years before that photo was taken, one of Whitey Bulger's rivals was gunned down on that corner by an unknown assailant. It was early evening, the time when it's hard to see because the sun is down but the streetlights are still off. And it was raining. The shooter fired four shots. Three hit the target and one missed. It struck a passing car. My brother's car. And it killed his ten-year-old daughter, my niece, riding in the backseat. She'd be nineteen today. A smart girl, probably in college." He bent down in front of me and locked his eyes on mine. "A personal crusade? You're damned right it's personal. And now I want Frankie Tyrell to know I'm coming for him."

Chapter Eighteen

Kevin just kept staring at me. I had no doubt that he'd pursue Tyrell to the ends of the Earth. I'd seen that look before when he and Tommy Lee sought the killer of a refugee from Vietnam, the son of the Montagnard man who had saved their platoon.

When I didn't say anything, he asked, "Are you going to tell Tommy Lee?"

I'd already made up my mind. What purpose would it serve other than to put Tommy Lee in a difficult position with his friend? I wouldn't have condoned planting evidence, but it didn't sound like the illegal search was leading anywhere.

"You swear to me you didn't find a weapon or plant any evidence?"

"On my mother and my grandmother's graves, I swear I didn't find a weapon or plant evidence in Tyrell's room." He backed away. "Are we good?"

I stood. "We're more than good. We're finished."

"What do you mean?"

"You don't think Tyrell's going to stick around after seeing you, do you?"

"He's paid his entry fee for the tournament. Believe me, he won't want to lose his money. But if I've overplayed my hand and he bolts, I'll be right behind him. What are you going to do?"

"See if Susan can ride back with my uncle tomorrow. Then follow up on Mack Collins and Luther. I want to learn why they're both here."

Kevin nodded. "Sounds like the right angle. I'll keep you posted on Tyrell."

I headed for the door.

"Barry."

I stopped and turned around.

"I know what I'm doing," Kevin said.

"Good for you. But I find taking shortcuts usually leads to a screw-up."

"And sometimes a shortcut is the only way to get ahead of your quarry. I'm tired of chasing the bastard. He's coming to me."

If Kevin meant to reassure me, he failed.

The next morning Susan and I found Uncle Wayne and Mayor Whitlock with Luther at the breakfast buffet. The room looked like a senior center with the early risers crowding the serving line as if the hotel would run out of food at any moment.

Luther attacked a stack of pancakes. He looked up and smiled. "Good morning, Barry. Susan. Your uncle said you were here. Grab some food and join us."

"I can't stay," I said, "but, Susan, why don't you have something before heading out?" I turned to Uncle Wayne. "You're leaving after breakfast, right?"

"I was hoping they'd stay with me," Luther said. "Sandra's not a gambler so she'll be doing other stuff."

I stared at my uncle, shooting lasers at him. At first, he seemed to waver from our plan.

"Uncle Wayne," I prompted.

"Sorry, Luther. I need to get back to the funeral home, what with Barry out of town." My uncle turned to Mayor Whitlock. "And I'm sure Sammy's too important to be out of the office two days in a row."

I relaxed. There was no way Mayor Whitlock would contradict his own importance.

"How long are you and Sandra going to be here?" I asked.

"We're booked through tonight." Luther's appetite suddenly disappeared. He set down his fork and pushed away his plate. "She was very sweet to bring me here, but I think she's setting me up for the talk."

"What talk?" I asked.

"The one where she says I shouldn't be living by myself. I'm seventy. Eurleen was younger."

"Seventy's not old," Uncle Wayne said. "It's the prime of life."

If my uncle were a hundred, he'd say it was the prime of life.

"I know," Luther said. "But Sandra looks at me and sees an old man living alone. She's been making noises that I should come live with her. She's divorced, big house, no kids."

"Then she should move back to Gainesboro," Mayor Whit-lock said. "What's Atlanta got that we don't?"

How about everything, I thought. But I bit my tongue.

"Nah," Luther said. "Her business is based there."

"What about your son?" I asked. "Would he come back?"

"From DC? No way. And boys are different. They don't worry about their dads like daughters do."

So, Luther still didn't know Darren had lost his job. Maybe that was going to be part of Sandra's little talk. Maybe that's why Darren was in Cherokee. To help his sister convince their father to move.

"Are Darren and Sandra close?" I asked.

"No. Not as close as I wished. Darren was always the little brother and Sandra the older bossy sister."

Mayor Whitlock nodded. I wondered if he was agreeing with the relationship of his niece and nephew or thinking about his own relationship with his sister Eurleen.

"Darren will probably push for the opposite of whatever Sandra wants," Luther said. "That's the way it's always been. But I'm going to do things my way. Probably sell the house and get a condo in town. That should keep Sandra off my back for a while."

"That's a good plan, Luther," Uncle Wayne said. "Get a fresh start."

Susan returned to the table with a bowl of cereal and fresh fruit.

I got up and gave her my chair. "I'd better get started myself."

"Barry," Luther said hesitantly.

"Yes?"

"Any progress? You know, on that killing?"

"Still gathering information."

"To think someone did that on my Eurleen's grave."

"Trust me. Tommy Lee and I will get to the truth."

Luther's eyes teared up. Everyone else stared at their food. I left them in silence.

Meeting Detective Sergeant Romero at eight was the first item on my agenda. We were going to make a surprise visit on Eddie Wolfe and ask why he'd gone to Jimmy Panther's lodgings immediately after speaking to us the previous day. Did he come to the same conclusion that Danny Swift might be hiding there? If so, why didn't he tell Romero and let the police handle it?

I had fifteen minutes to run up to the room, grab my notepad and revolver, and be outside before Romero arrived. I stepped out of the breakfast buffet and spotted Sandra Cransford hurrying toward me.

"Hi, Barry, I was hoping to catch you. Can we talk a moment?"

Her mourning clothes had been replaced by a pair of jeans and a gray turtleneck sweater.

I moved to the closest wall away from the doorway. "I'm afraid I've only got a moment. I'm meeting someone."

"I wanted to explain why we're here. I called my father after you spoke with me yesterday morning. He was awfully shaken up. Then after Sheriff Wadkins talked to him and Dad admitted he'd lied about Sunday night, I was worried he'd sit in the house and, well, I don't know what. He sounded so down."

"I understand. I just left him. He seems in better spirits this morning."

Sandra smiled. "Good. This is a place he's always enjoyed and he came here without Mom. Her absence wouldn't be conspicuous."

I edged forward, anxious to leave. "You were good to come up from Atlanta and bring him."

"It was his spontaneous suggestion, so I wanted to explain why I didn't mention it yesterday. I thought it might seem strange, the Cherokee man killed on Mother's grave and then we come to the reservation."

It did seem strange and had I not been so focused on the previous night's poker game and Kevin's invasion of Tyrell's room, I probably would have questioned Luther's motive for being here. "I just hope he has a good time. I understand you're staying another night."

She laughed. "That's the plan. If he doesn't lose all his money today."

"Are you going to see your brother while he's here?"

Sandra stared at me liked the question had been in some foreign language. "Darren?"

"Yes. I spoke to him yesterday. He said he's up here on business."

Sandra's face hardened. "Well, that's just great. Mack Collins is here too. If Darren sees him, he's just hotheaded enough to cause a scene."

"You saw Mack?"

"I ran into him last night. He has a meeting with the Cherokee gaming commissioner this morning. Mack said the man's uptight over the Catawba casino plans and needs some handholding." She eyed me suspiciously. "Did Darren say why he was here?"

I decided not to share Darren's plan to rally anticasino support from Panther's followers. Sandra would tell Mack, which would only add fuel to the fire burning between the two men.

"No. He just said business. I didn't press him since you'd told me about his job situation."

"If he's got any sense, he'll keep his nose out of tribal politics. Dealing with the state legislature is one thing, but the Cherokee Council is a whole different ball game."

You mean ball-play, I thought, and realized I was going to be late to meet Romero. "Sorry, I've really got to go."

Sandra stepped back. "Working your investigation?"

"Yes."

"Then if it helps clear my father of suspicion, I don't want to delay you." Her eyes moistened. "I know he had nothing to do with that man's death. And if Darren's mixed up in it somehow, that would just kill Dad."

"Why would you think Darren's involved?"

She raised her hands. "I'm not saying he knowingly played a part. It's just that Darren's easily manipulated and could be in something over his head."

"I'll bear that in mind."

"For God's sake, don't tell him I said anything."

"I won't."

She smiled. The tears were gone. "If you're still here tonight, perhaps you, Dad, and I can have dinner. My treat."

"Maybe. But don't count on it. I'll leave a note at the front desk if it looks like I can make it."

As I hurried to the room, I thought through what Sandra had said. She and her dad had been unaware that Darren was also here. She explained why Mack Collins hadn't gone to Raleigh. I figured the concern over the proposed Catawba casino must really have the Cherokee leaders on edge.

If my theory was correct that Panther planned to sacrifice his collection of artifacts to seed the site of the new Cherokee casino, then it would be a game-changer, the very words Panther had told Darren when he advised him to be prepared to press a new advantage. Panther's scheme would effectively halt all excavation and construction until the extent of the supposed archaeological find could be determined and the protective measures required by federal law be satisfied. That could delay the new casino for years. No wonder Skye said her brother seemed smug. He must have loaded his collection in the bed of his truck while she and his grandmother were at church. And Danny Swift had seen that load under the tarp at the ball-play game.

Another possibility hit me. Maybe Danny hadn't run off at all. Maybe he had seen too much and someone made sure he didn't talk about it.

As I walked toward my room, I glanced at Tyrell's door. The Do Not Disturb sign dangled from the knob. Kevin had been right. Tyrell wasn't spooked enough to bolt. He was still in the game. And I suspected either he or Kevin would soon up the ante.

"Your theory fits a lot of the facts." Detective Sergeant Romero made the assessment after I finished outlining my hypothesis. "You should also know the location for the original casino had to be moved because of relics."

"Really?"

"More shifted than relocated. The initial excavation uncovered some artifacts and remains. We didn't even determine if they were human remains because Jimmy immediately organized a protest. It was easier and cheaper to slide the casino closer to the bend in the adjacent stream. Actually made for a prettier setting."

"But if Jimmy were plotting to create his own archaeological site on a much wider scale, it doesn't narrow down the suspect pool."

We rode in Romero's patrol car on the winding road to Eddie Wolfe's mobile home. I decided to use him as a sounding board for my developing theory, especially since Danny Swift's involvement could mean a more ominous turn in Romero's investigation.

"What's Rooster think?" Romero asked.

"I haven't gone into the details I shared with you. Tommy Lee and I'll talk later today."

"I think he'll say you've cleared the Cransfords from any involvement. The whole graveyard scene strikes me as an attempt to divert attention from the casino site. Someone took advantage of the clash at the funeral to muddy the waters."

"If the phone records back their alibis. Tommy Lee should get those today."

"And this Tyrell guy. You think he's anything more than a paid assassin?"

"I don't have proof he's even that." I decided to keep last night's argument between Tyrell and Senator Collins to myself. Until Melissa Bigham found some connection, I wouldn't risk tainting Collins' name with that of a mobster.

"In some ways Tyrell narrows the pool of suspects," Romero said. "I'm sure his services don't come cheap. And someone had to know how to hire him. We might have fourteen thousand tribe members who will benefit from a second casino's profits, but I doubt you'll find any Cherokee who has that kind of cash. Are you monitoring his bank accounts for any big deposits?"

"No. That would be handled out of Boston. That's a good point, though. I'll ask for an update."

"Could be all cash," Romero said. "I understand they found Whitey Bulger with hundreds of thousands of dollars."

"Might be."

Romero's suggestion opened a new possibility. Tyrell was hanging around waiting on a final payment. I'd float that by Kevin.

Romero turned up the gravel road to Eddie Wolfe's mobile home park. "Way I see it, we're looking at building contractors, gaming machine manufacturers, or maybe some off-reservation investors, all of whom stand to lose a lot of money if this casino falls through."

"What do you mean off-reservation investors?"

"Not everything is built on tribal land. Only the casino itself must be located there. Since the site is right at the edge of the Qualla Boundary, hotels and restaurants will spring up on private property adjacent to it. Multilane roads will have to be constructed. It's a big project on both sides of the boundary."

"Any of those investors had a run-in with Jimmy Panther?"

"Not that I know. If it happened off-reservation, we wouldn't necessarily be informed."

"Would Eddie Wolfe know?"

"Now that's more likely. I think we need to press him harder. My turn to play bad cop."

The red Camaro sat in front of Eddie's trailer. An Infiniti sedan was parked beside it.

"Looks like he's got company," Romero said. "That's not Skye's car."

"DC plates," I said. "I think you're about to meet Darren Cransford."

Romero led the way up to the front door. It was ajar. He gave a single rap and entered without waiting for a response. Two steps inside, he froze. I had to move to my left in order to see around the hulk of a man.

Darren Cransford stood staring at us, his face pale as morning fog. The screen of the laptop on the counter behind him flashed a spasmodic display of tangled colors, broken by a spider web of cracks emanating from a hole in the center. With a stuttering motion, he slowly raised his hands. The palms were crimson.

At his feet, sprawled across the floor from the living room to the kitchen, lay Eddie Wolfe. Feathers covered his body like a dusting of snow. White snow and red snow. Snow as red as the blood beneath it.

Chapter Nineteen

Darren Cransford looked at his bloody hands. "I just found him. I swear."

Romero drew his service pistol. "Sir, step forward. Slowly."

Darren complied. Tremors visibly ran through his body. "I just got here."

"You good with him?" I asked Romero. "I'll check Eddie."

Romero waved his pistol, motioning Darren to move to the side. I crouched by Eddie's shoulders and felt his carotid artery. The skin was cool and the pulse nonexistent.

"He's gone. I'm going to check Darren's car."

"My car?" Darren asked. "Don't you need a warrant?"

"Not to see if the engine's still warm." Before Darren could reply I was out the front door.

Although the morning sky was sunny, the air temperature still held an autumn chill. I stood in front of Darren's Infiniti. Its gray surface was dry. I glanced at Eddie's Camaro next to it. Drops of dew beaded on the waxed red paint like sparkling sequins. I placed my palm against the middle of the Infiniti's hood. The metal felt warmer than Eddie Wolfe's body and the sporadic clicks from the engine confirmed it was still cooling down. Darren had been telling the truth about just arriving, but that didn't mean he hadn't shot Eddie earlier and returned to retrieve something.

I studied the adjacent mobile homes. Neither had vehicles parked in front. Up the hill, I saw Dot Swift's Toyota Corolla and figured she hadn't gone to her teaching job. Maybe her son was home. More likely, she sat by the phone waiting for news.

Inside Eddie's trailer, I found Romero and Darren exactly as I'd left them.

"Well?" Romero asked without taking his eyes off his suspect.

"Car's still warm. Probably hasn't been here more than ten minutes."

"Pat him down for me."

Darren kept his hands in the air while I checked for a concealed weapon. He wore a light windbreaker over a blue dress shirt, and other than car keys in one jacket pocket and a wallet in his pants, he carried nothing else. I stepped back. "He's clean."

Romero lowered his gun. "I'm going to check the rest of the trailer. Keep him here and standing." Romero squeezed past Darren, stepped over the body, and moved down the hall.

"I came to talk to him, Barry. Just like I told you yesterday."

"This is a case for the Cherokee police, but I'll help you sort it out with them the best I can."

Darren nodded, and then risked a quick glance at the body. "I knocked but no one came to the door. Since it was open, I came in."

"Detective Sergeant Romero will get a statement from you. You should save your account for him."

"But will you be with me?" His voice grew plaintive at the thought of being alone with the large Indian.

"Not my call."

Romero returned from the back bedroom. "No one here. Looks like the rooms were tossed or Eddie was extremely messy."

"Skye would know," I said.

"Yep." Again, he stepped over Eddie's body and checked the second, smaller bedroom.

Once assured that no one else hid on the premises, Romero moved into his investigative mode. "I'm going to the patrol car to radio for assistance. We could use the Swain County crime lab."

"Anything from our department?" I asked.

"Not unless you've acquired some high-tech forensic equipment I'm unaware of."

"No. We still call for support out of Asheville."

Romero turned to Darren. "You come with me. I'll get a preliminary statement while we wait in the car."

"How can I help?" I asked.

"Sit tight for now. Better for me to have our people interview the neighbors, in case testimony is required in court. But I don't mind your eyes going over the crime scene. There are shoe covers and gloves in the car."

I'd examined murder scenes before but not one where the victim had been coated in feathers. The source lay near his feet. A twisted pillow apparently had been pulled from a bed and used as a makeshift silencer. The implications were confusing. Had the killer been Tyrell, I would have thought he'd come prepared with a suppressor. But the fact that a pillow was used still showed a certain degree of calculation. Rounds weren't fired in the heat of an argument. The pillow demonstrated resourcefulness once the decision to shoot had been made. Someone had come from a bedroom. Could Jimmy's sister Skye be that someone?

And there was the amount of feathers scattered over the body. More than what I thought bullets ripping through the pillow casing would have disgorged. It was almost like someone had shaken the feathers out. Feathers. Was this some sort of payback for the broken feathers sent to Archie, Luther, and Mayor Whitlock?

I left the body and carefully moved through the bedrooms at either end of the mobile home. The smaller one had a rollaway without a pillow. Work clothes had been dumped out of the closet and onto the floor. Several footlockers along the wall had been opened. They contained heavy winter clothes and boots. Some camo hunting gear was mixed in, and everything seemed to have been tossed around by a whirlwind.

The main bedroom had a disheveled double bed with two pillows, a dresser with drawers pulled out, and a closet with nicer shirts and slacks. These had been unceremoniously dumped as well.

The bathroom was unscathed, meaning the toilet tank and cabinet under the sink must have been too small to hide the object of the search. I noticed two toothbrushes in the holder, and I suspected one belonged to Skye Panther. They were both dry.

I returned to the living room just as Detective Sergeant Romero entered through the front door.

"Where's Darren?" I asked.

"He's locked in the back of the patrol car. Reinforcements are on the way. We'll take him to the station for a formal statement. You think he's good for it?"

"No. I don't think he's stupid enough to come back here if he was the shooter. Darren's working PR for the Catawbas. He told me he came to Cherokee to rally support from Jimmy Panther's followers. Eddie Wolfe is the logical place to start."

"Maybe Eddie refused his support."

"Maybe. But I think the ME's going to find he's been dead a couple hours. Blood surface is congealing and body temp is down." I looked up the hallway. "There are two toothbrushes in the bathroom."

"Yeah. I noticed that," Romero said. "But I can't see Skye pulling the trigger or even owning a gun."

"Maybe it was Eddie's."

"And motive?"

I thought for a moment, trying to weave together the disjointed elements of my case. "If Jimmy planned to salt the new construction site, he would have kept that plan as secret as possible. But I don't think he would have undertaken the risk alone. How close is Eddie's workplace to the proposed casino?"

Romero's face lit with fresh enthusiasm. "Real close. Less than five miles. Eddie could have been there shortly after midnight."

"Or even earlier. Skye said Eddie told her they clocked out at midnight. But she said on cleanup detail, they finish when they finish."

"And I never checked," Romero said.

"You had no reason before now. But think about it. Danny Swift saw Eddie and Jimmy together at the ball-play game. The artifacts were already loaded in Jimmy's truck. Stands to reason Eddie knew about them. He might have been the only one. If Skye's put that together, and she knows someone betrayed her brother," I looked down at the body, "she has to figure Eddie Wolfe may have been that someone."

Riding to Eddie's with Romero meant I was stranded until an officer returned to town. Tommy Lee would wonder why I hadn't checked in. With no cell service and Romero constantly on and off his two-way, I was forced to cool my heels.

Eddie's Camaro was the only free vehicle, but asking to use the victim's car as a personal taxi would be extremely presumptuous, especially since forensics hadn't examined it.

The smaller beads of dew had begun to evaporate from the Camaro's hood. I thought of Archie and wondered if I would have checked Darren's car if Archie hadn't first made the dew observation on Panther's pickup. I walked around the Camaro and stopped at the trunk. The dew no longer existed in beads but had been transformed into narrow rivulets that had flowed toward the rear window. Someone had opened the trunk, forcing the heavy dew to roll off the back.

Romero got out of his patrol car.

"Hector, take a look at this."

The policeman joined me at the rear bumper. "Opened after the dew formed. But by Eddie or his killer?"

"If someone tossed the house, maybe he went for the car as well."

"Did you see any keys inside?" Romero asked.

"No. Maybe they're on the body."

Romero glanced at his patrol car. "I know you've got other things to do this morning. I was thinking of letting you drive my car back as soon as one of my colleagues arrives."

"What about my taking Darren to the station in his car? Can someone record his statement there?"

"Yes. That works. But he's not to leave Cherokee till I question him again."

"He asked about a warrant to search his car. Maybe we should trade his release from the scene in exchange for that search." I looked at the trunk. "In case he moved something from this trunk to his."

"Good idea. First, let me find a way into the Camaro." He pulled latex gloves from his pocket and went into the trailer.

I waited by the trunk. Darren Cransford gave me a pitiful look from the backseat of the patrol car. A few minutes later, Romero returned dangling a set of keys from his right hand.

"They were in Eddie's front pocket. Whoever shot him must not have searched him." He popped the trunk. "At least not after the feathering."

The Camaro's trunk was small. As pristine as Eddie had kept the exterior and passenger compartment, the trunk had an irregular coating of soil. Stuffed in one corner lay an overnight bag. Still wearing his gloves, Romero unzipped it and spread the two sides apart. A couple shirts, underwear, and jeans had been jammed inside. The detective plunged one hand into the clothes and retrieved a brown envelope. Like the bag, the unmarked envelope was also stuffed. With hundred dollar bills.

"The box-making business pays well," I said.

"Maybe we should both apply for jobs." He pulled the money free. "Watch me count it so I've got a witness before logging it in."

"One hundred fifty Benjamin Franklins," I said, as the last bill fell on the stack. "Fifteen grand. Nice round number."

"Yes." Romero placed the money back in the envelope. "And I doubt if Eddie withdrew it from a bank." He zipped the bag closed and set it aside, revealing a thicker coating of dirt beneath it. "What's this?" The edge of a stone appeared in the soil. Romero lifted it and blew on it like it was a cake full of burning candles. "An arrowhead."

"One of Panther's?" I asked.

"That's my guess. And if your theory's correct, this dirt is probably from the casino construction site. Eddie might have retrieved what Jimmy planted. And the money was the payoff."

"For that and for revealing Jimmy's plan that enabled Tyrell to get here ahead of time." I looked back at the wadded clothes. "Eddie was running, which means he was scared. I guess he was right because someone got here before he split."

"We need to pull a soil sample from that construction site. I suspect it will match this dirt and what you found on Jimmy's body."

"I'd like to see the location."

Romero nodded. "I'll catch up with you as soon as we wrap here. You think this is Tyrell's handiwork?"

"It doesn't strike me as Tyrell's style. Too sloppy. It's the way he should have killed Jimmy if he didn't want to be suspected. But I'm told he's a creature of habit, and I don't know what he'd be searching for."

"Maybe the money."

"But why would Tyrell pay a local guy?" I asked. "Let's say Eddie betrayed Jimmy. That would have been to the guy who hired Tyrell. Eddie didn't have the stomach for murder. He was Judas and told someone of Jimmy's plan. That person brought in a professional hit. Then the trouble at the cemetery gave them an opportunity to throw any investigation in a completely different direction. But there were two loose ends that could link the murder back to the casino construction. Danny Swift who saw Jimmy and Eddie with the artifacts and Eddie who might not have bargained for murder."

"Why not kill Eddie the same night as Jimmy?" Romero asked.

"Eddie was probably making the runs to get the artifacts away from the site. Skye said he didn't come back here when she expected him. He told her his cleanup shift ran long, but I think we're going to find just the opposite."

"So, maybe the search here was for the artifacts. If the plan was to get them back to Jimmy's, it didn't happen in time."

Romero's conclusion made sense. But there must have been quite a few boxes, given the size of Panther's collection and the span of empty shelves in his house. I looked back at the trailer. It sat on cinder blocks with latticework covering the gap between ground and flooring. Laurel bushes were spaced across the front.

"Come with me," I said.

Romero followed me around to the rear of the mobile home. The latticework continued along the side, but there was an open gap in the rear. Here, the ground had been dug out to provide more storage space for a lawn mower or other yard tools. The clear height was at least four feet.

A dirty blue tarp had been thrown across something stored beneath. Romero and I wrestled it free. Wooden apple crates were stacked three high. Those on top held pieces of pottery, some broken, some intact. We had found Jimmy Panther's collection.

"Now that soil sample is more important than ever," Romero said. "If we get a three-way match—Jimmy's body, these artifacts, and the construction site—we'll have a clearer picture of what happened."

"Yes. What, where, when, and why. But who?"

Romero turned and headed for the front of the trailer. "Let's see if we can avoid a warrant to search Cransford's car."

The first words out of Darren's mouth were, "I want a lawyer."

"Fine," Romero said. "But you're not being charged with anything, and I thought you'd like to be on your way."

Darren looked at me as if to say, "Is this guy kidding?"

"You and I can go back into town," I said. "You'll still need to make an official statement and answer any follow-up questions that might arise."

"You'll go with me?" Someone plucked from the deck of the *Titanic* couldn't have looked more relieved.

"That's right," Romero said. "As soon as we get your car cleared."

"Cleared for what?" Darren asked.

"Well, it's at the scene of a murder and owned by the man who was found next to the body. You were concerned about our having a warrant before searching your car, so I'd be irresponsible to allow the vehicle to leave the premises without checking it."

"How long will that take?"

"Hard to say. I've got to get a judge, then have the search warrant delivered for you to see, plus we've got our hands full here already." Romero looked at the Infiniti. "Of course, you could just open the car voluntarily and then you and Barry would be on your way in five minutes."

Darren's jaw worked back and forth as he thought about Romero's proposition. "I just didn't want people to know I brought them."

"Brought what?" I asked.

Darren pulled a remote key from his pocket and pointed it at the Infiniti. A short beep sounded and the trunk popped open. "Signs and placards I had made in Charlotte."

The trunk was full of poster boards and wooden rods.

"I thought Eddie could organize nailing the signs to the handles and then lead several carloads of protestors to Raleigh."

Romero picked up a stack of white placards. Red lettering spelled out short messages: Cherokee For Catawba, Casino Rights For Catawbas, Stand Up For Tribal Equality.

"Eddie Wolfe asked you for these?" Romero asked.

"No. Jimmy Panther. Since his death I've left voice messages for Eddie but he wasn't returning my calls. Yesterday I got his address from the Boys Club and came out to learn once and for all if he was serious about the Raleigh demonstration."

"Did he know you were coming?" Romero asked.

"No. I figured if I left that on his phone, he'd make a point of not being here."

I thought about the fifteen grand in Eddie's bag. "Were you paying Eddie to organize this rally?"

"No. The idea started with Panther and he never mentioned money. If there was even the slightest hint that the Catawba proponents were funding their Cherokee support, the effectiveness on the legislators would be severely compromised. They'd just be another group of lobbyists."

Darren and I watched Romero rummage through the trunk and then the car's interior. Other than the sign materials, he found nothing else of interest.

Romero opened the driver's door. "OK, Mr. Cransford. You can go with Barry to the station and write your formal statement. Be sure and leave a cell number with the duty officer and don't leave Cherokee until I call you."

Darren got in the car without comment.

"Do you have the manpower to collect that soil sample?" I asked.

"Yes, but probably not till this afternoon."

"I'd like to go with you."

Romero laughed. "Don't worry, Barry. I won't let you miss a single minute of this mess."

Darren turned the car around and we headed down the gravel road.

"Mess. This is a god damned nightmare," he said. "First I lose my job, then my mother, and now I'm a murder suspect."

"Do you know your dad's up here?"

"In Cherokee?"

"Sandra drove him up yesterday. He wanted to get out of the house."

Darren said nothing.

"Mind if I ask why you haven't told him about your job?"

"Because there's nothing he can do about it. He's upset enough without telling him Mack Collins ratted me out. What a weasel."

"He's up here too."

Darren snapped his head around. "Collins is here?"

"Yes." I started to say he was with an anxious Cherokee gaming commissioner, but I was afraid that might not be appropriate to mention to someone on the other side of the casino fight.

"Then I guess he's with Sandra and my dad."

"Not that I saw."

Darren pulled his eyes off the road a second time and studied me. "But they were all here last night?"

"Yes."

Sirens wailed up the hollow, forcing Darren's attention back to his driving. He edged near the right ditch as two Cherokee patrol cars rushed by.

When we hit the blacktop, we simultaneously returned to cell coverage. My phone emitted a string of vibrations signaling multiple messages had tried to penetrate what was literally a dead zone. One was from Tommy Lee. Four were from Kevin Malone and had all been left within the past twenty minutes.

I highlighted the most recent and pressed play. "Barry, I don't know why you're not answering, but call me immediately—and I mean immediately."

I pressed callback and Kevin answered on the first ring.

"Where are you?" He barked the words, his voice pitched high and tight.

"Headed with Darren Cransford to the Cherokee Police Station. Eddie Wolfe's been murdered."

"Cransford killed him?"

"No."

"What's your ETA?"

"Twenty minutes."

"I can't meet you there. The casino's also out. Somewhere else."

"There's Oconaluftee Islands Park," I suggested.

"Good. I'll find it."

I was surprised he didn't pepper me with questions about Wolfe. "Kevin, what's wrong?"

"I'll tell you when I see you." And then he added in a low whisper, "I overplayed my hand."

I felt the blood drain from my face. Those words from Kevin could mean only trouble with a capital T. Trouble that had to have started with whatever Kevin did in Frankie Tyrell's hotel room.

I accompanied Darren into the police station and made sure he connected with the duty sergeant. From the looks we received, the whole department was focused on Eddie Wolfe's murder.

When I stepped outside, it dawned on me that I'd either have to walk to the casino for my jeep or go directly to the park. I phoned Kevin.

"Where the hell are you now?"

"Just leaving the police station. I'm on foot."

"Fine. Just another tourist. I'm on the island. There's a stand of giant bamboo with a path cut through it. Looks like I'm back in Southeast Asia. Come there and I'll find you." He hung up.

I dialed Tommy Lee and started walking down the hill toward the park in the middle of the Oconaluftee River.

"Did you sleep in?" Tommy Lee asked, half-joking and half-annoyed.

"Eddie Wolfe was murdered early this morning."

Silence. Then Tommy Lee calmly said, "Give me what's important."

I highlighted the key points including the discovery of the fifteen thousand dollars and Jimmy Panther's missing collection of artifacts. Tommy Lee didn't interrupt.

When I finished, he said, "I want that soil sample from the construction site as soon as possible."

"I'm going out with Romero this afternoon."

"No. I'll get it myself. Then I want a sample from Eddie Wolfe's trunk and any dirt clinging to the artifacts. Have Romero prep it. Any word on that missing boy?"

"No. And Romero's worried. We've got two murders tied together and the kid might be in the middle."

"Anything come of last night's poker game?"

I wanted to tell Tommy Lee about seeing Kevin enter Tyrell's room, but decided to stick with my promise, at least until Kevin and I talked in the park.

"Not really. Except Kevin taunted Tyrell at the card table. Called him a loser."

"Good God. What's he playing at?"

"He's playing at drawing Tyrell out. Kevin thinks he killed his niece over eight years ago during a mob hit. Kevin wants Tyrell to come after him."

Tommy Lee's sigh whistled in my ear. "I knew there was something like this going on."

"You were right, but that doesn't negate the possibility that Tyrell was contracted for Panther."

"But not Eddie Wolfe?" Tommy Lee asked.

"That's my take."

"Are you going back to Wolfe's?"

"No. I'm meeting Kevin in a few minutes. Something's spooked him."

"Barry, I can't say this forcefully enough. Watch yourself with Kevin. There's nobody I'd rather have guarding my back, but when it comes to a frontal charge, he makes General Custer look like a conservative tactician."

"I'll be careful. You got anything for me?"

"Yes. Phone records came in this morning. Luther received a call on his home line from Sandra's cell at nine thirty on Sunday night just like he said. They talked for thirty minutes."

"How about Darren?"

"Triangulation of cell towers that Sunday night show his calls came from the Kings Mountain area. He definitely didn't go back to DC. There are no calls after eight and no indication he returned to Gainesboro."

"So, all the Cransfords were telling the truth." Tommy Lee's information reminded me I'd forgotten to report Mack Collins' encounter with Frankie Tyrell. I gave him what few details I knew.

"Wayne saw this?" Tommy Lee sounded more astounded by Uncle Wayne's undercover work than Senator Collins' clash with Tyrell.

"Yes. It's something Archie cooked up, but Uncle Wayne claims the two men exchanged heated words."

"I don't like that. Mack heads the state senate's Indian Affairs and he owns a company that does the big-ticket work that could benefit from casino construction."

"I asked Melissa Bigham to go through the newspaper's morgue and any other source she might have for a link between Collins and Tyrell."

"Let me know what she finds," Tommy Lee urged. "If we have to question Mack, I want to be sure we're on solid ground. No, make that pure granite. Understood?"

"As they say on the cop shows, copy that."

"Good. And next time let me know when you're going out of cell coverage for any length of time."

"I wasn't expecting to find Eddie Wolfe's corpse."

"And I'm sure Eddie wasn't expecting to be one. So take care." He hung up.

I crossed the wooden footbridge onto Oconaluftee Islands Park. On a Wednesday morning in late September, few people were on the small strip of land. I saw a stand of towering bamboo bordering the far side. I didn't see Kevin.

The bamboo grew so thick the sunlight couldn't penetrate the leafy canopy. I stepped into the gloom and saw the glow of the path's exit a good two hundred feet away. The stalks were several inches in diameter. If used for Cherokee blowguns, they would be classified as bazookas.

Kevin didn't appear so I kept walking. The path became more of a tunnel. Halfway in, I saw sudden movement on my right. I stepped back and Kevin emerged from a small break in the stalks.

He looked up and down the path. Satisfied we were alone, he pulled a manila envelope from inside his windbreaker and removed a photograph. "Do you know who this is?"

The familiar face stared at me, eyes wide with terror, cheeks pinched from the duct tape pulled tightly across his mouth.

Kevin Malone had overplayed his hand.

And little Danny Swift had been caught in his deadly game.

Chapter Twenty

"Where did you get this?" I demanded.

Kevin shook the photograph in my face. "Do you know the boy?"

"Yes. His name's Danny Swift. They call him Swifty and he was last seen Monday at noon. He's been missing nearly forty-eight hours. We think he witnessed something related to Panther's murder."

Kevin grabbed a thick stalk of bamboo with his free hand and shook it like a prisoner trying to break out of his cell. "God damn it!"

His contagious anger set my heart racing. I shoved him with all my strength. "It's Tyrell, isn't it? You screwed with Tyrell and now he's got Danny."

Kevin fell backwards, landing on his butt. The photograph and envelope fluttered to the ground beside him. At first he made an effort to get up, his hands balled into fists, his eyes flashing with fury. Then his face crumpled and he sat on the path, suddenly looking like an old man.

I stood over him. "What happened in that hotel room?"

"I didn't lie to you. I didn't plant any evidence, but I took a satchel I found tucked behind his suitcase in the closet. It must contain Tyrell's payment."

"Full of hundreds?"

"Yes. One hundred fifty thousand dollars."

Ten times what we found in Eddie Wolfe's Camaro. The reason for Kevin's "loser" taunt in the poker room became clear. Frankie Tyrell had just lost one hundred fifty thousand dollars and didn't know it. When he found the money missing, he'd come after Kevin. But Kevin hadn't counted on Tyrell matching the pot with a thirteen-year-old Cherokee boy.

How had Tyrell found Danny Swift? The connection had to be Eddie Wolfe. When Eddie learned Danny had Jimmy's ball-play stick, he was afraid Danny might know about Jimmy's salting scheme. More importantly, Danny could link Eddie to Jimmy and the artifacts. Either Eddie had found Danny hiding at Jimmy Panther's, or he'd intercepted the boy as he was returning home. Maybe Danny had come to Eddie with questions.

Multiple motives were at play. Eddie must have kept Danny in his trailer while he called for instructions. I didn't think that call went to Tyrell, but to whoever was paying both of them. That person could have silenced Eddie and abducted Danny Swift. Yet, Tyrell must have his own leverage over his employer if he was using the boy to get his money back from Kevin.

I picked up the photo and envelope. Kevin's name had been printed in block letters. "How'd you get this?"

"The envelope was dropped at the front desk. No one saw who left it. So I have no evidence it came from Tyrell."

"It's as good as a ransom note. We have to take action."

Kevin got to his feet. "I know. But if Tyrell even thinks I went near the police, he'll kill the boy."

"You are the police."

"I broke into his room. What legal standing do I have? Tyrell knows that and he's counting on me to deal with him."

"He'll kill you and the boy."

"And if I do nothing, he'll kill the boy for sure. This is my fault."

"But it's not a one-man operation. You try this solo and you're guaranteeing disaster."

Kevin paced up and down the narrow path. "I know. I've got to bring Tommy Lee in on this. But if his whole department or the FBI gets involved, then there are too many opportunities to spook Tyrell and sign this kid's death warrant."

"Any conditions for how an exchange will be made?"

"No." He pointed to the photograph in my hand. "That's all I got. I suspect he wants a reply in a similar manner. The fact that there's no deadline means immediately. Otherwise he'll cut his losses and move on."

"Tyrell doesn't know me or Tommy Lee, but that doesn't mean someone else in the conspiracy wouldn't recognize us. We've got to keep our distance."

Kevin threw up his hands. "I'm wide open to ideas. If people are already looking for the boy, then Tyrell will be careful how he transports him. He'll probably name a place close to if not the very spot where he's holding the kid."

"Maybe. Or maybe we can make that work for us. He's banking Danny Swift is worth more to you than the money. But he also knows you're now a rogue. Like him, you're outside the law. So, our gamble is how much he thinks you'll risk, that risk being the conditions for the swap."

"You mean if I think it's too risky, I'll walk away with his cash?"

"Yes. And because that's what Tyrell would do, he might not see it as a bluff."

Kevin nodded. "You got a place in mind?"

I looked up at the sparkling pieces of blue sky appearing and disappearing as a breeze blew through the upper reaches of bamboo leaves. Then I eyed the pathway's entrances at each end of the long strip of heavy growth. Kevin and I stood about a hundred feet from either opening. When I turned back to him, he grinned.

"I'll be damned. You bastard. You're putting me back in the jungle."

I shrugged. "If the Viet Cong couldn't kill you, what chance does Frankie Tyrell have?"

"When?"

"After dark. Two in the morning would be good. Tell him Danny's too hot to be shuttled around in the daylight. Say you don't want Danny to see you clearly because once he's free you're splitting."

"All right. Let me work it out from this point."

"No. We're making a plan together and we're following it. My neck's sticking out as much as yours."

"What do you mean?"

I stepped into the small enclave in the bamboo from which Kevin had emerged. "Because I'm going to be in here covering you. The weather's clear and there's a full moon. Under this canopy the brightest spots will be the entrances. Each of you will see the other's silhouette. You'll be alone, he'll have Danny. Tell him to enter from the end near the Qualla Arts Center and the Museum of the Cherokee Indian. You'll come in first from the opposite entrance closer to the Cherokee Agency for Indian Affairs. You'll set down his satchel here. Tell him you'll leave a flashlight by it and then you'll back off twenty or thirty feet. Enough to make a pistol shot difficult. Then he comes in with Danny, checks the satchel and lets the boy walk to you. Everybody exits and nobody in the village sees a thing."

"Except you grab Tyrell after Danny's safe."

"And we'll have him for kidnapping. Where the ransom money came from will be irrelevant."

Kevin looked skeptical. "You know he's going to check this place out ahead of time."

"I'm counting on it. So you need to watch it as soon as you've left your response at the hotel desk. I'm sure he's watching you, so he won't be surprised you're watching him. I need you to let me know when he's cleared this location. It had better be no later than dusk."

"OK," Kevin said. "Where will you be in the meantime?"

"Trying to find out who's really behind all this."

Kevin left the shelter of the bamboo first. From this point, we couldn't take the chance of being seen together. All communication would be through texting. I insisted on being the one to inform Tommy Lee and said I would contact Kevin if there were any changes to the plan.

The isolation of the bamboo was as private as any place I could find. Even the murmur of traffic on the roads running parallel to each bank of the river was muted by the rippling sound of running water. I leaned against a wall of stalks and dialed Tommy Lee's cell phone.

"What now?" he said.

"Tyrell's got Danny Swift."

"Christ almighty. How'd that happen?"

I gave him a summary of Kevin's stunt to bring Tyrell after him. I neglected to mention I'd seen Kevin cracking the code to Tyrell's room lock. I would confess later, but at the moment I didn't need Tommy Lee second guessing my judgment.

"I don't like it," he said. "Two in the morning is too isolated a time. Any backup will be more likely to be spotted."

"And that's the reason Tyrell may go for it. We're balancing risks to keep him in the game. One hundred fifty thousand dollars is a big pot to walk away from, but Kevin's convinced Tyrell will do it if he thinks it's too risky."

"What's the closest I could get?"

"Probably the parking lot of the Bureau of Indian Affairs. As long as it appeared empty, an official-looking vehicle could park there overnight."

"How far is that?"

"Probably three hundred yards. We passed it when you missed the turn to the police station."

Tommy Lee said nothing for a moment.

"This is about saving the boy," I said. "I'll take the chance."

"OK." The sheriff must have spoken to himself because he said the word so softly I hardly heard him. He cleared his throat and raised his voice. "I'll borrow some kind of appropriate car. How's cell coverage there?"

"I'm calling from the middle of the bamboo stand."

"Good. Then make sure your battery's fully charged. I'll phone you no later than one forty-five. We'll keep an open line because I want to hear everything."

"All right. I'll be in place long before then."

A car horn sounded through the phone. "Where are you headed?" I asked.

"To the casino construction site for those soil samples. Have you asked Romero to prep the ones from Eddie Wolfe's trunk and the artifacts?"

"No. I just finished with Kevin. I'll have to contact Romero through their dispatcher. He's probably still in the dead zone at Eddie's trailer."

"Well, make it as soon as possible."

I decided it was time to ask Tommy Lee what had been gnawing the back of my mind. "How much do you trust Romero?"

"What do you mean?"

"That second casino represents a lot of money, not only to vendors and contractors, but the Cherokee per capita payments. Every institution, every individual will be touched by the outcome of this controversy."

"There's a difference between being touched and being corrupted. Hector Romero is a good cop. He's as solid as he looks."

"Then that's all I need to know." My phone beeped with an incoming call. Melissa Bigham's name flashed on the screen. "Gotta go. We'll talk later." I switched over and said, "What have you got for me?"

"Well, hello to you too," she said. "What have you got for me?"

"Nothing. But keep your phone by your bed tonight."

Melissa eagerly jumped on my tease. "What's going down?"

"I can't tell you, but it's more than Panther's killer."

"Then I'll sit in my car with the motor running."

"I'm serious, Melissa. Not a hint to anyone that something's about to break. This is a heads-up only to you."

"Should I hold the front page?" she asked.

"No. If it happens, it will be too late for your press run. I'm rewarding you in advance for whatever you're about to tell me."

"First of all, I only got two hours of sleep last night after working the Internet and then working the phones this morning."

"You were careful?"

Melissa laughed. "As careful as you can be and still be a reporter. I said I was doing a profile piece on one of our senior legislators. And that's what this might turn into if your investigation goes nowhere."

I was getting stiff standing amid the bamboo and started walking to the police station. "Anything surface that looks unusual or questionable?"

"No hint of a scandal in Collins' elections or his conduct in the state senate. He's been careful to make sure his construction company goes through open bidding for any state contracts, and he doesn't bid on projects he supports in his own district."

"What about the pending casino?"

"This morning I reached the chair of the senate committee overseeing roads and highways, figuring since that's Collins' primary business it would more likely fall under public scrutiny if tied to the road improvements around the new casino."

"Who's that?"

"Senator Gerald Eckles," Melissa said. "He's out of Wilmington representing several coastal counties and has no connection to the Cherokee. He gave the most pushback when I asked about Collins and state contracts related to the casino construction. He challenged the question as to being pertinent to a personality profile."

"Was he defensive or just trying to write your story?"

Melissa thought a moment. "Neither. He was protective, either of Collins or their relationship. He told me the major road contracts were most likely going out of state and that Mack Collins hadn't bid on them. Eckles said Collins was supporting the second casino on its own merits and refused to be considered for any opportunity to benefit financially."

I couldn't see how Mack Collins' position was any different than his general policy as Melissa first described it. "Sounds like he kept everything aboveboard."

"Yes. But Eckles went to such great lengths to champion Collins' integrity that I wondered why he felt the need to go into such elaboration. Then Eckles said something that caught my ear. He said Collins won't even talk to the Department of Transportation about projects he knows the state legislature is funding. He keeps his North Carolina company at arm's length from any inside information he might have."

"North Carolina company?"

"Yes," Melissa said. "I thought that was odd too. So, for the last hour I've been researching any Internet links for Mack or Maxwell Collins to other construction companies. One of the paper's database subscriptions kicked up a Maxwell Collins in New Jersey thirty years ago."

"He's from New Jersey. He told me himself."

"Did he tell you he was indicted for a bid-rigging scandal?"

That stopped me right in the middle of the footbridge over the Oconaluftee River. "Our Mack Collins?"

"Yes. I saw the photo that ran in the Trenton newspaper. Definitely Mack, although he had to be no more than thirty-five."

"Was he convicted?"

"No. The case never came to trial. Get this, Barry. The prosecution's key witness committed suicide. Convenient, huh?"

My blood ran as cold as the mountain water beneath me. "And then he came here."

"Not immediately. A follow-up article reported he closed the New Jersey company and returned to his business interests in South Boston."

I whistled under my breath. "Hometown of Frankie Tyrell and Whitey Bulger."

"Yep. And what better way to launder money than through a construction company. You can always be low bidder because you're flowing extra cash through the project."

"Why wouldn't this have come to light during his election campaigns?"

"Come on. A local election of a state representative for rural mountain counties? By then, Collins had lived here twelve years. I'm sure the *Vista* didn't do any deep background investigation of him. And after that first election, he's run unopposed."

My whole perspective of Mack Collins suddenly shifted. "Thirty years ago, Bulger must have sent him south to get out from under the microscope and start a new operation. Along the way, Collins pursued political clout as well."

"A sweet setup," Melissa said. "And it would explain why he's never run for higher office. The Charlotte and Raleigh papers would have scrutinized everything from his birth certificate on. What are you going to do now?"

"That's going to be Tommy Lee's call. And you know what you're going to do."

"Who are you? My assignment editor?"

"No, thank God." I heard the clatter of typing on a computer keyboard. "So, you're on it?"

"Yes, Deputy Clayton. My task is to learn what out-of-state construction companies are finalists for casino-related projects and then uncover Mack Collins hidden inside one of them. Now let me go to work." Melissa hung up.

I stood on the bridge, thinking through the implications of her discovery. Mack Collins knew Frankie Tyrell. He may have come to Cherokee with the satchel of cash to pay Tyrell off. If so, then why the argument witnessed by Uncle Wayne? At that point, Tyrell didn't realize Kevin had stolen his money. Was it because Collins had expected Tyrell to leave immediately? That he didn't want their paths to overlap any longer than necessary?

They say there are no secrets in a small town. Senator Mack Collins, the person respected by our mountain community for so many years, was at best a criminal and at worst a murderer. Would he also condone the killing of an innocent child?

I pulled the photograph Kevin had given me and studied it in the sunlight. My first look within the gloom of the bamboo had focused on Danny's face, the sheer terror in his expression. Now I examined the whole picture. The colors were muted and blurry because the photo had been printed on ordinary computer paper. Danny appeared to be lying on a carpet. It wasn't a carpet I'd seen in Eddie's mobile home. The dark gray fell away into shadows like Danny was on his back in some kind of container.

In the lower corner, a bent piece of metal gleamed in the brightest section of the photograph. I held the paper closer. The partial view revealed enough for me to identify a tire iron. Danny Swift was in the trunk of a car. A large car.

I flashed back to Mack Collins at the funeral home, asking me to keep him informed of the progress of my investigation, asking as he leaned against the trunk of his big Lincoln.

Chapter Twenty-one

Conducting a funeral follows a procedure. I know the family is in a highly emotional state of grief, maybe even shock. My job is to walk them through a ritual which might have variations in its details but usually has the same destination—a country hillside cemetery.

Conducting a murder investigation follows a procedure. There is also a body and most likely a family in shock and grief. In this case, my job is to collect evidence, interview witnesses and persons of interest, and follow that evidence and those interviews wherever they may lead. At the beginning, I might have a hunch as to the final resolution, but twists and turns can bring me to a completely unexpected and unanticipated destination, one that I couldn't have imagined. And instead of ending at a country hillside cemetery, this investigation began there.

Now an unpredictable yet inevitable showdown loomed—a showdown with a powerful state senator and a Boston mobster. At the conclusion of a funeral, the dead are remembered and buried. I was facing an unknown conclusion where life and death still hung in the balance, and the only certainty was that someone in the game was going to lose.

I slid the photo back in the envelope and hurried up the hill to the Cherokee Police Department. Although I would stay clear of Kevin, there was no reason for me to halt my investigation. On the contrary, if anyone were watching me, a sudden shift in my behavior could be alarming. I should be ignorant of the kidnapping, but moving forward with Jimmy Panther's murder inquiry.

I'd become such a familiar face at the police station that I was buzzed through without having to say who I was seeing. I made my way to the dispatcher, a Cherokee woman in her late twenties, who looked at me with a harried expression. Her morning had already been a long one.

"Is Detective Sergeant Romero still at the Eddie Wolfe scene?" I asked.

Even though I wasn't in uniform, she must have known my role.

"Yes, Deputy Clayton."

"It's urgent I speak with him. Can you patch the two-way through to my phone?"

"Yes, but the connection might be better coming into our system. You can use his desk and I'll buzz you with the line."

I walked down the narrow hall to the office where Tommy Lee and I talked with Romero only two days earlier. I sat in the worn desk chair whose squeak was barely a whisper compared to the tortured screech under Romero's weight.

The dispatcher's voice came through the speaker phone. "Deputy Clayton, Romero's on line two."

I thanked her and punched the flashing button. "Hector, are you close to leaving?"

"Not really. What's up?"

"An extremely urgent situation has arisen and I need to meet you as soon as possible."

"What situation?"

I didn't want to go into details on an open police frequency. "My sheriff has new information you need to see in person regarding Jimmy Panther. The timing is critical and he wants your eyes to review it in case there's something his two eyes missed."

The radio patch went silent a moment as Romero digested the obvious lie. Then he said, "OK. What if we meet someplace between us?"

"Sounds good. Where?"

"I'll call you from the road in about fifteen minutes. Maybe we can make lunch."

Romero understood something critical was in the air and a cell phone-to-cell phone connection would be the most secure.

"All right. My treat. See you soon." I dropped the receiver on the cradle and realized my jeep was still back at the casino. Romero would need to pick me up, but we could work out those details when he phoned again. In the meantime, I'd walk down to the village and look for a spot we could rendezvous. And, more importantly, I'd call Tommy Lee and alert him we might be arresting one of Gainesboro's most prominent citizens.

He answered the phone with an order. "You're going to wear a Kevlar vest. I'll bring it tonight."

"All right. But you might want to delegate that errand. Our agenda may have changed."

"I'm near the construction site," Tommy Lee said. "Are you having trouble getting the soil samples from Romero?"

"I forgot to ask him."

"You're kidding?" The sheriff was clearly annoyed.

"Melissa Bigham discovered Mack Collins' roots go back to South Boston, and he may have been laundering money for Whitey Bulger."

Tommy Lee Wadkins was a man of few words. Now he was a man of no words. Without waiting, I updated him on Melissa's phone call and her new efforts to find a connection between Collins and out-of-state companies in the running for contracts.

When I finished, he asked, "Melissa will sit on this?"

"Yes. I told her something was going down tonight and that I would call her. She knows the Collins information is tied in somehow, but she's unaware it involves a kidnapped child."

"Where's Mack Collins now?" Tommy Lee asked.

"I assume he's either meeting with the gaming commissioner or he's headed across state to Raleigh."

"I wish I knew if he was still in Cherokee. If he's staying, then that looks like he's up to his armpits in this plot."

"I can call him. He gave me all his numbers when he said he wanted to be kept informed about the case."

"Do that. Tell him you're in Cherokee and you thought you saw him at the casino last night. You couldn't speak then, but you'd like to bring him up to speed on the investigation."

"What if he just wants to do it over the phone?"

"Tell him you have some documents involving Darren Cransford that might or might not be significant. You need to show him in person. We know there's a rift between the two of them so Mack will be curious."

"And if he's on his way to Raleigh?"

"Then I think he has no immediate play in tonight's events and we'll see what Melissa uncovers."

"What documents am I going to show him?"

Tommy Lee chuckled. "It's what I'm going to show him. I'm going to have Melissa fax those newspaper articles to the Cherokee Police Department. Then you and I will confront him together."

"Don't you think he'll warn Tyrell?"

"No. He knows nothing about our connection to Kevin. We're going to say the articles were supplied by Darren Cransford. He'll believe that because if Darren can discredit him, the opposition to the Catawba casino will be weakened."

"What's your goal?"

"To see if he's rattled. See if he gives more information than he gets and hope he realizes that we're developing links that could be damaging, especially if something happens to Danny Swift."

"What time do you want me to set it up?"

"Try for late afternoon or early evening. I'd like to keep him guessing till then. Meanwhile, go on with your investigation. Call me with whatever you can work out."

I stopped along the side of the road and pulled out my wallet. Tucked behind a couple of twenties was the card with the litany of Mack Collins' phone numbers. His cell would be the most likely choice since he was either here or on the road.

"Collins here," he said brusquely. My number was unfamiliar.

"Senator Collins, it's Barry Clayton."

His tone immediately brightened. "Hello, Barry. What can I do for you? Is your uncle ready to testify?"

"I think we'll all be better off if you keep Uncle Wayne in reserve. I was wondering if you were still in Cherokee."

For a few seconds there was no response and he must have been calculating how I knew where he'd been. I pressed on. "I saw you at the casino last night. I'm here working the Panther murder and meeting with the Cherokee police. Sorry I wasn't able to speak with you."

"No problem. I was there to see the gaming commissioner, but I'm headed back to Gainesboro and on to Raleigh tomorrow."

"That's too bad. Something's developed that I think you should see."

"Really? Is it related to Luther?"

"It might be. It's definitely related to you and Luther's son Darren."

Silence again, but this time I let it go on.

When I didn't elaborate, he asked, "Can't you fax it to me?"

"No, sir. It's potential evidence and shared jointly between us and the Cherokee police. I'm afraid I'm dealing with their chain of custody, however, as long as I've signed for it, I could review it with you. I'm sure it's nothing, but I have no control over what my counterparts here might do. As we discussed the other night, we don't want you to be blindsided."

"All right. I suppose I can be back in an hour."

"I'm afraid I'm not clear till around six. You might not know but Jimmy Panther's colleague Eddie Wolfe was murdered early this morning."

A rush of air sounded in my ear as if someone had punched Collins in the stomach.

"Who?"

"I guess you could say he was Panther's lieutenant. Everyone expected him to pick up the mantle of leadership in the fight against the new casino."

Collins' voice rose to an angry bark. "Is that what Darren's claiming? That I'm tied into these killings?"

I sidestepped the question. "Is six good, sir? Then I can bring you up to date on the whole day."

He sighed. "Yes. Where?"

"I've still got a room at the casino hotel where we can talk privately." I gave him the number and he promised to be there.

After a quick call to Tommy Lee to confirm the meeting with Collins and insure he would have Melissa Bigham fax the articles in time, I walked down the hill to the Cherokee museum. The redwood carving of Sequoyah towered over the front of the building and appeared much larger than when I first saw it from Tommy Lee's car. I circled the base where blocks of stone had been etched with the names of the seven Cherokee clans. Some were animals I'd expect. Wolf, Bird, and Deer. But others were significant in their unlikeliness. Long Hair Clan, Paint Clan, Blue Clan, and my favorite, the Wild Potato Clan.

My cell phone rang and I recognized Romero's number.

"Sorry to be so vague. I couldn't trust that we wouldn't be monitored by a scanner."

"I gathered that," he said. "What's happened?"

"I have evidence Danny Swift's been kidnapped. It's absolutely critical we keep it quiet."

"Who's we?"

"You, me, Tommy Lee, and Kevin Malone, the friend of Tommy Lee who gave us the lead on Tyrell. I'm at the museum. Can you pick me up?"

"Yes. But then where?"

"What was your next move?" I asked.

"I was going back to Jimmy's. I called Cherokee Boxes and learned Eddie Wolfe didn't stay at work till midnight last Sunday. They finished at ten."

"So he lied to Skye."

"Or they were in it together," Romero said. "I wanted to go through both Jimmy's summer lodge and his winter asi for any sign Swifty hid there. But a kidnapping changes everything."

"Not necessarily," I argued. "We can't have too much information. Just get me as soon as you can. I'll be the little guy standing beside Sequoyah."

I briefed Romero on the way to Jimmy Panther's. The picture of Danny Swift unnerved him and he had serious doubts about the exchange I'd set in motion. I emphasized that we knew Danny had seen Jimmy and Eddie with the artifacts. If Eddie had taken Danny, then maybe Tyrell found the boy to be convenient leverage to get his money back.

Two points posed delicate handling with Romero. The way Kevin got Tyrell's money could undercut the Cherokee's acceptance of Kevin as the agent for the exchange. I told Romero that Kevin had somehow intercepted a payment drop and I left it at that.

The second sensitive issue concerned our suspicions regarding Mack Collins. He was well liked by the tribe and an advocate for their causes. Bringing him in as the possible mastermind of two murders would put Romero in an awkward position should our suspicions be unfounded and Mack Collins carry a grudge.

When we arrived at Emma Byrd's house, I saw an extra car in the front yard.

"Skye's here," Romero said.

"Does she know about Eddie?"

"I didn't talk to her." He opened his door. "We'll learn soon enough."

"Nothing about the kidnapping," I said.

"I understand. We can say we're here to notify Skye, and you'd like to look one more time for traces of Swifty."

This time Romero headed for the front porch, not the rear door. I kept pace a few yards behind him. As he reached the first step, Emma emerged from the door. She wore another shapeless dress, this one blue rather than brown, and it hung to the tips of her moccasins.

She nodded to me, and then spoke to Romero. "Are you here for Skye?"

"Yes."

"You were good to come, but she learned about an hour ago."

"I'm sorry," Romero said. "I've been tied up trying to figure out what happened."

She beckoned us on the porch with a single wave of her thin hand. "She's in the kitchen. I fixed her some potato soup. Would you join us?"

I looked to Romero for the proper response because I didn't know if it would be an insult to refuse her hospitality.

"Thank you, Miss Emma, but it will be better if Skye finishes and then we can talk. Meanwhile, we'd like to take one more look at Jimmy's. The Swift boy's still missing and I want to make doubly sure he didn't come here. We should be back in about twenty minutes, if that's all right."

Emma studied the big man a moment, as if sensing there was more going on. Then she shrugged. "Take your time. I'll keep Skye here till you return." She turned around and disappeared into the house.

As we walked up the path, I asked Romero, "When you were here yesterday, did you notice anything different from when we searched the day before?"

"No. But if Swifty had heard us coming and didn't want to be found, he wouldn't be found. He'd melt into the forest like his ancestors. He had a gift."

"Like with the blowgun?"

"Yes. If I believed in reincarnation, I'd say he was an old soul who had walked these hills many times."

Old soul wasn't the way I'd describe the frightened boy in the photograph, but I kept that thought to myself.

When we reached the summer lodge and neighboring asi, Romero retrieved the key from beneath the rock and opened the padlock. The interior didn't appear any different from my previous visit. The one wall of empty shelves reminded me of the trove of boxes we found stashed underneath Eddie Wolfe's trailer. The chairs seemed to be in the same position. Closer examination showed a thin layer of dust had been undisturbed.

The asi had an unlocked door and no windows. The cone-shaped structure looked like an upside-down basket. Mud appeared to coat the sides, and in a few chipped places I could see vines and wood strips underneath. The round roof had been constructed of bark shingles. Stepping into the dark interior, I saw a small fire pit illumined by a beam of light shining through a vent in the center of the roof.

"What's the main construction material?" I asked Romero.

"Wattle and daub. It's woven sticks, the wattle, and mud mixed with straw and grass, the daub. Holds the heat in the winter, although it's smoky as hell."

He pulled a flashlight from his duty belt and searched the earthen floor. Nothing.

"We know Eddie was here," Romero said, "but it looks like he didn't disturb a thing."

"Maybe someone else got Danny, or Eddie saw him coming up the road to his home."

"Maybe. Don't know where else he'd know to find him."

It dawned on me one thing was missing from both structures. "How about the bathroom. The outhouse should be separated from the house a decent distance. Did you check that?"

Romero's lips tightened. "No. I didn't think of it. Should be in the back somewhere."

We walked around the asi and saw a trail curving along the side of the ridge. About fifty feet after the bend hid both lodges from sight, we found a simple plank shell set on a flat inset in the hill. A once interior door hung askew on rusty hinges.

"Not exactly Bed, Bath and Beyond," Romero said, "but it gets the job done." He opened the door.

An unpainted wooden toilet seat sat in the middle of a frame about the size of a loading palette. The smell emanating from the dark hole in the center left no doubt as to the outhouse's active status. Again, Romero flipped on his flashlight, leaned in, and directed the beam into the hole.

"What you'd expect to see," he reported. He moved his light to the space between the seat and the back wall. "What's this?" He leaned over and retrieved something.

A half-used roll of duct tape.

He pushed me aside as he quickly backed out. He cast the light across the dirt just inside and out of the doorway. Gouges could be seen in the soil. "Somebody jumped him here. Swifty had no chance to run."

"The tape was probably already cut into strips," I said. "In the struggle, the whole roll got knocked free. Eddie probably thought it fell into the latrine."

"Eddie?"

The voice came from behind us. Both Romero and I jumped.

Skye Panther grabbed Romero's arm and physically wheeled the big man around. "For God's sake, tell me what's going on!" She was not crying. Her eyes locked on Romero's and burned with anger. "Eddie got my brother killed, didn't he?"

She released Romero and snatched the duct tape from his hand. "And he took that boy."

Skye looked at me for confirmation, but I said nothing.

"We don't know that," Romero said.

"Come on," she screamed. "I'm not a fool. You either tell me the truth or I'll find someone who will."

Romero glanced at me.

I nodded to Skye. "Let's go to your grandmother's. It's time we started working together."

Chapter Twenty-two

We sat in the front room of Emma Byrd's house. The furnishings were modest. Emma sat in a rocker nearest the stone fireplace in which seasoned, split logs had been stacked, prepared to ward off the fall chill of evening. A small table by her side held needlepoint work and a cup and saucer.

Romero occupied two-thirds of her floral print sofa. Skye sat at the other end, tight against the armrest, putting as much distance between herself and the detective as possible. Each balanced a cup and saucer in their laps, Romero's lap making the china look like it came from a dollhouse.

I sat in a straight-back, cane-bottom chair that was probably made by a local craftsman. My cup and saucer were on the floor beside me because I held my pencil and notepad ready to jot down anything either woman might say.

Emma had offered hot sassafras tea. This time Romero accepted and he added I would like some as well. I didn't argue. The herbal concoction was known for its calming powers and the Cherokee used the root and leaves for medicinal purposes. The taste was akin to warm, flat root beer, and I hoped it would settle Skye down for our conversation.

Romero drained his cup and smacked his lips. Then he turned to Skye. "When was the last time you saw Eddie?"

"Late yesterday afternoon. I was here. Since Monday I've spent the nights with Emmama."

"He came by to see you?"

"Not entirely. He said he wanted to check Jimmy's for the boy. Swifty."

"Did you go with him?"

"No. Eddie thought two of us would double the chance of being heard. He didn't want Swifty running away."

"How long was Eddie gone?" Romero asked.

"About forty-five minutes. I thought he might have found the kid and was talking to him."

"What did Eddie say when he returned?"

"That there was no sign of Swifty. Eddie said he was late for work, but he would call me this morning."

"And he didn't call."

She nodded, but she didn't cry. Instead she reached into a handbag at her feet and pulled out a cracked leather wallet. "This is Eddie's. Emmama found it this morning when she went for a walk."

"Found it where?"

"On the gravel road," Emma said. "Where Jimmy parked when he didn't want to disturb me. Where the stream noise muffles the car engine."

"Was that where Eddie parked yesterday afternoon?" Romero asked.

"No," Skye said. "He pulled up into the yard."

"How do you think the wallet got there?"

"He came back after his shift. The Camaro's seatbelt was bad to snag his hip pocket. I think it slid free when he got out of the car."

Romero looked at Emma. "Did you hear anything?"

"No. And I was restless."

Romero shifted on the sofa, angling to face Skye.

"I spoke to Cherokee Boxes. Eddie never showed for work yesterday. They also confirmed that the cleanup detail on Sunday finished at ten, not midnight."

Skye's cheeks flushed. "He told me midnight."

"How did you learn Eddie had been killed?"

"When Emmama found the wallet, I tried to call but got his voicemail. I assumed he was at home and out of coverage. So, I called one of his neighbors who has a landline. She told me the police were there and that Eddie was dead."

Romero glanced at me to make sure I was getting things down. When he said nothing further, I realized he was encouraging me to pick up the questioning.

I laid the pencil and pad in my lap. "Skye, what do you think happened?"

"The same person who killed Jimmy killed Eddie."

"And before that. Why did Eddie come back last night?"

"Maybe he thought Swifty would bed down for the night in one of Jimmy's lodges."

"You were angry when you saw the roll of duct tape. Why?"

She stiffened, hesitating to tell me.

"Go on, child," Emma said. "Tell them what you told me."

Skye licked her thin lips. "I thought Eddie had found Swifty and come back for him. Maybe that was a condition Swifty wanted. Not to be seen. Not wanting his friends to think he went crying to Jimmy's. But when I heard Eddie was dead, I thought more was going on. Eddie wasn't Jimmy. He wasn't as confrontational. But he'd gotten into something over his head."

Skye turned to me. "I saw that roll of duct tape on Jimmy's shelf Monday. It was there yesterday morning when Emmama and I went through his things." She looked at Romero. "You came by after Eddie yesterday afternoon so I walked back up to make sure everything was locked up. The duct tape was gone. I thought you'd taken it."

"Now what do you think?" I asked.

"That Eddie used it to bind Swifty until he could return after dark and move him. He must have left him in the outhouse."

"And why do you think Eddie got your brother killed?"

"Because he'd become secretive the last few weeks. I thought he had another girlfriend. Several times I'd walk into a room where he was on the phone and he'd abruptly hang up. Or he'd get calls when we were out and he'd excuse himself to answer." Tears finally welled in her eyes. "Did he kill Jimmy?"

"I don't think so," I said. "Sunday night I think he transported Jimmy's artifact collection from the new casino property to his trailer."

"He stole Jimmy's collection?" Skye asked.

"No. Jimmy's collection was never stolen." I summarized our theory of Jimmy salting the site of the second casino and his alliance with the Catawbas. Emma and Skye listened without interrupting until I got to the part about someone knowing what Jimmy intended to do and leaking the plan.

Skye began to tremble, clutching her arms across her chest and bending forward to stifle her sobs. "It was Eddie. It had to be Eddie. He used me, Emmama. Used me to bring him to Jimmy."

Romero and I sat there, unable to say anything that would ease her grief.

Emma knelt in front of her granddaughter. "You can't blame yourself for the evil in another's heart, child. You trusted him and Jimmy trusted him. Eddie might not have pulled the trigger, but he was worse. He betrayed a friend." Her face softened. "He betrayed you, Skye. He wasn't worthy of you." Her eyes narrowed as she swept her gaze from Romero to me. "I'm glad he's dead."

"Did you find a cell phone at Eddie Wolfe's?" I asked the question as soon as we were back in the patrol car.

"No," Romero said. "I was just thinking about that."

"If the killer took it, he's concerned either incriminating texts or phone messages might be on it. We should get the number from Skye."

"Let's not," Romero said. "Remember Emma found the wallet. Who's to say Skye didn't meet Eddie after dark?"

"You don't believe that, do you?"

"Doesn't matter what I believe. With Swifty's life on the line we have to consider all possibilities. I'll get the cell number from his employer. Then what?"

"I'll give it to Tommy Lee. We don't need the physical phone to check a call log with the carrier."

"Won't that take days?"

"I think Tommy Lee's leaning on his niece at the FBI."

Romero laughed. "Hell, the NSA's probably monitoring the calls as it is. Rooster should ask them." He pulled the mike from his two-way and instructed his dispatcher to get Eddie's number.

Five minutes later, we had the information and I relayed it to Tommy Lee. I also gave him the update on the duct tape and the suspicion that Eddie Wolfe had trapped Danny Swift in the outhouse.

The sheriff asked me to put him on speaker phone. "Hector, I'm going to bring some soil samples from the site. Would you prepare some from Eddie's trunk and the artifacts?"

"You got it. What do you want me to do tonight?"

Romero and I hadn't discussed his role at the exchange. Although we were working well together, he would probably be more amenable to an assignment from Tommy Lee.

"I'll be in the parking lot of the Bureau of Indian Affairs," Tommy Lee said. "With night binoculars, I'll cover the entrance to the bamboo forest used by Kevin. Can you get into a safe and invisible position to watch the other end where Tyrell and the boy should enter?"

"Yes," Romero said. "What's the communication plan?"

"Since Barry's going to be inside at the exchange point, I want him in place early. We're opting for cell phones and earpieces. I can merge you in if you'd like. I don't want radio chatter."

"You got it. Will Barry have night goggles?"

"No. I don't want to chance a reflection off the glass. How are you at camo?"

Romero winked at me. "I'm an Indian, Rooster. Once you see me, it's too late."

"Well, Barry's not. He's a funeral director used to standing where he can be summoned on a moment's notice. I'm bringing him a vest, but help him find something that will make him disappear."

Romero glanced at his watch. It was nearly two. "I've got just the thing."

"Good. Get it to him before five. Barry, that's when I want to meet you in your hotel room."

"You need me there?" Romero asked.

I started to object. I didn't want Romero crossing paths with Mack Collins.

Tommy Lee spoke first. "Not necessary. I'm going over some information from the Gainesboro side of the investigation. In fact, I took the liberty of faxing it to your department. They're going to hold it in an envelope for me. I'll pick it up with your soil samples."

"Sounds good, Rooster. See you at the station."

"All right," Tommy Lee said. "Barry, I'll see you in your room at five. And charge your damn phone."

The rap on the door came at five fifty-five. I cracked it open, saw Mack Collins, and motioned him inside. As he passed me, I took a quick look up and down the hall. No one was in sight. I wondered if Mack had come from the elevators or from Frankie Tyrell's room.

Behind me, Collins said, "Tommy Lee, Barry didn't say you'd be here."

I closed the door and turned to see Collins stopped at the foot of the bed, hesitant to venture nearer the sheriff.

Tommy Lee pointed to the chair I'd just vacated. "Sit down, Mack. We have some things to discuss."

I walked closer, blocking Collins' return to the door. Tommy Lee and I had rehearsed how the scene would play. On the coffee table in the small conversation area, he'd laid out the New Jersey newspaper articles and the photo Kevin Malone had taken of Frankie Tyrell outside the Cherokee casino. Facedown was the picture of Danny Swift gagged in the trunk of a car. Tommy Lee would play that card if and when the time seemed right.

Collins glanced at the table as he moved toward the chair. His step faltered and he grabbed the armrest to steady himself. "Where did you get these?" he hissed.

"That's not important," Tommy Lee said.

"The hell it isn't. Darren Cransford would say or do anything to bring me down, even stoop to digging up thirty-year-old dirt. And that's all it is. I wasn't convicted of anything."

"The way I understand it a key witness went into the dirt." Tommy Lee tapped the photo of Tyrell. "And this isn't thirty years old."

"I have no idea who he is," Collins snapped.

"I have a witness who saw you arguing with him last night. I'm in the process of pulling the surveillance footage now."

Collins' face went red. "Do you have someone following me?"

"No. But the FBI is following him." Tommy Lee said the lie easily enough.

Collins sat. He looked at the documents in front of him, his eyes lingering on the turned-down sheet of paper. "I have nothing to do with that man."

"Which man would that be?"

"So, this is the way you're going to play it? Not a conversation but an interrogation?"

"That depends on you, Mack. If you want to lawyer up, then I'll have to bring the FBI into it. And you know the death of two Indians who opposed the second Cherokee casino will bring federal scrutiny, particularly when the leading legislative advocate for the project is seen talking with a Boston hit man." Tommy Lee waved his hand over the documents. "And the New Jersey stories alone are enough to embolden anyone who might challenge you for your seat."

Collins seemed to shrink in the chair. "I knew Tyrell a long time ago. I didn't like him then and I don't like him now."

"You're denying you brought him down here?" Tommy Lee asked.

"Of course I deny it. Look, I'm not admitting to any wrong-doing in the past, but I am saying I came to Gainesboro thirty years ago to make a clean start. I've done that, and I've worked hard for our community and this region."

If Collins was telling the truth, a new possibility arose in my mind. "But did they let you?" I asked. "As you became successful, you had more to lose. What did Whitey Bulger and Frankie Tyrell extort from you?"

At the mention of Whitey Bulger, Collins' head jerked around. "Nothing. I refused to give them one red cent."

Whether that was true or not, Tommy Lee and I didn't have the resources to delve back through years of the financial records of Collins' company. But his statement confirmed Frankie Tyrell had tried extortion.

"Is that why you argued with Tyrell?" Tommy Lee asked. "You thought he'd come here to cut himself in on the casino expansion."

"I saw him, I didn't know why he was here, and I told him to leave. That's it. End of story."

"You're saying Tyrell wasn't here for a piece of the action?" Tommy Lee said. "I find it hard to believe you ran into him by coincidence."

"Believe what you want."

"Then I'll take your cell phone, please."

"What?" Collins puffed himself up with indignation. "You have no warrant, you have no right."

Tommy Lee looked at me. I moved closer, better to see Collins' face.

"I'm not worried about a warrant." Tommy Lee leaned over the table and flipped up the photo of Danny Swift. "Not when it involves a child's life."

Mack Collins stared at the image. His jaw dropped and his face paled as if every ounce of blood had drained from his body. "Who is that?" he managed to whisper.

"You don't know?" Tommy Lee asked.

Collins studied Danny's terrified face. He genuinely seemed confused. When he looked up, I saw fear in his eyes.

"I have no idea," he said.

"A thirteen-year-old boy who witnessed something he shouldn't have. Your buddy Tyrell has him, and I'm taking your phone so that you have no chance to warn him that we're coming after him."

Collins reached into his suit coat pocket. Tommy Lee and I stiffened.

He slowly laid a cell phone on the table. "Now I understand why you're doing this to me." He pointed to the phone. "You'll find one call from an unidentified source. It was Tyrell and he said his phone was a prepaid. He came out of the blue."

"When?" Tommy Lee asked.

"Yesterday morning. He told me to meet him at the casino. He had information he was sure I'd be interested in."

"What information?"

"He didn't say, but that was Tyrell's code for something he thought I'd pay to keep quiet."

"But you didn't pay before," I said.

"I know. Back then I called his bluff. He would gain no advantage by floating some old newspaper stories. I suspect Whitey ordered him to back off and wait till I had something more to lose. Now Whitey's out of the picture and Tyrell's greedy. He's also stupid and arrogant. Thinks he can run some of Whitey's old operations."

Arrogant. The same way Kevin described him.

"And what more do you have to lose?" I asked.

"Nothing. That's why I told Tyrell to leave Cherokee. I used a meeting with the gaming commissioner to explain my presence here."

Tommy Lee confiscated the phone. "That doesn't add up, Mack. With a potential kidnapping and murder charge on the line, why would Tyrell risk bringing you into his game? He hasn't survived this long being completely stupid."

Collins stared at Danny Swift's photo. "I don't know. Ask him when you catch him."

Senator Eckles' words resounded in my head. His North Carolina companies.

"You do have something to lose," I said. "You have out-of-state companies at play in the bidding."

"Do I? That's news to me."

Tommy Lee looked at me with surprise. Melissa Bigham hadn't gotten back to us with a name or proof linking Collins to any such company. I was flying blind. I wanted to say Senator Eckles had told me so, but Melissa and I had inferred that conclusion from his remark. Eckles had made no such accusation directly.

"Couldn't that be Tyrell's assumption? The revelation of which could both embarrass you and cost you money."

"God damn it, I don't know what Tyrell's assuming. But I'm telling you my hands are clean." He pointed to Danny. "And I have nothing to do with this child. I suggest you worry about his safety."

I tried a Hail Mary pass as a last resort. "That child's in a trunk. Can we search your car?"

"Knock yourself out." Collins leaned closer to the photograph. "The carpet in my trunk is beige. This is char—"

He stopped midword.

"What?" Tommy Lee prompted.

"It's charcoal," he said softly. "Like the lining of Luther Cransford's Cadillac."

Chapter Twenty-three

Luther Cransford's Cadillac. The vehicle he'd driven Sunday night when Jimmy Panther was killed. And now Luther was in Cherokee at the same time Eddie Wolfe was murdered and Danny Swift kidnapped. Had our investigation come full circle and wound up at our original suspect?

"There are other Cadillacs on the reservation," Tommy Lee said. "Why would you think this is Luther's?"

"I hope it's not," Collins said. "Were both the murdered Indians at Eurleen's funeral?"

"Yes," Tommy Lee said. "And Eddie, Jimmy, and Jimmy's sister Skye came to the site of the Cherokee remains. Luther was there and saw them."

"But that doesn't explain the connection to the boy," I argued. "Tyrell had to be linked to Eddie Wolfe. If Luther's involved, what's his connection to Tyrell? Tyrell was in Cherokee before the funeral protest occurred."

"We're not talking two things here," Tommy Lee insisted. "I'm convinced it's one thing and it's one motive." He leaned closer to Collins. "Does Luther have something to gain from the construction of the second casino?"

"Not that I know of," Collins said. "Not Luther." His eyes lost focus as some new idea crossed his mind. "Sandra," he whispered to himself.

"Sandra Cransford?" I nearly shouted. "What's a dental equipment company have to do with anything?"

"Dental equipment?" Collins looked as confused as me. "G. A. Bridges builds bridges and roads. It's word play on Georgia bridges. You thought it was dental bridgework?"

"God damn it," Tommy Lee said. "Reece screwed that up. Why didn't we double-check?"

I felt blood rush to my cheeks. "My fault. Wakefield checked her out, but just for her alibi. I didn't ask him about the business."

Tommy Lee sighed. "And we weren't looking for construction companies at the time."

"Her alibi held up and we moved on," I said. "When you checked on Luther's claim that Sandra called him at nine thirty last Sunday night, did you pull GPS information on her location?"

"No," he growled. "I was focused on Luther."

"She could have left Gainesboro at three in the morning and still made her eight o'clock breakfast in Atlanta." I sat on the edge of the bed, my mind racing. "Does Sandra know Frankie Tyrell?" I asked Collins.

"I never introduced them." He paused. "But Tyrell made contact with my daughter at Wellesley. He sent me a picture of him, Cheryl, and Sandra. My daughter and Sandra were roommates."

"What kind of picture?" I asked.

"They were at some Irish pub. Tyrell was sending me a message that he could touch my family any time he wanted."

"So, Sandra's potentially known Tyrell over twenty years," I said. "How did she get into the construction business? It's not the kind of career I'd expect of a Wellesley graduate."

"She worked summers in my office. All through high school and college. I thought maybe she'd stay with my company since my own children weren't interested. She said she wanted a bigger city. Gainesboro couldn't compete with Atlanta."

"Where'd she get the capital to launch her business?" I asked.

"Corrine and I gave her a personal loan. She said other funds came from friends and bank loans. I assumed Luther helped her. She paid us back within five years and I've never had any say or input into her company."

"Could Frankie Tyrell or Whitey Bulger have been those friends?" I asked. "Could she have laundered money for them? What you refused to do."

"Anything's possible. If they were moving some operations south, Atlanta's a logical choice."

"And if you loaned Sandra money, she could stretch the truth and claim you were involved with her business," I said. "Senator Eckles seems to have that opinion, and it had to come from someone."

"Eckles knows I keep arm's length from state projects."

"Yes. But if Sandra pretended to be your backdoor channel, would he nudge things her way?"

Collins' eyes narrowed. "Only if there was something in it for him. Eckles is slippery, especially if Sandra were making campaign donations to grease the process."

I looked at Tommy Lee and saw his nod. He must have been thinking the same thing. One hundred fifty thousand dollars is a lot of grease. Kevin hadn't stolen Tyrell's payment for executing Panther. He'd taken the cash payoff for Senator Eckles and others like him. If Tyrell got that cash from his Boston loan sharks, then they would want it back with exorbitant interest. Everything depended upon winning that construction contract.

"Well, Darren claimed to have a connection to you," I said. "Why wouldn't Sandra also try to exploit that?"

Collins licked his lips. He seemed shaken to his core. "She'd be looking at the largest contract the Department of Transportation would award. The road and bridge expansions slated to improve access to the casino."

"Millions?" I asked.

"Multimillions," Collins said.

"All in jeopardy if the Catawba succeed or the new Cherokee site becomes mired in archaeological controversy."

"Yes," Collins said. "And I expect this state contract is crucial. If Tyrell and Sandra are laundering money, then the company has to have work to generate the reportable income. The recession years have been tough on all construction. They might be close to broke and owe money to the wrong people. They're desperate." Collins picked up Danny's photograph. "What about this boy? What's happening to him?"

His obvious concern lent credibility to his innocence. But he had the proven connection to Frankie Tyrell, and too much was at stake to take a chance.

"We have a plan," Tommy Lee said. "At this critical point, I can't let you out of my sight."

Collins hung his head. "You still don't believe me."

"I believe you. But the circle of people involved is so small that if you're outside that circle and something goes wrong, you'll be vulnerable as the leak. This is for your protection as well as the operation's."

"So, what now?" Collins asked.

Tommy Lee smiled. "We order room service, we rehearse, and we send Barry out as soon as it's dark."

While we waited for dinner, Tommy Lee set things in motion to check Sandra Cransford's and Collins' phone records. He also instructed Deputy Wakefield to speak with the security guard at Luther Cransford's gatehouse to let him know if anyone signed in or out as Luther's guest. And to inform Wakefield whenever Darren's, Sandra's, or Luther's vehicles came and left.

I called Detective Sergeant Romero and we tested the three-way conference feature merging Romero and me with Tommy Lee. Romero assured us he would be in position without being seen and set to move at my signal.

At seven, the room service cart arrived with our dinner. Tommy Lee and Mack Collins had ordered the prime rib. I was too nervous for such a heavy meal and ate a grilled chicken salad. I hadn't wanted anything, but Tommy Lee told me the whole operation could be compromised if my growling stomach gave me away. I realized I was no longer a deputy. I was a member of his platoon.

Collins removed the silver cover from his plate. The prime rib and mixed vegetables steamed. "I must say you feed your hostages well."

"You are a state senator," Tommy Lee said. "And I hope you remain one."

Collins sliced into the thick cut of meat. He looked up at me before eating. "When I saw you at the funeral home and asked for updates on the case, I set myself up, didn't I?"

"Not at the time," I admitted. "But as the politics of the casino and the Catawba petition came to light, yes, your name started surfacing. I had to wonder if your interest was more than concern for Luther."

"Well, I hold no hard feelings. I was angry at Darren because I think the Catawba casino is a mistake and a dangerous precedent. It's being spearheaded by a video poker mogul in South Carolina who can't get what he wants in that state. We have a good relationship with the Cherokee and they have a good casino operator in Harrah's. I have grave doubts about the direction the Catawba tribe is taking."

I felt my phone vibrate. A four-word text message appeared. "It's from Kevin," I said. "He reports, 'Tyrell checked bamboo, gone.'"

"Kevin?" Collins asked.

"One of my men." Tommy Lee clearly chose not to tell Collins that Kevin was from Boston.

"Finish your meal and then change," Tommy Lee told me. "Tyrell will be back early and I want you in place."

I ate rapidly while Tommy Lee and Collins made small talk over their dinner. I set my empty plate on the cart, and said, "I'm going to step out and phone Susan. Back in a moment."

Tommy Lee nodded. Collins looked grim. Both understood I might be making the final call to my wife.

I walked to the stairwell from where I'd seen Kevin break into Tyrell's room. The Do Not Disturb sign still dangled from his door. On the fourth-floor landing, I leaned against the railing and speed-dialed Susan's number. Seven thirty. She should be home.

"Barry. Is everything OK?"

I could hear the TV in the background. Then Democrat's bark as he heard Susan say my name. I wanted to say no. I wanted to say I was scared. That I was going into the dark against a professional killer to help a rogue cop who had shot his own partner. And at the center of it all was a child I hadn't met and didn't know. But if "Protect and Serve" meant anything, it meant Danny Swift. I was ready and willing to lay my life on the line for him.

"Everything's fine, honey. I hope to be home tomorrow."

"So, you've had a break in the case?" She sounded excited.

"A real possibility. We've identified a company that stands to make a lot of money from the new casino construction. We've uncovered some questionable practices and we're running phone and wire transfer checks that should tie everything together." Truthful, yet vague enough to make the investigation appear to be nothing more than paperwork.

Susan audibly exhaled. "I can't tell you how relieved I am. The cold-blooded nature of the murder has set me on edge. And then after seeing Tyrell in person. Barry, I didn't want you to know how worried I was. I'll just be glad when it's over."

"Me too." I hadn't told her about Eddie Wolfe or Danny Swift. If she was worried before, that knowledge would ratchet up her fear exponentially. "I love you, Susan."

"I know. I love you, too."

I parked my jeep behind the Cherokee museum where it was out of sight of both the main and side roads. Romero had lent me a camera and large camera bag, and I looked like a photographer interested in some night shots of the village and river.

At eight thirty, the full moon crested the eastern ridges, and even though my afternoon run to a discount store provided me with black jeans and a black turtleneck large enough to fit over a Kevlar vest, I would be visible as a three-dimensional walking shadow.

Fortunately, I didn't stand out as an isolated figure because I wasn't the only person outside. Cars drove by, some headed to the casino, others returning to one of the many mom-and-pop motels scattered nearby. Couples strolled along, enjoying the fresh air and moonlit landscape. I crossed the footbridge and stopped midway to take a high-angle picture down the length of the island. With the Carolina moon in the upper frame, the scene was quite nice and I took several shots.

The island park seemed deserted and I was careful to project no particular destination as I walked along the shore. Up ahead, the tall stand of bamboo cast a long shadow from the low-hanging moon, and when I stepped across its dark edge and into its depths, I was confident I had disappeared.

I stayed close to the left edge of the interior path where I would be a less visible silhouette if anyone happened to look through the bamboo tunnel. Feeling my way along the wall of stalks, I trod softly on the carpet of brown leaves that had fallen from the canopy high overhead. As I reached the midpoint, I slowed, dragging my hand across the tightly packed bamboo. A gap opened just wide enough for me to slip through, and I left the path for the confines of a space not much larger than a casket.

I sat on the leaf-covered ground, opened the camera bag, and retrieved the camo-painted ground cloth Romero had supplied me. I set it aside and pulled out the nine-millimeter Glock Tommy Lee had given me. I'd brought a thirty-eight caliber service revolver for my shoulder holster, but he insisted I carry more firepower. Next I unpacked a high-beam flashlight, a black ski mask, and stick of black greasepaint both courtesy of Romero, and the coiled earpiece for my phone. Then I placed the camera into the empty bag and set it in a corner of my self-imposed prison.

Before donning the mask, I smeared the greasepaint around my eyes where the skin would still be exposed. With the earpiece and mask in place and the Glock and flashlight tucked close to my side, I lay down and spread the ground cloth over me.

Buryin' Barry was buried and would remain so for the next five hours.

Chapter Twenty-four

I never served in the military and so I'd never been posted to sentry duty or a sniper position or what I guess could have been a hundred other assignments requiring absolute silence and stillness. I'd been on a few stakeouts when I was a uniformed patrolman in Charlotte and done similar duties as a Laurel County deputy. But I'd never been entrenched so close to my quarry or under such dangerous circumstances.

My main concern was staying focused and not letting my mind wander. I didn't have a bag of tricks like a trained soldier might have. In the funeral business, I tried to stay in the moment, listening for the cue words from a minister that would move the ritual onto its next event. The danger is I'm so primed for action that I'm listening only for those cue words and not the entire context.

Once, during a service at a small Baptist church in a mountain hollow outside of Gainesboro, I sat patiently on the back pew while the preacher's remarks transformed into a full blown sermon. Suddenly, he shouted out the word, "Undertaker." I leaped to my feet. The congregation turned around and the preacher's face went red as he backed away from the pulpit. He said, "I'm sorry, Barry. I didn't mean you personally. You'll be there." Laughter rippled through the pews.

I later learned the preacher had been extolling the virtues of eternal life and proclaimed with fervor, "Death will be no more. You'll see no undertaker in heaven."

Now, for five hours, I hoped no one would see this undertaker on the earth either. As the time passed, I felt my limbs grow stiff and the ground chill start to seep into my bones. Traffic noise diminished until only the occasional rumble of an engine rose above the river's gurgle. Crickets, hoot owls, and sporadic dog barks replaced the human sounds.

My phone vibrated. To me it crashed like thunder. The screen glowed like a lighthouse beacon.

"Yes?" I whispered.

"How you doing?" Tommy Lee asked, tension flowing through the words.

"Good. Ready."

"I've got Mack in the car with me. Kevin called a few minutes ago, checking in at midnight. As far as he knows, Tyrell hasn't been back to the casino."

"Hardly expect he'd keep Danny in his room."

"He could be at one of the smaller motels with external doors," Tommy Lee said. "Easier to get Danny in and out."

"Any word from Wakefield?"

"No activity to or from Luther's house. He and Sandra are still registered in separate rooms at the casino."

"You're able to see the spot where Kevin will enter the bamboo?"

"Yes. It's a distance, but I've got a clear view. If there's trouble, I'll come in as fast as I can."

"And Romero?" I asked.

"I haven't heard from him."

"That's a surprise. You call him?"

"Yes. No answer."

The chill from the ground was replaced with cold fear. If Romero was AWOL, who would cover Tyrell and Danny as they entered the bamboo? And where was Romero?

"I'll call again in ninety minutes," Tommy Lee promised. "That's approximately one forty-five and we'll keep the line open. Romero knows that's when we'll merge our phones."

"And if he's not there?"

"He will be. And you'd best not speak, just connect to my call."

"Trust me. This is one time I won't hang up on you."

The next ninety minutes passed like ninety days. I slowly shifted position every five minutes as if I was engaged in some prone Tai Chi session. I would need to be ready to quickly get to my feet and shed the ground cloth, the flashlight in my left hand and the Glock in my right. I was counting on Kevin to leave his flashlight by the satchel of cash so that I would have a clear view of Tyrell. If I could avoid using my own light, then I would be a voice in the darkness and not a target.

My phone buzzed and I accepted the call.

"Tap the phone," Tommy Lee said.

I drummed my fingers on the plastic casing.

"Good," Tommy Lee confirmed. "I should be able to hear anything."

I slipped the phone into the sheath on my belt.

"Barry, I still haven't heard from Romero. Probably some glitch with his phone, but…"

He let the thought hang and I knew he was worried. Had we made a mistake in bringing the Cherokee detective into the exchange? The cards were dealt, and folding now wasn't an option.

The crickets abruptly ceased chirping. Somewhere to my right a twig snapped. I lifted a corner of the ground cloth and peered through the vertical bars of bamboo. The pathway ended in a cool blue oval of moonlight. Glints reflecting off the shore rocks and river were visible beyond.

A shadow moved across the opening. A shadow with a brief-case. The figure flattened against the stalks. Kevin Malone had arrived ten minutes early, maybe to check that I was well hidden, maybe to be in a position where he could watch his back.

I turned my head to the opposite end of the path. That opening was brighter with an unobstructed view of the river. If Tyrell stayed with the plan, he and Swifty would be clearly silhouetted against the moonlit background—not necessarily two distinct silhouettes because I expected Tyrell to hold the boy in front of him as a shield.

"Figure approaching footbridge." Tommy Lee's alert meant either Tyrell was coming alone or an unknown person was making an inopportune visit to the island.

A few minutes later, Tommy Lee added, "Definitely a man looping around the island to the far end of the bamboo. Should be coming into Hector Romero's view."

Romero. Who wasn't with us.

The man suddenly appeared in the opening. He wore a dark windbreaker and his ball cap was pulled low on his head. His arms were out to his side at forty-five degree angles. His left hand held an envelope or sheet of paper. I looked back at Kevin. He had moved to an identical position with the briefcase in one hand and flashlight in the other. The scene was a bizarre parody of an Old West duel on Main Street in Dodge City.

Kevin started walking at a slow, measured pace. Tyrell stood motionless. It became clear to me that Danny wasn't with him. Tyrell had changed the rules and I had no idea what new game we were playing.

When Kevin was about a quarter of the way into the bamboo tunnel, he stopped. "Where's the boy, Tyrell? Produce him or I'm walking away with my money."

"I'm not a fool, Malone." Like Kevin, Tyrell spoke in a calm, relaxed voice. "He's safe and you'll get him. Here are the terms." He strode forward, arms still away from his side. "You give me my money that you stole, and I give you the address where you'll find the kid."

He stopped and waved what I now clearly saw was an envelope.

"How do I know the boy's alive?" Kevin asked.

"I don't kill children."

Kevin moved forward again, I thought for a second he might rush the other man but he stopped beside me. Tyrell was still fifty feet away. From ground level, all I could see of Kevin were his shoes.

"Tell that to Erin Malone." Kevin's voice constricted with rage.

"Who?"

"The ten-year-old girl passing by in a car when you gunned down Paddy Connelly."

"Erin Malone." Tyrell emphasized the last name, recognizing the significance. "Sorry. I was three hundred miles away in New York when that tragedy happened."

"Yeah. Playing cards with the Lombardi goons. How convenient."

I kept my eyes on Tyrell. He was far enough away that I could see him without lifting my head too high.

"If this is about misplaced revenge, Malone, then you're going to get the kid killed. If I don't walk out of here in ten minutes or if you fire your gun, he's dead. My associate is close enough to hear a shot."

Associate. Like he was talking about a damn business partner.

Tyrell started walking closer. "So, set down the briefcase and back away like you planned."

We had run out of options and the clock was ticking.

Kevin set the satchel in front of him and then angled the flashlight against it, throwing the beam toward Tyrell.

Safely out of the light's backwash, I slowly rose to my feet. Tyrell's eyes were locked on Kevin and he kept coming.

"The child will be dropped five minutes after I leave you. You're a good cop, Malone." He tossed the envelope toward Kevin. "And the only good cop…" His right hand whipped to the small of his back.

The bamboo behind him rattled like a discordant wooden xylophone as a wall of stalks crashed across the path. Whirling around, the mobster raised a pistol with a suppressor. I lifted the Glock just as a sharp cough pierced the air. I thought Tyrell had fired a silenced shot, but the gun fell as he threw both hands to his head and collapsed to his knees, twisting toward me. A fluff of white stuck to his right eye.

Then Hector Romero filled the path. He wore a camo shirt and pants and his broad face was splotched with green and black paint. He held a pistol in one hand and a cut stalk of bamboo in the other. No. Not simply a stalk of bamboo. A blowgun whose dart was embedded in Frankie Tyrell's eye.

"I'm coming in. I'm coming in." Tommy Lee's voice sounded in my ear.

"Stay back, Tommy Lee," I urged. "You'll spook whoever's watching. Give us a minute here."

Kevin stood over Tyrell. Blood coated the gangster's face. The dart must have penetrated several inches into his brain. He made no sound although his limbs twitched in spasmodic jerks like a robotic toy with a dying battery.

"Jesus, Mary, and Joseph." Kevin looked up at Romero, more startled by the giant standing before him than the body at his feet.

"I couldn't fire my gun," Romero said. "And I couldn't let him fire his. Not if it meant Swifty's death."

I stepped from my hideaway and looked at the body. Tyrell's pants were dark like mine. So were his shoes. The blood from his punctured eye had soaked the thistledown on the exposed end of Romero's dart and run down into the collar of his windbreaker. "Strip off his cap and jacket."

"Why?" Kevin asked.

"I'm the closest to his height and weight. I'll walk out of here with the briefcase and head in the reverse direction of how he came in. Tommy Lee can monitor me. You and Romero will have to stay here. Maybe we can flush out his partners."

"Maybe they're going to drop Swifty off somewhere like he promised," Romero said. "What's in the envelope?"

Kevin picked it up, opened the end, and pulled out a piece of paper. I picked up the flashlight and held it so we could see the message. It wasn't an address. Just four words: "Is a dead cop."

"He wanted to taunt us," I said. "Just like with Jimmy Panther. No doubt he was the executioner."

Kevin snatched the cap off Tyrell's head. Above the bill was the logo of the New England Patriots. "At least the bastard didn't pollute a Red Sox cap." He put the cap on me, angling the bill down as Tyrell had worn it.

"Help me get into the jacket," I said. "We must be close to ten minutes."

"As if you could trust the son of a bitch to tell the truth." Kevin yanked one sleeve off, not caring how it twisted the lifeless arm. He rolled Tyrell on his face with the dart still in his eye and pulled the second sleeve free. He searched the jacket pockets and held up a set of keys ringed to a yellow tag. "A rental." He held the keys in the beam. "Chrysler 300."

"So, someone might be waiting in his car," Romero said.

"Or is some other place entirely," Kevin argued. "This prick would lie about the color of the sky."

I ripped off the ski mask and slipped the jacket on, ignoring the warm blood wetting my neck. "We can't take that chance." I looked at Romero. "Why weren't you on our call?"

"I couldn't risk answering. And I knew Rooster wouldn't want me in here."

"Rooster?" Kevin asked.

"Rooster Cogburn. That's what I call Tommy Lee."

Kevin bent over, nearly choking as he tried to stifle the spontaneous swell of laughter. "God damn, Chief. I don't know who you are, but I like you."

I realized Kevin and Romero hadn't met, but there was no time for introductions. "Tommy Lee," I said, knowing he was still monitoring my cell phone. "Call Hector again and this time he'll join. I'm going out as Tyrell. Keep your ears on and keep your distance till we know who's waiting."

His response was immediate. "Barry, you cut and run at the first sign of trouble. I'm too old to break in a new deputy."

I grabbed the briefcase, received a nod of respect from Kevin and Romero, and walked out of the bamboo in search of Danny Swift.

Chapter Twenty-five

Walking into the open moonlight was like coming out of a cave into the noonday sun. The river, the shore, and the footbridge all seemed illuminated by a floodlight. I'd chosen to emerge from the dense bamboo at Kevin's point of entry. It was closer to the footbridge and the logical exit for someone who had dispensed with an enemy and could move freely.

I tried to mimic the swagger I'd seen in Tyrell as he'd pushed past me on the casino stairs. But I kept my head down, hoping the camo on my face and the long bill of the cap would cloak my features in shadow.

"Can you see me?" I whispered.

Through my earpiece, Tommy Lee answered. "Yes, but only as a shape. You look enough like Tyrell that someone would need a light in your face to determine otherwise."

"Where'd he come from?"

"I first noticed him walking down the road parallel to the river."

"That's Tsali Boulevard," Romero said.

Tommy Lee had merged the detective sergeant onto the line.

"The main intersection with Tsalagi Road," Romero said. "There's a KFC on the corner and opposite it is Cherokee Baptist Church. The church has some parking in the rear next to the EconoLodge."

"There's an EconoLodge?" Tommy Lee asked.

"Yes," Romero confirmed. "Someone could wait there or in the church lot."

"Or be in one of the motel rooms with Danny," I said. "Close enough to hear a gunshot."

"Keep walking, Barry," Tommy Lee instructed. "First look for an occupied car or Luther's Cadillac. If you don't see either, look for a Chrysler 300 that's a likely rental."

"Got it." As I neared the intersection, I could see the glow of the EconoLodge sign about a hundred yards beyond. One had to be headed straight for the motel before noticing it. I crossed against the light. There was no traffic or even the sound of traffic in the distance. The KFC and church lots were empty. I kept my head down like I was carefully watching my step. Only when I walked along the dark side of the church did I risk looking ahead.

The EconoLodge parking lot was about three-fourths full. There stood a sprinkling of pickups, more minivans, and an abundance of SUVs. Sedans were in the minority and sometimes hard to see between the higher vehicles. If someone was waiting for Tyrell, the next few minutes were critical. I would be expected to know the location of the car and head toward it, not sneak around the lot.

My best guess was that anyone waiting for Tyrell would be parked close to an exit but outside the radius of a direct streetlamp. I walked toward the darkest corner. There was no Cadillac, no occupied vehicle. However, fifty feet away, I recognized the distinctive trunk of a charcoal Chrysler 300. Could this be the trunk where Danny Swift had been confined? Was he still inside?

I couldn't see into the depths of the dark interior. I approached the rear straight on so that an armed occupant would have to either get out of the car or shoot me through the back window. Then I thought of my advantage. I transferred the satchel to my right hand and pulled the remote key lock from Tyrell's jacket. With the Glock and satchel against my right side, I clicked the key with my left hand. A sharp beep sounded. Head and tail lights flashed and multiple front and rear courtesy lights illuminated the interior like a high school football stadium. The Chrysler was empty.

"Frankie?" Sandra Cransford's question, laced with fear, came from behind me. "What are you doing?"

I shifted the satchel in front of me to hide the Glock. I didn't know if Sandra suspected I wasn't Frankie or was simply curious as to why I'd stopped at the trunk. I didn't want to spin around, gun in plain sight, in case she had a pistol cocked and aimed at me. But speaking would give me away for sure.

I turned slowly. The glow from the car's interior courtesy lights revealed her standing about twenty feet away. She must have been behind the church and emerged from hiding when she saw me enter the EconoLodge parking lot. She looked confused, but she held what appeared to be a thirty-eight pistol rock-solid in her hand. I knew I was facing Eddie Wolfe's killer.

Sandra took a step closer. "Whoever you are, don't move!"

"Sandra. It's over. Put down the gun."

"Barry?"

Immediately Tommy Lee whispered through my earpiece, "Keep her talking. We'll come as quickly and quietly as we can."

"Tyrell told us everything," I lied. "Eddie Wolfe's role, the need to stop Jimmy Panther, and Danny Swift's abduction because of what Eddie thought the boy saw."

"Eddie Wolfe was a god damned fool. He panicked when he heard the kid saw him with Jimmy and the artifacts. The kid knew nothing. Nothing until Eddie snatched him. And then that crooked cop took our money. Frankie said the kid was the best way to get it back."

"The cop wasn't crooked." I took a gamble. "We know the money was meant for Senator Eckles."

Surprise flashed across her face. "Frankie told you that?"

I didn't press my luck with another lie about Tyrell. "No. Eckles got caught in a sting this afternoon. He's singing like a canary."

"That bastard. If we go down, he goes down."

She grabbed the pistol in both hands. "I'll take my chances with the money and the car. Set the satchel and keys on the pavement and step to the side. When I'm safely away, I'll text you where you can find the boy."

"No. You take me to the boy now. Then I hand over the money."

She said nothing, her face a mask hiding the cold-blooded calculations racing through her brain. I hoped she believed Tyrell was still alive and talking. What good would it do to kill me? Not if she got the car and money, which was the best she could hope for. I was betting she wouldn't shoot me in the parking lot if I willingly went with her.

She inched closer. Her eyes dropped and squinted in the low light. "What's that on your neck?"

"Nothing."

"Blood. Smeared blood." She studied the wide, damp splotch running from the collar across my chest. "Frankie's jacket." Her face went feral and her lips curled into a snarl. "You killed Frankie."

Her finger tightened on the trigger. I flung the satchel aside and for a split second her eyes tracked it.

Two shots sounded almost as one. The powerful impact of the forty-five slug knocked Sandra flat on her back. My ears rang with the boom of the Glock. By the church, headlights flashed on as Tommy Lee abandoned his stealth and raced toward us.

He braked a few feet from Sandra's body. Bright red blood pooled on the asphalt around her. In the glare of the headlights, I checked myself. Somehow Sandra's shot had missed. I must have been the one who fired first.

Tommy Lee jumped from the driver's side. "Are you hit?"

"No." I was aware of lights coming on in the windows of the motel. A few frightened faces peered through cracks in the curtains.

Tommy Lee knelt beside Sandra. Mack Collins stepped behind him. The state senator's eyes were wide.

Tommy Lee shook his head.

"Did she tell you where to find the boy?" Collins asked me.

"No." I turned to the trunk. Beside the lock was a round bullet hole. Sandra's wild shot had traveled in a downward trajectory into the center of the trunk's interior.

Romero and Kevin pushed close beside me. Both gasped for air after running from the island.

"Swifty?" Romero squeezed out the word between breaths.

"I don't know. Step back." I lifted the remote key, found the icon for the trunk, and pressed it.

The latch popped and the lid rose. All of us peered inside. The trunk was empty.

"Maybe he's tied up in one of the motel rooms," Kevin said.

I looked at the EconoLodge. A motel was a risky place to hide a boy bound with duct tape. "No. If he's still alive, they've left him in a place they control. Most likely where Sandra knew they wouldn't be disturbed." The obvious answer came to me. "We only had her word that Luther was the one who wanted to come to Cherokee. What if she got her father safely out of the way in the casino hotel so she could use his house?"

Tommy Lee nodded. "I'll send Wakefield to watch the entrance to the development. But we can't be sure that's where he is."

"And if he is there, we can't be sure he's been left unguarded." I turned to Romero. "I know this is difficult, but do whatever you can to keep the press away from here. We don't want news breaking that tips someone off that the game is up."

Romero glanced at the EconoLodge lobby. "Their night duty man might have already called in the gunshots. At least Tommy Lee's in uniform for anyone watching. I'll call in men by phone and keep it off the scanner. We should wrap this scene and Tyrell's fairly quickly. Even though I agree with Barry about the motel, I'll check the registry just to make sure they didn't get a room with Swifty."

"Better safe than sorry," Tommy Lee said. "Then I think you and Mack should go to the casino and see if Luther's there. Mack, he's going to need to lean on you. He's lost his wife and now his daughter. He should hear it from you rather than a hotel employee."

Collins blinked back tears. "I know. But it was my past that brought Sandra into this."

Tommy Lee stepped close to the state senator. "You're wrong. From what we heard her say, Sandra willingly chose her path. She and Tyrell were lovers and losers. They created their own desperate situation, and they created their own destruction. It was none of your doing." He paused, and then added, "That is true, isn't it, Mack?"

"Yes. You have my word."

Tommy Lee nodded.

"What's our plan?" I asked.

Tommy Lee looked at the Chrysler and then at Sandra's body. "We squeeze this car by her and you drive it to Luther's house. Kevin and I'll lead in my car till we get to the gatehouse. Then you go in ahead. We'll use the cell phone connection again. I hope you'll pass for Tyrell long enough to draw out whoever might be on guard." Tommy Lee turned to Romero. "You good with that?"

The big man's face tightened. "Whatever you think, Tommy Lee. Just get Swifty safely away."

I noticed it was the first time Romero didn't call the sheriff Rooster. He was worried.

"Any questions?" Tommy Lee asked.

"Just one," Kevin said. He looked up at Romero. "Why the hell did you bring a blowgun to a gunfight?"

The question broke the tension and Romero smiled. "In case I was discovered and disarmed. What would be more invisible in a cluster of bamboo than a weapon made of bamboo? It would be like searching for a needle made of hay in a haystack. I had no idea I'd need it while I still had my pistol."

"Better than a pistol," Kevin said. "That was one wicked shot."

"Yeah. Wicked. I was aiming for his throat."

The 300 in Chrysler 300 was probably some automotive horsepower designation or elite-sounding marketing invention. Keeping up with Tommy Lee turned it into a NASCAR race. The Chrysler 300. The luxury sedan took the twisting roads better than I did. Even belted in, I had to cling to the steering wheel to stay upright. The normal travel time from Cherokee to Luther's gated community in Gainesboro was about an hour and fifteen minutes. We made it in forty-five.

Tommy Lee's car screeched to a halt just inches from the crossbar and caused the guard to jump to his feet, spilling a cup of coffee over his desk. I rolled down my window to hear.

"I'm Sheriff Tommy Lee Wadkins. We need your help."

The startled guard had short gray hair and a coffee-soaked, brush mustache. He quickly regained his composure. "Joey Abbott, Sheriff. Retired south from the NYPD. Your instructions to notify your deputy were passed on to me. No one's come from the Cransford house since I went on duty at eleven."

"Good. We're going in. I'm bringing Deputy Wakefield here. He'll stop every vehicle entering or exiting. You back him up."

"Shouldn't be any traffic this time of night," Abbott said.

"That's right. So if there is, the occupant could be armed and dangerous. Let Wakefield handle it."

Tommy Lee walked back to me. "I'd posted Wakefield about a hundred yards from the entrance, but I'll call him up to the gatehouse. Drive slowly and Kevin and I will follow with our lights out. Stop just before you come within sight of the house. We'll park and go ahead on foot. I wish your damn courtesy lights weren't so bright. Be careful getting out of the car. And have your gun ready."

Abbott raised the bar and we entered Glendale Forest, domain of the cultured, the well-to-do, and a possible killer.

I thought I'd remember the terrain from our visit to Luther the previous Monday. But at night the landscape of moon-cast shadows became foreign territory. Tommy Lee's instructions to drive slowly proved to be a practical course of action. I saw a corner of Luther's house just in time to stop.

In my rearview mirror, I watched Tommy Lee and Kevin disappear into the shadows of a row of fir trees. A minute later, my phone vibrated.

"We're in position," Tommy Lee whispered through the earpiece. "I'm at the front corner and Kevin's by the garage. Luther's

Cadillac is parked up against it. There's one light burning in the house, but no sound of an occupant."

"So, Sandra brought her father's car here," I said. "Maybe Danny Swift's still in it."

"Kill your lights and pull all the way in," Tommy Lee said. "Kevin, you cover him."

Tommy Lee had merged Kevin's cell phone as well.

"Copy that. Barry, if the kid's there, you load him in the Chrysler and get the hell out of here."

"I agree," Tommy Lee said. "Barry, take it when you're ready."

I cut the lights, unfastened my seatbelt, and laid the Glock in my lap. Then I eased my foot down on the accelerator.

I turned into the driveway and saw Luther's Cadillac snug against the door of the garage exactly where it had been when Wakefield and I were here Monday. I inched forward, following Tommy Lee's advice to park as far in the driveway as possible. Not only would I be in the darkest spot near the house, but I would barricade the Cadillac from any chance of escape.

As I stopped, the flaw in the plan hit me. How was I supposed to get into the trunk of the Cadillac? I didn't have a key. Had it been on Sandra's body?

I pressed the flashlight app on my cell phone. Tyrell had probably been driving so I leaned over the console and swept the beam over the passenger's floorboard. The gold clasp of a small black purse gleamed in the light. I found the Cadillac's key on top of its contents.

I was out of the car in two seconds, and, as feared, the courtesy lights turned the Chrysler into a giant light bulb. I ran to the Cadillac, pressed the trunk release, and pushed the rising lid up as fast as I could.

Danny Swift lay on his side, his arms and feet hog-tied behind his back. Duct tape still covered his mouth. His eyes were shut and he didn't appear to be breathing.

"Oh, God, no," I muttered.

His eyes flickered open and he twisted his head toward me. It was three thirty in the morning. The boy had been sleeping.

As his eyes focused, a tremor ran through his body. I must have looked a sight with my camo-painted face and bloody jacket. He might have thought I was Tyrell.

"You're safe, Danny. I'm getting you out of here." I lifted the boy over my shoulder and ran to the Chrysler.

"Godspeed," I heard behind me, and turned to see Kevin crouching, pistol drawn, positioned between me and the house. I tossed Danny across the backseat, jumped behind the wheel, and slammed the transmission into reverse.

Chapter Twenty-six

Wakefield's patrol car sat broadside across the exit lane to the right of the gatehouse. A pickup truck that must have belonged to the guard barricaded the entry side. If a co-conspirator managed to elude Tommy Lee and Kevin, he'd have to crash through the decorative stone fence bordering Glendale Forest's landscaped entrance.

Wakefield stood behind the hood of his vehicle and held up his left hand like a traffic cop. He kept his right close to his holstered revolver. I braked and cracked my door enough to activate the interior courtesy lights.

"It's me," I shouted. "I've got Danny Swift."

Immediately, Wakefield ran to assist me.

Joey Abbott emerged from the corner of the gatehouse. "What do you need?"

"A knife to cut his ropes."

Abbott hustled toward his pickup.

I spoke into my phone. "I'm with Wakefield. Advise if you can." I cupped my hand over my ear to block out any other sound.

"About to enter the house," Tommy Lee whispered. "Take the boy to the hospital. Use Wakefield's car."

"Copy that. Be careful."

I looked at Danny who was bent like a pretzel on the Chrysler's backseat. "You're safe. We'll get you out of those ropes."

The boy just stared at me, eyes wide with fright.

"Will this do?" Joey Abbott handed me a Marine Corps KA-BAR knife, handle first.

I slashed the cord pulling Danny's bound feet and hands together. He groaned as his strained muscles relaxed.

"Lie still and I'll cut your hands and feet free." Carefully I wedged the black blade between his wrists. The yellow nylon rope was tinged with dried blood where Danny's struggle had cut deep into his skin. I sliced upward and severed the cords. Then I repeated the action with his ankles, noticing that dried blood also caked his socks.

"I'll carry you to the patrol car. We're going to the hospital."

"What about the duct tape across his mouth," Wakefield asked.

The broad strip of gray tape stretched from earlobe to earlobe.

"I'd rather take care of it at the emergency room. They might have some kind of solvent to remove it without ripping his skin." I looked at the boy. "Understand? We'll get that tape off you at the hospital."

He nodded and the panic that had possessed his face melted away.

"Good. Wakefield, open your front passenger door. He'll ride beside me."

This time I more carefully slid my arms under Danny's shoulders and knees and carried him to the patrol car. When he was securely belted in the seat, I handed Wakefield the keys to the Chrysler. "You let me know as soon as you hear something from Tommy Lee."

"Will do. You want me to call ahead to the ER?"

"No. I can do it from the road. You stay ready to help Tommy Lee and Kevin."

I gunned the patrol car and we left the tense scene at Glendale Forest in the rearview mirror.

During the six-minute race to the hospital, I managed three calls. The first went to Susan telling her to alert the ER and find a pediatrician in the middle of the night.

The second call was to Detective Sergeant Romero reporting Swifty was safe and headed for medical evaluation. I knew he'd want tell the boy's parents, but I advised him to wait till I had more information before he suggested they drive to Gainesboro. I promised to give him an update as soon as I could. Romero said his check of Sandra's room in the casino hotel found evidence that Tyrell spent time there. Sex and money—always a recipe for disaster.

My third call fulfilled a promise. Melissa Bigham was sitting by her phone at three thirty in the morning. We spoke for twenty seconds and she was on her way to Cherokee.

As I pulled up to the door of the emergency room, three medical personnel hustled out with a wheelchair. I stood back and let their expertise take over. The nurse, physician, and orderly looked familiar, probably because Susan must have introduced them at some point in the past.

The nurse smiled reassuringly. "Barry, just park your car at the end of the building. I'll tell the desk you're to come back to the examination room."

Before I could move the car, my cell phone rang. Tommy Lee's number flashed in the screen.

"Just got to the hospital," I said without bothering with a hello. "They're examining Danny now. You OK?"

"There was nobody there," Tommy Lee said. "Sandra and Tyrell left him unguarded. Kevin and I figure they didn't kill him in case something went wrong at the exchange and they needed proof he was still alive. But I believe if Tyrell had shot Kevin, Danny would have been dead within the hour."

"What are you going to do now?"

"Unless you need me, I'm heading to Cherokee. Looks like Sandra and Tyrell concocted this whole god damned nightmare on their own. But the threads might lead elsewhere. I'm going to bring in Lindsay Boyce and the FBI. We've got evidence of an interstate crime of bid rigging between State Senator Eckles and G. A. Bridges. Always better to have the feds hit a state politician. It will be very difficult for Eckles to squash that investigation."

"Did you happen to record my confrontation with Sandra?"

"Every word. I think the FBI techs will be able to boost her voice. What's your next move?"

"Wait on Danny's medical evaluation."

"If they need to keep him, you go home and get some rest. You did a hell of a job tonight."

Maybe it was the phone connection, maybe not, but Tommy Lee's voice broke on his final sentence. I could receive no higher praise.

I found Danny Swift sitting on a gurney in a small, curtained-off area. The staff had already removed his clothes and dressed him in a hospital gown. The doctor and nurse were carefully pulling the duct tape free, liberally applying some clear liquid to Danny's skin during the process. In the brighter light, I was able to read their ID badges: Alexander Holden and Barbara Spellman.

As soon as the strip of tape cleared Danny's lips, he said, "I want to see my mom and dad. I want to go home." His voice was high, not yet deepened by puberty.

"Well, tiger," Dr. Holden said, "we want you to do just that. But we've got to check you out first."

Danny looked to me for help.

"Let them do their job, Danny, and I promise you'll get another ride in the police car when it's time to leave."

The curtain pulled open behind me. Susan entered followed by an older man wearing a wrinkled shirt under a lab coat.

"This is Charles Marsh," Susan said. "He's a pediatrician."

Holden stepped back. "You want to take over, Charles?"

"No, Alex. You keep on." He smiled at Danny. "You're in good hands, kid. I'll get Barry to brief me on what happened." Marsh held open the curtain. "Why don't we talk down the hall?"

"Don't go," Danny pleaded.

I crossed the room and placed my hand on his head. "I'm not going anywhere they can't reach me faster than you can run, Swifty."

A faint smile appeared on the boy's bruised lips.

I gave Marsh and Susan the story of what we thought had happened, and that we wouldn't officially talk with Swifty until he'd been medically cleared. My hope was that the exam would conclude he was physically fit enough to go home. After the trauma of abduction and separation, his parents and familiar surroundings were what he wanted most.

"I agree," Marsh said, "provided he hasn't suffered any physical abuse other than what I saw on his hands and feet. Let me confer with Dr. Holden and talk to the boy a few minutes. I suggest that when you do interview him officially, you have a child psychologist sit in. He or she is trained to spot signs you might miss." He turned to Susan. "Why don't you and Barry go to the waiting room? I'll be out to brief you shortly." Without waiting for an answer, he left us in the hallway.

"Does he know his stuff?" I asked.

"Absolutely. When we have kids, I wouldn't want anybody but Charles to be their doctor."

"Then that answers that question."

"Good, because I have one for you."

"What's that?"

"Why do you have camo paint smeared all over your face?"

I took her by the arm and escorted her down the hall. "Let me tell you an interesting story, Doctor Clayton."

Twenty minutes later, Dr. Marsh and Dr. Holden entered the deserted waiting room with visible proof of their evaluation. Each of them held a handle of Danny Swift's wheelchair. The boy was back in his clothes with bandages wrapped around his wrists and ankles. The doctors wore the brightest smiles I'd ever seen at four thirty in the morning.

Again, Danny sat beside me in the patrol car. Susan joined us and rode in the back.

Danny was silent, leaning his forehead against the side window and staring into the darkness, probably reliving all he'd been through. I didn't push him to talk.

Clouds started moving in from the west. The full moon, now setting behind the ridgeline, grew fuzzy. Shadows merged into uniform darkness and soon my vision ended at the outer boundaries of the headlights.

"A woman killed Eddie Wolfe." Danny made the unprompted accusation in barely a whisper.

"Did you see it?"

"No. Eddie had me tied up in a bedroom. She came to check on me and took the pillow. She shot him. The noise was loud, but not loud enough. No one came. My mom and dad were just up the hill, but they never heard. She pointed the gun at me and made me get in her trunk. It was still dark. No one saw."

For the first time, a sob broke his voice. I couldn't image what it would be like to be forced into a trunk less than a hundred feet from your home.

I needed to say something, but I struggled for the appropriate words.

Susan came to my rescue. "You were very brave, Danny. She was a bad person. She can't hurt you anymore."

He sniffled. "Eddie was bad too. The lady was mad that he'd taken me. She said now they had no choice. That was just before she shot him."

No choice. Eddie was the link to Sandra, and Danny was the link to Eddie. With both Eddie and Danny dead, the final connection would be broken.

"They?" I let the question hang.

"I guess her boyfriend. Someone named Frankie."

"You saw him?"

"No. But she was on the phone a lot with him. Once she said, 'I love you.'"

"They talk about anyone else?" I shifted my eyes from the road for a second and saw Danny's tear-streaked face in the glow of the dashboard.

He thought a moment. "Someone named Malone. She said, 'We'll wait till you settle with Malone.'"

As Tommy Lee suspected, waiting to kill Danny had been the plan in case Kevin had balked and demanded proof the boy was still alive.

"And she talked about someone named Mack," he said.

I slowed the car, not wanting to lose any concentration on his words. I sensed Susan lean forward behind me.

"Was Mack part of the 'they' she mentioned?" I asked.

"I don't think so. She said Mack was an old fool. A fool with power he wouldn't use to help her."

So Mack Collins had refused to be manipulated by Sandra or her brother Darren when each had pressed him from opposite sides of the casino battle. If Collins played no role, then I didn't think he should pay a consequence. I suspected Tyrell had gotten Sandra to do what Collins refused to do—launder money for Whitey Bulger through a construction company. And if that money stopped during the Great Recession, Sandra and Tyrell were left with a house of cards, a company desperate to stay afloat but without the criminal mastermind to save it.

"I don't want to talk about it anymore," Danny said.

"You don't have to. You'll be home soon."

When we passed Oconaluftee Islands Park, I saw lights flashing from within the bamboo. Romero must be back at the scene with his team.

I was wrong. When I pulled into the small lot in front of the police station, the door flung open and Romero emerged like a bear from his den. He started clapping. Tommy Lee followed and Melissa Bigham was right behind him, her camera at the ready. Other officers appeared, lining the walkway and joining in the rhythmic applause.

Danny Swift strained against the seatbelt and pressed his face close to the windshield. I left the headlights burning so that he could see the rousing welcome. Mack Collins and Kevin came out side by side. Kevin started doing an Irish jig. Mack managed a smile.

Then Dot Swift and the man who must have been her husband stepped into the light. Danny squealed and tore off his seatbelt.

"Go on." I unlocked the doors.

True to his name, Swifty flew into the arms of his parents.

Chapter Twenty-seven

"Read them and weep, gentlemen. Read them and weep." Archie Donovan Jr. watched the hole cards flip over and fill out Uncle Wayne's full house of aces over jacks. Archie sat motionless as my uncle raked the pot away from him.

"I'm out," Mayor Whitlock exclaimed. "At least I lost to somebody different for a change."

Everyone looked at Archie and the purple Crown Royal bag that had been plump with coins and now lay before him like a deflated balloon.

"Maybe you can pay Wayne to give you some pointers," Pete Peterson said.

"Or pray for the state legislature to adjourn so that Mack can return," Taylor Hobbs advised.

Taylor had been the person I replaced at the game two months earlier when I'd been ambushed with the cemetery expansion. Now I was sitting in for Luther while my uncle replaced Mack. Neither of us was interested in becoming regulars, even though it was uncertain if Luther would return.

All of Gainesboro had rallied around Luther, no one more than Mack Collins. But the magnitude of his daughter's crimes weighed on Luther like an unbearable stone of grief and sorrow. The evidence against her was undeniable. Her thirty-eight revolver and pillow feather traces found in the Cadillac tied her to Eddie Wolfe's murder.

Furthermore, soil matches confirmed Jimmy Panther had been at the casino construction site, and the recheck of Sandra's cell phone call to her father the night of Panther's murder placed her in Cherokee, not Atlanta. Tommy Lee admonished himself for not scrutinizing her location as closely as he should have. But, at the time, he'd been focused on Luther's alibi and only looked where he thought he should look. All that aside, Danny Swift's testimony would have been the nail in Sandra's coffin.

The investigation had spread to the state level, and the FBI snared Senator Gerald Eckles in a bribery scandal after tracing cash withdrawals from G. A. Bridges that matched deposits in accounts tied to Eckles. The payments began during the Great Recession when public works projects became the primary source of revenue for construction companies. Several state DOT staffers in charge of bid reviews were also feeling the heat.

Mack Collins had so far proven to be squeaky clean. Melissa Bigham had withheld his name from her story, a story that went national, because she had no proof that Tyrell and Sandra hadn't come together on their own. Collins appeared to have left his old life behind and rebuffed every effort to entice or threaten him back into the mob, including what I suspected was Tyrell's final attempt to intimidate him in Cherokee. We'd enough victims as it was.

Frankie Tyrell had improvised Panther's execution at the cemetery. When Sandra told him about the confrontation and Panther's threatening notes and feathers, Tyrell saw a way to introduce a new motive for the crime. He didn't care if it threw suspicion on Luther.

I think of all Sandra's wicked deeds, the one Luther couldn't bear was his daughter's desecration of his wife's grave. He would carry that abominable atrocity for the rest of his life.

Romero received proper credit for the rescue of Danny Swift. When I asked him if he'd been worried Tyrell might have spotted him earlier in the day mounting his camouflage blinds in

246 Mark de Castrique

the bamboo, he said he hadn't carried them in. The screens of bamboo had been created in Oconaluftee Village and he'd had some children bring them to the river to use as rafts. If Tyrell spotted them, he'd see them only as rafts and not realize they could have another function. In his mind, they would always be rafts. The kids left them hidden in the bamboo and all Romero had to do was reposition them.

The issue of a second Cherokee casino still divided the tribe. The shock that Jimmy Panther was murdered to further its construction halted the pro-casino momentum. But, the revelation that Panther was planning to fraudulently plant artifacts undercut some of the moral high ground claimed by the opponents. The potential money, both in per capita payouts to enrolled tribe members and in the contracts and ancillary business growth, was a dangling carrot that refused to go way.

To Darren Cransford's credit, he severed his ties to the Catawba efforts and worked to reconcile his relationship with his father. I hoped that would bring Luther comfort amid the great despair Sandra had caused him. Both men faced a hard road ahead.

However, the challenge from the Catawba casino intensified as Sandra Cransford was held up as an example of unscrupulous efforts to deny the Catawba their rights. The logic was spurious, but emotions ran high.

I hoped whatever the outcome, it would be decided by the tribe and not the outsiders manipulating and jockeying to get their way. But hadn't that been the case for centuries? Termination, not preservation.

The luck of the Indians couldn't be confused with the luck of the Irish. Kevin Malone returned to Boston unscathed. The illegal entry into Tyrell's hotel room was never revealed because no one doubted Kevin's version of how he intercepted the satchel in a public drop between Tyrell and Sandra. Tommy Lee and I said nothing, and Romero had the good sense not to ask us. Kevin did say at our parting that I'd pulled his potatoes out of the boiling pot and he would make it up to me. Given his track record, I'd prefer to call it even.

Mayor Whitlock got up from the table. In his customary orange Clemson warm-up suit, he looked like the Great Pumpkin rising out of the pumpkin patch. "Well, boys, it's been fun."

I slid back my chair.

Whitlock raised his hand. "Hold up a minute, Barry. A little town business."

The queasy churning returned to my stomach. "Wayne and I rode together."

Uncle Wayne made a show of checking his watch. I was thankful he would get me out of there.

"It's only ten thirty. We've got time."

My jaw dropped. An alien had taken possession of his old body. Uncle Wayne considered post-nine o'clock to be populated only by insomniacs.

"Grand, that's just grand," Whitlock proclaimed. "I'll show the others out and be right back. Make yourselves at home." He led Archie, Pete, and Taylor up the stairs.

"Uncle Wayne, what's going on? You can't stand being around the mayor any longer than I can."

My uncle frowned. "Now that's not true. Sammy's gotten mellower in his old age. He's got some good ideas."

"Well, retiring from office would be the best one."

Multiple footsteps came down the stairs. Mayor Whitlock and Archie wore grins as wide as a piano's keyboard.

"This is going to be grand," Whitlock said again.

"Grand," chorused Archie and Uncle Wayne.

I looked at my uncle with disbelief. He was in on whatever was about to happen. Betrayal. An Eddie Wolfe in my uncle's clothing.

"And what is so grand?" I asked.

"Why, the new opportunity you've given us," Mayor Whitlock said. "Archie, you tell him. He's your best friend."

Not even on Facebook, I thought.

Archie slid into the seat beside me. "Barry, you know how much I appreciate your bringing me into the Jimmy Panther case."

Bringing him in because Kevin Malone had hoodwinked me into keeping Francis Tyrell occupied.

"And you said I did a good job," he continued.

"Yes. You did a good job." I looked at the eager faces of my uncle and Mayor Whitlock. "You all did."

"Well, I've got some spare time," Archie said. "We all do. And we've decided to open up a detective agency."

"A what?"

"A private detective agency. I can run it out of my office. We were so successful on your case, we figure we can do it professionally."

"There's not another one in town," Whitlock said.

"You're the damn mayor. How can you go undercover?" I turned to my uncle. "And you put people under a cover of dirt. Everybody knows you." I threw up my hands. "They know all of you."

"They only think they know us," Archie said. "That's the beauty of it."

Suddenly, Romero's voice rang in my head. "If Tyrell saw it as a raft, then in his mind it would always be a raft."

"Fine. Fine." The whole thing was too ridiculous to argue. "And where will you get these cases?"

"From you," Archie said triumphantly. "Not the big murders, of course. We'll handle the kind of things the department doesn't have the time or manpower to investigate. Shoplifters. Cheating spouses. Maybe a cold case."

"They show them on TV," my uncle said.

"I know what a cold case is. But that's not my call. Tommy Lee has to authorize any referrals to private detectives."

Their smiles withered. Archie and Whitlock looked at my uncle.

"Well," Uncle Wayne said, "we were hoping you would ask him for us."

"You know him as well as I do."

"Yeah, but we just asked him for a favor," Mayor Whitlock said. "Some extra security for a town event."

"What town event?"

The mayor pressed his hands on my shoulders. "You remember Barry Clayton Day?"

Archie grinned. "It's next Saturday."

Acknowledgments

Although the plot and characters of this novel are fictitious, the background events are based on actual issues confronting the Eastern Band of the Cherokee.

After much debate, a second casino is under construction on the edge of the Qualla Boundary Reservation, which some tribe members believe will diminish the number of visitors to the cultural and artistic centers that tell the Cherokee story.

The attempt by the Catawba tribe of South Carolina to buy land in North Carolina for the sole purpose of building a casino is currently under debate and faces strong opposition from both the Cherokee and elected representatives in the North Carolina Legislature.

I am grateful to the members of the Cherokee tribe who shared their perspectives on the impact of both the second casino and the Catawba proposal. I'm also grateful to Mary Walker for her insights into Cherokee heritage and her support of the Richard "Yogi" Crowe Memorial Scholarship Fund to further postgraduate education for Cherokee students.

I'm indebted to attorney Tom DeMille for sharing his knowledge of the legal issues involved with Native American gaming and to retired Boston police detective William DeMille for providing his law enforcement expertise. Unlike Kevin Malone, Billy went by the book.

The writing and publishing of a novel is a team effort. Thanks to Robert Rosenwald and the entire staff of Poisoned Pen Press, and to my editor Barbara Peters for her ongoing guidance. Also thanks to my wife, Linda; daughters, Lindsay and Melissa; and son-in-law, Pete for reviewing the manuscript.

Last but not least, I am grateful to those booksellers and librarians who share my stories with their patrons, and to you, the reader, for spending some time in the mountains with Buryin' Barry.

Mark de Castrique
April 2014
Charlotte, North Carolina

To receive a free catalog of Poisoned Pen Press titles, please
contact us in one of the following ways:

Phone: 1-800-421-3976
Facsimile: 1-480-949-1707
Email: info@poisonedpenpress.com
Website: www.poisonedpenpress.com

Poisoned Pen Press
6962 E. First Ave. Ste 103
Scottsdale, AZ 85251